ALSO BY RICHARD MASON

Natural Elements

Us

The Drowning People

HISTORY OF A
PLEASURE SEEKER

HISTORY OF A PLEASURE SEEKER

A NOVEL

RICHARD MASON

Alfred A. Knopf
NEW YORK
2012

THIS IS A BORZOI BOOK PUBLISHED BY ALFRED A. KNOPF

Copyright © 2011 by Richard Mason

All rights reserved. Published in the United States by Alfred A.
Knopf, a division of Random House, Inc., New York, and in
Canada by Random House of Canada Limited, Toronto.

www.aaknopf.com

Knopf, Borzoi Books, and the colophon are registered trademarks of
Random House, Inc.

Originally published in Great Britain by Weidenfeld & Nicholson,
an imprint of Orion Publishing Group, London, in 2011.

ISBN: 978-0-307-59947-6
LCCN: 2011942615

Jacket image: La Reproduction interdite (Portrait d'Edward
James) by René Magritte, 1937. © 2011 C. Herscovici, London /
Artists Rights Society (ARS), New York. Museum Boijmans van
Beuningen, Rotterdam, The Netherlands. Photo: Banque d'Images,
ADAGP / Art Resource, New York

Jacket design by Carol Devine Carson

Manufactured in the United States of America

First American Edition

THE GILDED CURVE

AMSTERDAM, 1907

The adventures of adolescence had taught Piet Barol that he was extremely attractive to most women and to many men. He was old enough to be pragmatic about this advantage, young enough to be immodest, and experienced enough to suspect that it might be decisive in this, as in other instances.

As he stepped from the Leiden train into the whirling hustle of the Central Station, several passers-by turned discreetly to look at him. He had an open face with amused blue eyes, a confident nose and thick black hair that curled around his ears. He was not much above middling height but he was muscular and well fashioned, with enormous gentle hands that made people wonder how it felt to be caressed by them.

In one of these hands on this cold February morning was an envelope too large for the pockets of his English suit. It contained a copy of his degree certificate and a letter of recommendation from a professor who owed his father a favor. As Piet crossed the traffic on the Prins Hendrikkade, he reaffirmed the decision he had made immediately on receiving Jacobina Vermeulen-Sickerts' invitation to interview: that he would knock at the front door of the house, like an equal, and not at the servants' entrance.

The family lived on the grandest stretch of the grand-

est canal in Amsterdam. Piet knew from the newspapers
that Maarten Vermeulen-Sickerts dispensed bread to the
slum dwellers and had been instrumental in bringing clean
drinking water to the city's poorest districts. He knew he
owned the country's most lavish hotel and a number of
similar establishments across Europe. His daughters, Constance and Louisa, were familiar to Piet, too, as was their
leadership of the "smart young set" and the rumor that they
alarmed their mother, Jacobina. Taken together, the family
had a reputation for being colorful and modern and very
rich: three qualities Piet felt sure would ease the tedium of
teaching a spoiled little boy.

He sauntered down the Blauwbergwal and crossed onto
the Herengracht Canal. On both sides of the water, houses
built for the magnates of the seventeenth century surveyed
the world with the serenity that comes from surviving the
upheavals of three hundred years unscathed. They were tall
but slender, with none of the grandiloquence of the rich
men's houses his mother had shown him in Paris, and yet
the fact that they *were* rich men's houses was indisputable,
and subtly advertised by the profusion of their windows.

Piet turned left, and in his head he was walking away
from Leiden, from Herman Barol's dark little house on the
Pieterskerkhof and the life of the university clerk that went
with it. For four years Piet had been assisting his father in
sanctioning undergraduates who had omitted to pay their
library fines or cheated in their exams or been caught in the
company of women of ill repute. From these young men he
had learned to affect the nonchalant swagger of the rich, but
he had no intention of chasing them up forever.

He put a freshly laundered handkerchief over his mouth
and inhaled deeply. The canal stank with a virulence for
which life in the comparative simplicity of a country town
had not prepared him. Within the odor's complex depths

lurked cheese rinds, rotting shoes, rats' urine, human def-
ecation, oil, tar, and a consignment of industrial chemicals
that had leaked from a ship in the harbor. The combined
effect was choking, but the people who passed him paid no
attention to it. He was sure that he, too, would get used to
it in time.

He continued more briskly. As the house numbers
increased, so did the emphasis of the architecture's whispered message: that people of wealth and distinction lived
here. The narrower dwellings, two or three windows across,
that dominated the earlier stretches of the canal grew rarer.
As he crossed the Nieuwe Spiegelstraat, they all but disappeared. Soon the narrowest house was four windows wide.
Which one was theirs? He looked at his watch. He was still
twenty minutes early. To avoid being seen, he crossed the
canal and continued his walk up the farther side.

The appearance of a house with six windows on its ground
floor signaled a further elevation of status and the beginning
of the Gilded Curve. He felt a pricking of panic. He had not
always been a diligent student and there was little sincerity
in the recommendation his professor had given him, a fact
that would reveal itself to a sensitive reader. Piet was far
cleverer than many who had more to show for their clever-
ness, but this was hardly an argument he could advance.
He did speak perfect French—his mother Nina had been
a Parisienne and his English and German were adequate;
but his piano playing was only competent, and the adver-
tisement had stressed Egbert Vermeulen-Sickerts' musical
genius and the desirability of a tutor who could match and
extend it.

He sat down on a wrought-iron bench between two trees
and collected himself. He did not have the best credentials
but was wise enough to understand—even at twenty-four—
that symbols on paper are not the only grounds on which

people make up their minds. A tutor, after all, was more than a servant. The successful candidate would dine with the family, not wait on them, and though the Vermeulen-Sickertses had not specified this requirement, he was sure that people so à la mode would prize amusing conversation. This he was very good at making, having learned the arts of charm at his mother's knee.

He took out Jacobina's letter and began to sketch on the back of the envelope the austere, imposing façade of a house opposite him. When he had captured the tricky perspective of water and bricks, he felt calmer and more optimistic. He stood up and walked on; and as the canal curved again he saw the house at number 605.

The possibility that he might soon sleep in one of the rooms on its upper stories made Piet Barol shiver beneath his cashmere coat with its velvet collar, bought secondhand from a well-off student with urgent debts. The house was five windows wide and five stories high, with hundreds of panes of glass that glittered with reflections of canal and sky. The front door was on the first floor, achieved by a handsome double staircase of gray stone, and the façade of small rectangular bricks was relieved of sternness by pretty white stucco scrolls. Despite its size there was nothing showy about it, nothing over-ornamented or insecure.

Piet approved wholeheartedly.

He was crossing the bridge towards it when a man in his late twenties emerged from the servants' entrance beneath the staircase. He was not well dressed and his suit, which had been bought in slimmer days, was too obviously "Sunday best." He looked a little like a young man who had pursued Piet doggedly the summer before: dark and slouched, with a drooping chin and an oily nose. Piet had not let that chap have his way, and he did not intend to let this one prevail either. As his competitor made off in the direction of the station, Piet saw that he was slightly out of breath by the time he had gone a hundred yards. The spectacle cheered him.

He straightened his tie and crossed the bridge. As he prepared to mount the steps to the front door, the servants' door opened, and a woman with a severe chin said: "Mr. Barol? We are expecting you. If you'd be so good as to step inside."

The stink of the canals vanished at once and was replaced by the sweetness of an apple cake browning to perfection, which underscored the scents of polish and clean hair and the fragrance of a large bucket of orange roses that stood on a table by the butler's pantry. "I am Mrs. de Leeuw, the housekeeper. Please follow me." The lady led him into a kitchen devoted to quiet, choreographed efficiency. An enormous icebox stood in one corner, its oak door lined in white glass and held open by a handsome blond fellow of about Piet's age to facilitate the entry of a polished jelly mold. "Careful, Hilde!" Piet's guide spoke without tenderness. "May I take your coat, Mr. Barol? Mr. Blok will take you upstairs."

Mr. Blok now appeared at the door in a dark tailcoat: a waxy man in his late fifties with a scrupulously shaven chin. Something in his glance suggested an awareness of Piet's charms—which Piet thought problematic, since he felt no answering inclination. On the rare occasions Piet Barol went with men, he preferred them athletic and close to his own age. The butler was neither. "This way, Mr. Barol," he said.

Mr. Blok left the room and went up a narrow staircase. Piet did not wish to appear provincial, and his face gave no sign of the impression the entrance hall made. Panels with quotations from the Romantic painters surmounted a wainscot of marble shot with pink and gray. On a half-moon table was a silver bowl filled with visiting cards. Mr. Blok turned right beneath a gilt lantern and led Piet towards an open door at the head of the passage, through which tall French windows were visible.

As he passed the dining room Piet glimpsed olive-green-and-gold wallpaper and a table set for five—a family dinner, which meant that Constance and Louisa would be dining in. He knew from the newspapers that they did so rarely and read this, quite correctly, as a sign of their interest in their brother's new tutor.

He longed to meet them and be their friend.

The staircase to the upper floors was carpeted in soft red wool and surveyed by a trio of statues beneath a glass dome. Mr. Blok led Piet past it and ushered him into the room with the French windows, which was nothing but a tiny octagon, constructed of glass and stone and furnished with two sofas of extreme rigidity. It told him plainly that the splendors of the drawing room were reserved for men better and grander than he; and because Piet Barol had a strong sense of his innate value, he took exception to this judgment and resolved to conquer the person in whose gift the freedom of the house lay.

The butler retreated. Piet placed the envelope containing his references on a table so slender it barely bore this burden and settled to wait. Above him, a chandelier of five gilt griffins observed him disdainfully, as if each of its winged lions could see into his soul and disapproved of what they found there. Mrs. Vermeulen-Sickerts' first name conjured images of hairy patriarchs and he hoped she wouldn't be too ugly. It was harder to flirt with an ugly woman.

He was pleasantly surprised when a light step sounded on the tiles and Jacobina appeared. Although approaching forty-six, the legacy of an athletic youth was evident in her

neat waist and quick, fashionable movements. She was wearing a day dress of apple-green wool with a high lace collar
and a small train: an impractical garment in many respects,
but Jacobina Vermeulen-Sickerts had no pressing need to be
practical. "Good afternoon, Mr. Barol." She extended a hand
and shook his firmly. "Please don't get up." But Piet was
already standing, and he smiled shyly as Jacobina sank onto
one of the sofas and said: "Do excuse the uncomfortable
furniture. My husband is very fond of Louis Quinze and the
fabric is too delicate to have the seats resprung. Would you
drink some tea with me?"

"Gladly."

Jacobina ordered refreshments on an extravagantly ornamental telephone. "And now, may I see your references?"

It was as well to get these out of the way at the beginning.
As Piet handed them to her, his eye caught Jacobina's and
he understood that he had made a favorable first impression.
Indeed, Piet's smell, which was the smell of a gentleman,
and his clothes, which were a gentleman's clothes, reassured
Jacobina in ways of which she was not at all conscious. She
glanced at the pages in her hand, saw that Piet had the
university degree the position required, and said: "Tell me
about your family. Your father is a clerk in the university at
Leiden, I believe?"

"He is, ma'am." Herman Barol had a respectable position in the administration of Holland's oldest university.
Piet conveyed this without mentioning that such posts are
generally held by petty autocrats unable to achieve influence
elsewhere.

"And your mother?"

"She died when I was seventeen. She was a singing
teacher."

"I'm so sorry. Do you sing?"

"I do, ma'am."

"Excellent. So does my husband."

It was, in fact, thanks to his mother the singing teacher that Piet was able to read in Jacobina Vermeulen-Sickerts the subtle traces of an interest that was not wholly professional, long before she became aware of it herself. Since her son could walk, Nina Barol had spoken to Piet as though he were a cultivated and delightful intimate of her own age. She had discussed the personal situations of her students with a candor that would have horrified them, and later, as a boy accompanist, Piet had had ample opportunity to look for evidence of what his mother told him. He was now unusually sensitive to indications of private emotion. As he answered Jacobina's questions, he absorbed a wealth of detail about the woman who might be persuaded to change his life. She had a strong sense of propriety, that was clear. But it did not seem to be stronger in her than in other respectable women Piet knew, who had happily abandoned it for him. "And what of Master Egbert?" he said.

Tea was brought in and Jacobina poured. "My son is extremely intelligent, but sometimes intelligence of that sort can be a burden. He has always had a vivid imagination. Indeed, I have encouraged it. But perhaps I have been overly lenient with him. My husband believes he needs sterner treatment, though I am looking for a tutor who can combine authority with gentleness."

Jacobina had made this speech to each of the sixteen people she had so far interviewed; but as she spoke the word *gentleness* to Piet Barol her eyes flicked to his hands, as if they were the perfect expression of what she sought. "Egbert completes his schoolwork very well. He speaks English and German and French and dedicates himself to the practice of his music with commendable discipline. He has long outgrown any music teacher I have been able to find. But—"

"He is shy, perhaps?"

"Not unusually so, Mr. Barol. If you met him you would not think anything much out of the ordinary. The problem is—he will not leave the house."

"Will not?"

"Perhaps cannot. We have had to obtain a special permit to educate him at home. He last went into the garden a year and a half ago but has refused absolutely to go into the street since he was eight years old. We tried to coax him at first and then to force him; but I am afraid the tantrums were so affecting I put a stop to my husband's efforts. Perhaps that was wrong, but it is very hard for a mother to see her child afraid and do nothing."

"Of course."

"So there you have it. We need a tutor who is capable of—of finding Egbert, wherever he has lost himself, and bringing him back to us."

It was the fourth time that day, and the twelfth that week, that Jacobina had been obliged to debase herself before a stranger with this frank rendition of her maternal failings. It was not an experience she enjoyed. But Piet's expression was one of such thoughtful concern, and contrasted so well with the embarrassment of the other candidates, that she was inspired to further revelation. "I cosseted him too much when he was little, Mr. Barol. I should have made him be braver, but I did not and now he lacks the courage even to venture onto the steps outside. Have you experience of difficult children?"

Piet had no experience of any children whatsoever. "Life in a university town acquaints one with many brilliant eccentrics," he said judiciously.

Jacobina smiled to disguise the fact that she might also have burst into tears. She loved each of her children fiercely, but Egbert most fiercely of all because he had greatest need of her. She took a sip of tea. "It is also essential that any tutor is able to communicate with him musically. He is devoted to music."

"I was *répétiteur* for my mother and her students from the time I was nine."

"Excellent. Perhaps you would play for me now?"

"With pleasure."

Jacobina rose. "Let me take you to the schoolroom. Egbert's sisters, my daughters Constance and Louisa, have banished him to the house next door. Fortunately it belongs to my aunt, who now spends most of the year at Baden-Baden. We have had a door specially constructed so that Egbert needn't use the street. I suppose it was the wrong thing to do, but he can be—obsessive, at times, about his playing, and Louisa in particular has a sensitive ear. In my aunt's drawing room he can make as much noise as he likes without disturbing anyone." She led Piet into the dining room and he saw that on one side of the fireplace the shape of a door was cleverly hidden in the wallpaper. Jacobina opened it to reveal an entrance hall tiled in white and black and rather smaller than the one at Herengracht 605.

He held it for her as she passed through.

Jacobina Vermeulen-Sickerts had taken many men to her aunt's house to hear them play the heavy Bösendorfer that was Egbert's closest confidant. She had taken them alone and never felt at all awkward; but when the secret door clicked behind the handsome Piet Barol she felt suddenly that she was doing something improper. She crossed the hall and opened the drawing room door. "Egbert's in bed today. He catches colds easily—that's why we keep it so hot in here." It was, indeed, very hot. Heavy gilt radiators burbled beneath windows hung in midnight-blue velvet. "Do remove your jacket if you're too warm."

Piet did so and sat at the piano, wondering what he should play. He was no virtuoso, and the possibility that an oily-nosed overachiever would snatch this chance from him made his stomach clench. He opened the instrument, waiting for inspiration, and the memory that came to him was of his mother telling him that the only key for love is E flat major. He glanced at Jacobina. She did not look like a woman whose sensual appetites were well catered for, and the room was certainly the temperature for tenderness.

What would she permit?

The idea of finding out reignited old temptations, for this was not the first flirtation Piet Barol had conducted from a piano stool. He hesitated, weighing the dangers. But already the adrenaline of risk was pumping through him and would not be disobeyed.

Mrs. Vermeulen-Sickerts wanted a tutor with authority and gentleness. He should play her something slow and sentimental and not too difficult, preferably in E-flat major. But what? Jacobina moved past the piano and turned to face him, just as his mother's students had done. As she passed he caught her scent—of rosewater and musk and hand-laundered underwear—and it came to him that the second nocturne of Chopin fulfilled all his criteria.

Nina Barol's edition marked this piece *espressivo dolce*—to be played sweetly and expressively—and Piet began to play it softly from memory, at a slow *andante*. The piano was first rate and recently tuned, and it lent his performance a finesse he did not often achieve on his mother's upright.

He was correct: it was many years since anyone had touched Mrs. Vermeulen-Sickerts with the aim of giving her pleasure. Jacobina had almost ceased to mourn this sad fact, but in the presence of such a beautiful young man it struck her forcefully. She stepped closer to see him better. Piet's face was manly but graceful, with succulent red lips that prompted thoughts of her husband's dry little kisses.

Jacobina looked away.

Piet tripped in a run of semiquavers, but the piano forgave him and hid all traces of the jarring note in folds of rich harmony. As he played he sensed the atmosphere responding to the music's enchantments. Indeed Jacobina's nostalgia for the lost opportunities of her youth increased with every note. Watching Piet, she was not unaware of the muscles of his shoulders nor of the way his perfectly laundered shirt clung to his back as he leaned over the keys. It was a long time since she had heard any music but her son's relentless exercises, and the gentleness with which Piet's huge fingers elicited these hushed sounds from the piano was bewitching.

It was a secret she no longer shared with anyone, but Jacobina Vermeulen-Sickerts was very different from the woman her family and closest friends thought they knew. In her deepest self she was more like Louisa than Constance and had spent her girlhood imagining a life not at all like the one she now enjoyed. A change in her breathing made Piet's pulse quicken. He looked up, caught her watching him, and held her gaze until she looked away. He was used to enlivening the lessons of Nina Barol's prettiest pupils in this fashion and since his seventeenth birthday had grown steadily bolder—though he had never yet employed his stratagems on a lady of rank, or in a situation so laden with potential disaster.

Piet played the last bars of the nocturne very delicately and the piano's ringing made the air between them tingle. He did not silence it by lifting his foot from the pedal.

When Jacobina said "Play me something more modern, Mr. Barol," he was ready for her. His choice was the entr'acte to the third act of *Carmen*, also in E-flat major, which had been useful in similar situations before. Its pure, beguiling melody rose from the embers of the nocturne and the rumbling arpeggios of the bass line showed his hands to advantage. As he played, he thought of the smugglers who appear onstage at its close, whispering that fortune awaits if only they will tread carefully. This was exactly how he felt as he drenched his quarry in sweet, permissive magic.

Jacobina Vermeulen-Sickerts' social position protected her from the lascivious stares of men. The possibility that she had encountered one now left her flustered, but not disagreeably so. She looked away, deciding that she had been mistaken, but when her eyes flicked again to Piet Barol's she found that his were ready to meet them, and this was joltingly erotic. Jacobina rode twice a week but otherwise took very little exercise. She had recently begun to worry that this showed and to feel rather let down by her once sylphlike body. To receive an admiring glance from a young man was exhilarating.

She stared out of the window as Piet finished playing.

"What a touch, Mr. Barol." She spoke the compliment to the street outside and when she turned to face Piet he was smiling at her, and did not stop.

Piet Barol's smile often got him what he wanted. On this occasion it was full of charming hopefulness, and under its influence Jacobina made a decision. "You are welcome to take your meals with us, or dine out as you wish. You will find us an easy-going family. My daughters delight everyone they meet. And Egbert . . ." But she left this sentence unfinished. "Mrs. de Leeuw will show you to your room."

"I will give of my best, *mevrouw.*"

"I am sure my husband will wish to see you before dinner. I'll have some shirts and socks of his sent up. We can arrange for your bags to come tomorrow."

"Thank you, Mrs. Vermeulen-Sickerts."

"Je vous en prie."

Naomi de Leeuw did not approve of tutors as a breed, nor of their ill-defined place in the household hierarchy— neither servant nor guest. One or two of Piet's predecessors had used this blurred distinction to their advantage and she had no intention of allowing this cocky young man to do the same.

"You will share the attic floor and a bathroom with Mr. Blok and Mr. Loubat," she said stiffly as she led him to his room. "I thank you not to visit the basement, where the maids' rooms are, after five p.m. We have high standards of cleanliness. You are permitted to take two baths a week and will have shaving water every day. Shirts are to be worn three times at a maximum. Hilde Wilken will do your laundry." She opened a door and ushered Piet into a small, comfortably furnished bedroom with a window that looked over the garden. "There is no smoking in the house, and no drinking unless you are offered refreshment by a member of the family. The bathroom is two doors along. You are required to attend church on Sunday mornings but may spend Sunday afternoons at your leisure. Do you have any questions, Mr. Barol?"

"I don't think so, Mrs. de Leeuw."

"Very well. I do hope you'll be comfortable here."

When she had gone, Piet sat on his bed and loosened his tie. He was half alarmed by the suddenness of the change he had wrought in his fortunes. Gone at a stroke was the tiny alcove, separated by a curtain from his father's room, in which he had slept since leaving his cradle. Gone was the outside toilet, the rusting plumbing, the vile university food to which he and Herman had become accustomed since his mother's death. The ambitions he had nursed so privately—of travel and comfort and elegance, of escaping forever the straitened gentility of his youth—were plausible now, seized from the realm of fantasy by his own determination to act on his instincts. To have a room of his own at last! To be able to bathe without laying a fire and boiling the water; to shit without shivering in the little wooden hut beside the back door! He started to laugh as the nervous energy of the afternoon drained from him. He felt light and triumphant, capable of anything.

There was a knock at the door. It was Didier Loubat, the footman, with a pile of shirts and collars and a little box of studs. He was taller than Piet and blond, with a strong jaw and sharp sea-green eyes. "The old man wants to see you in forty-five minutes. His office is at the front of the house, on the first floor. D'you want me to come and get you, or will you find it on your own?"

"I'll find it."

"Good man. The whole family's gathering to vet you at dinner. *Bonne chance.*" Didier's friendliness was a relief after Mrs. de Leeuw's chilly formality. "My room's next door if you need anything, and the bathroom's down the hall. A little tip: don't let Blok see you in a towel. He's a terrible old lecher."

"I thought he might be."

Didier grinned. "You need your wits about you in this house, but you'll get used to it. There's a towel in the cupboard."

The towel in the cupboard was of vast size and fresh-smelling fluffiness. Piet took it with him to the bathroom, which was tiled in white porcelain and deliciously clean. In the corner was an eight-foot bath, and when he turned the tap the suddenness with which boiling water gushed from it took him by surprise and scalded him. That such quantities of hot water could be obtained so effortlessly was miraculous to him. He filled the tub very full and undressed and got in and stretched back at full length, baptizing himself in his new life. He would cable to his father tomorrow, but Herman had never shown much concern for his whereabouts and Piet doubted that his absence tonight would alarm him. He lay in the hot water, feeling very pleased with himself, but as it cooled so did his triumph and the complexities of his new situation stole in and replaced it.

Piet had sufficient experience of female unpredictability to know the risks of forming a liaison with his new employer's wife. As he washed, he decided that he would never again allude to the unspoken communications of the afternoon. Emigration to America and the making of a considerable fortune were the next stage of his plan. He would take no chances until he had saved the money to fund them. He submerged himself again, and it came to him that his efforts with Mrs. Vermeulen-Sickerts had left him in a powerful negotiating position with her husband. The salary advertised was sixty guilders a month. It was clear from the establishment at Herengracht 605 that the man who owned it could afford considerably more. Piet got out of the bath and began to dry himself. Unless he was very much mistaken, Jacobina would make sure he was employed whatever the salary. His experience of wealthy undergraduates had shown him that many rich men prefer to pay more, rather than less, on the grounds that quality is closely correlated with expense.

He dressed slowly and carefully, and by the time he was

finished he had decided to add a further challenge to the many he had risen to that day.

He had decided to ask for more.

The office of Maarten Vermeulen-Sickerts was protected from disturbance by a small anteroom. Piet knocked twice at its door before gathering the courage to pull the rope of twisted vermilion silk that rang a bell above Maarten's desk. He heard its far-off tinkle, then vigorous steps, and then his new employer stood before him: a powerfully built, square-shouldered man with a full head of hair, silver at the temples, a prominent nose, and small dark eyes that bored so deeply into him he almost lost his nerve.

"My wife speaks very warmly of you, Mr. Barol." He gripped Piet's hand with a force that made many men wince. Piet did not wince. Maarten gestured for him to enter a handsomely proportioned room, papered in lemon yellow and cluttered with objects in silver, crystal, and gilt.

"You are a collector, sir."

"When I have the time. Sit down, if you please."

Piet sat on a chair made of dark wood, upholstered in pale blue and gold.

"That was made for the palace of Louis Napoleon, when he was king of Holland. This one is from the Palace of Fontainebleu." He sat down on it emphatically. "I enjoy fine furniture. But I'm also fond of china and porcelain and silver, anything that is made by hand and of rare quality. I value human endeavor, Mr. Barol, and the achievements our machine age cannot hope to emulate."

"We have something in common there, sir."

"Indeed?"

"I have less opportunity to pursue my interests, and of course I cannot buy. But I like to draw objects of beauty.

There are several fine collections in Leiden. I have spent many wet afternoons sketching them."

"You draw well?"

"Tolerably well, sir."

"Would you be kind enough to draw something for me? Something in here."

Maarten was a man who believed in putting the claims of other men to the test, and his wife's enthusiastic commendation of the handsome young chap before him made him rather wish to find fault with Piet Barol. He went to his desk and returned with a miniature silver model of a man on a tightrope, balancing precariously. "Eighteenth century Dutch. Let me get you some paper, Mr. Barol."

The detailing on the miniature was extremely fine. The way the man was about to fall off his rope, and yet never would, seemed to Piet to speak to his own situation. Indeed, it was precisely this quality that had persuaded Maarten Vermeulen-Sickerts to part with one hundred guilders for it twenty years before—when such a sum was meaningful to him. Like Piet he was accustomed to putting himself in dangerous situations and emerging from them unscathed. It was he, after all, who had seen the potential in his neighbor's barren farms, he who had sunk everything he had into purchasing the equipment to dig up their peat bogs, transport the fuel to Amsterdam, and refill them as lakes that froze in the winter. This had provided the raw material for his first fortune, built on selling ice around the world. Quite 30 percent of his first cargo had melted on its way across the Atlantic to the convenience-obsessed shores of the United States. Everyone had said he was a fool; that it would never work. And yet it *had* worked. Like the little silver man teetering on the silver rope, high above the silver plate that bore his weight, he had not fallen off.

Piet succeeded in capturing the miniature with such skill,

and so quickly, that Maarten was impressed despite himself. He did not show this but embarked instead on a detailed examination of Piet's history, which lasted longer than it would have done had his wife not already decided to hire him. But she had, and Maarten did not disagree with the women in his life if he could help it. Piet's was not the most distinguished record he had ever seen, but Egbert's last two tutors had been highly distinguished and had nevertheless failed utterly.

"My son needs to learn to leave the house without having hysterics."

"I understand that, sir."

"Very well. You have impressed my wife and I am prepared to retain you. Have you any questions?"

"I do, sir."

"What are they?"

The moment had come and Piet steeled himself to seize it. "They concern the remuneration." He spoke as though the subject were infinitely distasteful to him.

"Sixty guilders a month, Saturday afternoons and two Sundays off, free board and lodging, and two weeks' holiday."

"I am content with the other terms, Mr. Vermeulen-Sickerts. But I am afraid the salary prevents me from accepting the position."

"I beg your pardon?"

"My father is elderly and I wish to marry one day. I am not in a position to work for sixty guilders a month."

The effrontery of this astounded Maarten, but it also impressed him. He approved of people who valued themselves highly, provided they had valid grounds for doing so. "It is an excellent rate, Mr. Barol. You would be hard-pressed to equal it elsewhere."

"As a tutor, perhaps, sir. But I am young and have other opportunities."

"That pay more?"

"That could, in time, pay a great deal more." A trickle of sweat ran down the inside of Piet's left arm. He will not dismiss me now, he thought.

He was right.

Maarten hesitated, then said, "Very well, Mr. Barol. You drive a hard bargain, but that does not count against a man in my book. What sum do you propose?"

"A hundred, sir."

"One hundred guilders!"

"Yes, sir."

There was silence. Piet held it. Maarten thought of a similar incident in his own twenties when he had stubbornly refused seventeen offers for his ice, even as it lay melting in New York harbor. He was prepared to spend large sums on those he loved and had larger sums at his disposal than all but five or six men in Amsterdam. "Very well, Mr. Barol," he said, at last. "But I will expect the best of you, young man."

"You shall have it."

"I will not tolerate lateness or immorality. We keep an orderly, respectable, God-fearing establishment."

"Which is the position's chief attraction for me, sir."

While this exchange was taking place, Agneta Hemels took a perfect curl of blond human hair from a drawer lined in peach-colored velvet and went to pin it to Jacobina's head. "Up tonight or down, madam?" She asked the question as though its answer were a matter of grave concern to her.

Jacobina contemplated herself in the dressing table mirror and changed her mind. "Down, I think. Simple and young. The way Louisa had her hair for the de Jongs' last month."

Agneta's heart sank: Louisa's hairstyles, though simple in

effect, were far from simple to achieve. "Has madam found a tutor for Master Egbert?" She took the tortoiseshell comb and teased apart the strands for the first braid of the first plait.

"I suppose so."

"We all pray for his success." Agneta had learned that the easiest way to avoid an overfamiliar curiosity in her superiors' lives was to have no genuine interest in them whatsoever. This allowed her to remain composed, whatever she saw. "Was madam able to lunch between so many appointments?" Her tone was superbly solicitous.

Like Piet Barol, Agneta Hemels did not intend to work for the Vermeulen-Sickertses forever; like him, she wished for herself a comfortable life and was determined to get it. Their ambitions varied only in their scope. Agneta wanted to be a housekeeper with a large staff under her, somewhere out in the country, away from the stinks of Amsterdam, a place where others would bring her tea in her own private room and she would never have to rise before 6:00 a.m. unless the roof was burning.

"No time for lunch. I'm famished."

"Would madam like a little bouillon before dinner to keep her strength up?"

"No, no. Just attend to my hair." Jacobina was thinking about what she would wear. Her evening dresses suddenly seemed matronly. "Is the blue flowers on gold in a state to be seen?"

"All madam's dresses are kept ready, for whenever madam wishes them." Agneta was responsible, among many other things, for the maintenance of Jacobina's wardrobe. She was aware that the garment in question no longer fitted its owner. "Madam might be cold in that dress! What about the green velvet with the embroidered leaves? That's very becoming for winter."

But Jacobina had her mind set on the blue flowers.

"Of course, madam." Agneta finished Jacobina's hair, refusing to draw any connection between the arrival of a young man and her mistress' choice of a low-cut dress. She went into the dressing room next door and returned with a silk garment bag, from which she removed the gown Jacobina had asked for.

"You'd better bring a corset." Like her elder daughter, Constance, Jacobina Vermeulen-Sickerts was an enthusiastic champion of form-enhancing undergarments and had absolutely refused Louisa's request that they be banished from the house on grounds of health and female self-respect.

"Which one would madam like?" Ten years in service had taught Agneta Hemels that when the vanity of fine ladies is wounded, it is their servants who suffer. She did not wish to be responsible for selecting a corset that failed to squeeze Jacobina into the dress she had chosen.

"The blue one, with the red ribbons. It's the tightest, isn't it?"

"What a memory madam has." Agneta fetched it and took the silk dressing gown from Jacobina's shoulders, helped her into her drawers, knelt at her feet, rolled the stockings up her legs and fixed them to the garter belt. Then, making one last effort, she said, "Is madam sure she wouldn't prefer—"

"I'm wearing the blue flowers. Lace me up."

Agneta did her best. She was a delicately made woman in her early thirties with pale hair and freckles, not overly strong. She tugged as hard as she could while Jacobina blew all the air from her lungs; then she laced up her employer, hoping she wouldn't pass out, and arranged the dress on the floor. Jacobina stepped into it and succeeded in getting her arms through the correct holes, but only by bending almost double. The narrow waist required several violent tugs to fit over her thighs and there remained inches of corset visible between the back buttons, which would not fasten. Even Jacobina could see it was impossible. For a moment she was gripped by a wild fury, but with an effort of will she laughed off the attempt and gave Agneta the dress, which she never wanted to see again.

Agneta Hemels was not invited anywhere where the wearing of such a thing would be appropriate. Nevertheless, she knew precisely what she could get for the fabric if she sold it to a cushion maker and her gratitude was real enough.

"Perhaps I will wear the green velvet," said Jacobina, to silence her maid's effusiveness. "It is chilly tonight, after all."

Maarten led Piet to the dining room himself. The ladies had not yet come down and he used the interval before they did to tell Piet, at some length, about the objects it contained. The table was Georgian, bought at an auction in London; the chairs were Louis XVI, resprung and upholstered in olive green and white. The gilt salt cellars came from Hamburg, the clock on the mantelpiece from Geneva, the figures beside it from the Imperial Porcelain Factory in St. Petersburg. None of this detail was lost on Piet, who had a fine and instinctive appreciation of beauty. He showed this by judicious questioning that began to ease his employer's mistrust of good-looking young men.

The arrival of Constance Vermeulen-Sickerts was preceded by a clattering of high heels and a potent aroma of lilies of the valley. She was twenty-one years old, short and blond and confident, and her glance took in the cut of Piet's suit and the elegance of his shoes—his only pair, bought like everything else he owned from a cash-strapped undergraduate of means. She was a kindhearted person, though apt, like Louisa, to make snap judgments; and she felt rather sorry for Piet that her sister should have chosen the evening's menu with the aim of testing the new tutor's table manners. "Do sit down, Mr. Barol. We are not ceremonial in this house." She took a chair next to the fire as her mother and sister entered the room.

Louisa Vermeulen-Sickerts was dark and grave and looked older than her nineteen years. She was wrapped in a twist of pale gray muslin that made her mother's green velvet look fussy and uncomfortable. "Good evening," she said, with neutral friendliness.

Jacobina rang a bell, and Didier Loubat appeared, carrying a silver stand of oysters on crushed ice. They all sat down. Piet took in the handwritten menu in front of him, the four crystal vases of orange roses that decorated the table, the two silver dishes piled high with blood oranges on the sideboard, and felt wonderfully proud of himself. If Louisa had expected him to be confounded by the oysters or the langoustines or the quail *à la minute*, she was disappointed—because Nina Barol had foreseen just this eventuality and twice a year had served Piet the delicacies of her youth so that he might dine in sophisticated company one day, without shame.

They were waited on by Agneta Hemels and Hilde Wilken, who handed the dishes while Didier Loubat poured the wine and Mr. Blok carved the beef that followed the quail. Piet fielded the girls' questions about his life in Leiden truthfully but without revealing that indoor plumbing was a novelty for him. When he ate the pickled asparagus with his fingers, as he knew from his mother was proper, he detected a silent exchange between them and felt that he had passed a further test. He noticed that both girls were offered the Château Margaux and that they spoke to their parents without formality. Constance was the voluble one, but Louisa appeared to appreciate her talkativeness and not resent it. She laughed with everyone else at her sister's wicked account of a young man's tumble on the van Sproncks' ballroom floor the night before and only joined the talk when it turned to the guests' clothes.

"Louisa is in revolt against impractical female fashions," said Constance, "and abhors killing animals to embellish them. She intends to open a shop."

"She'll have crowned heads for clients one day, mark me." Maarten Vermeulen-Sickerts spoke in the genial tone of a man who applauds his child's spirited imaginings, without remotely believing in them. He loved having two rich daughters. Watching Constance and Louisa converse with Piet across the table, he felt enormously blessed. That two such soft young women, whose sole labor was to dance and dine with their friends; to wear pretty clothes and flirt and enjoy themselves; who spent money with such innocent disregard for its value and were capable of being moved to tears by something as insignificant as a rabbit skinned for its pelt; that they should be his; that they should live in this house that was his, with its distinctions and taste, its furniture and china and carpets and clocks and exquisitely trained staff, the best-paid servants on the Herengracht—all this was a source of deep satisfaction to him.

Such achievements might have led to the sin of pride, had it not been for Egbert. But as he looked at the young man who was now his tutor, who asked such intelligent questions and whose manners were commendably amiable and discreet, he began to feel optimistic about his son's chances. Surely he must look up to a fellow like this, he thought; and he felt a twinge of relief that responsibility for Egbert's developing masculinity was no longer his alone.

They took coffee in the private salon on the first floor. It was a cozy room with a piano and piles of illustrated magazines and an Aubusson carpet that caught the colors of the ceiling, which showed heaven glimpsed through parted clouds.

"Jacob de Wit. *Dawn Banishing the Figures of Night,*" said Maarten, when Piet admired it. He had bought the canvas three years before and paid a fair price although its owners were bankrupt and would have settled for less. He had altered the whole room to accommodate it. "Rather fine, don't you think?"

"Very fine, sir."

Constance and Louisa sat together on a cushioned daybed between the bookcases. Once Hilde Wilken had handed round the petit fours and deposited the tray of Meissen cups and steaming pots before Jacobina, Constance said, with a note of friendly challenge in her voice, "Entertain us, Mr. Barol."

Piet could play bridge and discuss with authority the paintings of several "Living Masters." He read very well, with a deep sonorous voice equally suited to Scripture and fiction. He also had a number of well-turned anecdotes, refined by repetition; such a range, in fact, that the introduction of one to the general conversation rarely seemed forced. Tonight he sensed instinctively that music was required, not words. With a little bow he rose and went to the piano.

Nina Barol had taught Piet not only to accompany her students but to sing with them, too. As a little boy he had taken the soprano role in duets with aspiring tenors and when his voice broke had continued to sing these parts in a sweet falsetto. This facility had developed into a party trick of proven impact. Piet knew that the spectacle of a man like him singing in the high, true voice of a boy was alluring, that it delighted women and pacified the competitive instincts of other men. He sat down on the piano stool and told the touching anecdote of how his adored mother, now dead, had taught him to sing the female parts of the great operas.

"Why don't you give us something from *Carmen*, Mr. Barol?" said Jacobina, hardly looking up from her embroidery.

"Oh do!" cried Constance. "I adore Bizet."

Nina Barol had seen the premiere of *Carmen* and been conquered for life. She had sung Piet to sleep after child-hood nightmares with Micaëla's song of a mother who loves her child and sends him money and forgiveness and a kiss. But it was not maternal affection the situation called for. Piet looked at his new employer, beaming by the fire-place as Didier Loubat poured him a brandy, and felt a pulse of thrilling, compulsive guilt. He liked Mr. Vermeulen-Sickerts. He felt instinctively that they could be friends, but the inspiration sparked by Jacobina's sly suggestion was too brilliant to ignore.

He sat down at the piano, paused once to pacify his con-science, and began the aria Carmen sings to Don José, in which she promises to take him carousing on the ramparts of Seville if he risks prison for her sake. "Yes, but it's dull to be alone," he sang, devilishly. "True pleasure requires a pair."

Didier Loubat replaced the decanter of brandy on the cocktail tray and stood silently by the door, his face abso-lutely expressionless. Hilde Wilken took an empty coffee cup from Constance's hand and curtsied. She looked at Didier, whom she loved desperately; to whom she had ren-dered her carefully preserved virginity. She did not speak French and did not understand the words Piet sang. But she caught the erotic charge of the music and when Didier did not return her glance, as he so easily might have done, she knew suddenly that he did not love her back; that he was bored of her. It was a certainty that had been creeping up on her, stealthily, for some time. As it sunk its claws into her back she thought she might faint. Instead she picked up the tray and left the room, digging her nails into the flesh of her palms to guard against tears.

On the other side of the door, Piet was singing, "My poor heart, so easily consoled, my heart is as free as the air." He was giving it beautifully and he knew it. "I have admirers by the dozen, but none of them are to my taste."

It was a devastating choice, because the words gave form to feelings within Jacobina of which she had been quite unaware even six hours before. Her heart *was* poor and worthy of consolation. She longed to feel as free as air. She thought of the dozens of suitors who had adorned her youth and glanced at her husband. Then she looked at Piet, a young *galent* entirely to her taste; and though she knew that she should be ashamed of herself for inviting this peacock into her nest, in fact she felt as though life had taken an exciting turn.

Maarten coughed. The sound brought echoes of his snoring and reminded her that he had done no more than kiss her—and that all too rarely—since Egbert's birth. For ten years she had submitted to this denial of affection and after one explicit rejection on the night of their eighteenth wedding anniversary had not again sought to arouse her husband's interest. What Jacobina Vermeulen-Sickerts did not know was that Maarten had woken on many nights to find himself stiff with dreaming of her and feasted his eyes on her warm body beside him. It was not because he did not wish to touch his wife that he did not touch her.

It was because of a promise he had made to God.

Maarten Vermeulen was twelve years old when he found in the ruins of a burnt-out farmhouse a charred section of beam in the shape of a cross and took this as divine confirmation of that morning's sermon. It was a winter's day of uncompromising harshness and the flames of hell had been vividly evoked by the charismatic young vicar of the Johanneskerk. This gentleman had read every word John Calvin ever wrote and had no time for spineless modernists who softened his teachings. Walking home from church, Maarten said nothing to his parents; but as soon as they had eaten he set out across the dunes of Drenthe to look for a sign.

He was at first reluctant to believe that God had decided, long before his birth, whether he was to be saved or damned; but the burned beam convinced him that the vicar was right. God *had* decided. Moreover, His decision was final and irrevocable. This begged the further question: what was the Almighty's judgment in his, Maarten Vermeulen's, specific case? When he pressed for an answer the following Sunday he was informed that such mysteries are not revealed before the End but that clues might be deduced from his behavior through life.

From that day, the question of whether or not he was predestined for salvation consumed a significant portion of Maarten's time and energies, and though he searched for a sign and detected many, none was ever as unequivocal as the charred cross he had found.

His career and the good works he went to great lengths to perform gave him some cause for comfort—as did the delectable Jacobina Sickerts' decision to marry him, though she had grander suitors. God had smiled on his idea of transporting ice great distances to slow the decay of perishable food. The fledgling concern had often come close to failure, but each time God had intervened and rescued it. Once he was reliably prosperous, Maarten had given 12 percent of his profits away each year: 20 percent more than the Bible instructed. He hoped his generosity was a sign that he was destined for heaven, but to make sure he went further than passive philanthropy. He threw his considerable energies into improving the lot of the less fortunate. He built bread factories and founded societies for land reclamation. He extended the city beyond the Singelgracht and built safe, watertight houses for the poor. He gave his workers a week's annual holiday and paid for their care when they fell sick and was rewarded by God with two healthy girls—but no son. When he still had no male heir after fifteen years of marriage he began to take this as evidence of heavenly disfavor, and when Jacobina fell pregnant for the third time he fasted for three days and made a bargain with God.

If the child were a boy, he would abstain forever from the pleasures of the flesh.

The child was a boy, and for a time Maarten felt serenely secure. But he was soon punished for this presumption. His boy did not behave as other boys did. Egbert did not like to run and play. As he grew bigger he slipped further into a world others could not see. When he began to refuse to venture beyond the house, Maarten took this to mean that the future of his own soul hung in the balance. He continued to fight against his sexual desires, with no thought for the impact his self-restraint would have on his wife. But though his business prospered greatly, his heir's behavior grew more, not less, odd; and sometimes he woke in the night from lurid dreams of hell and its eternal fires.

In many respects Maarten Vermeulen-Sickerts was a rational man, but the doctrine of predestination, once absorbed, proved impossible to shake; and because he shared his fears with no one, he was compelled to face them alone. Piet's polished performance, superior in every way to the embarrassed awkwardness of Egbert's previous tutors, was deeply reassuring. After the party had broken up and he had said his prayers, he went to sleep feeling calmer than he had in years.

Piet took off his tie and began to unbutton his shirt, standing in front of the mirror in his comfortable new bedroom. He felt giddy with relief.

There was a knock at the door. Didier Loubat put his head round it. "Did you survive?"

"I think so."

"You did much better than the last man at his first dinner. It's important not to cross the girls. D'you want a drink?"

"I thought it wasn't allowed."

"Blok's in bed, and the witch doesn't come up here after lights out. I've got Chartreuse."

"I'm in, then." Piet spoke nonchalantly, but in fact he had never tasted Chartreuse and was eager to try it.

"I'll get it. I suppose you'll need nightclothes, too."

Didier disappeared and returned with two chipped tumblers and a bottle containing five inches of emerald liquid. He had taken his tie off and opened two buttons on his shirt. "Borrow these till yours arrive." He handed Piet a pair of blue-and-white-striped pajamas, sat on the edge of the bed and poured the drinks. "I'm glad you've come. The last few tutors have been stuck up beyond belief."

Though Didier Loubat was a footman, he was a good footman and did not consider himself beneath anyone else who earned an honest wage. When he saw that there was no condescension in Piet's manner, he decided to reward the beauty of his face by giving him the benefit of an insider's experience. "You'll enjoy yourself here if you're sensible." He handed Piet his cup. "It's much the best house in Amsterdam and the family's all right once you know how to handle them. The one to watch out for is Constance. She expects every man to fall in love with her." He raised his glass in a silent toast. "But you mustn't. If Vermeulen catches you with one of his daughters you'll finish at the bottom of the Herengracht with lead weights tied to your balls."

"I'll remember that."

"Gents as handsome as us need to be wary, that's all." Didier made this observation without embarrassment. He had a lean, athletic frame, high cheekbones and a seductively crooked smile. The simmering arousal of Piet's interview with Jacobina remained and he wondered briefly whether Didier might help him relieve it. *No.* He was in the great city now. It was time to put away the habits of boyhood. He drained his glass in one manly swig and coughed.

Didier looked horrified. "That's last year's bonus. Treat it politely or you'll miss it." He poured Piet another inch. Consumed sparingly, the Chartreuse was delicious. Didier smiled to show that he did not judge Piet for his lack of experience with exotic liqueurs.

Piet was touched by this and relieved to have made an error so early on in their acquaintance. It removed the necessity of feigning sophistication. "What about Louisa?" he asked.

"Never says a word, but she's sharp as a dagger. Nothing escapes her."

"Do the sisters get on?"

"They adore each other. But if they decide you're affected or stupid, beware. Don't let their politeness fool you. They're vicious when they choose."

"How so?"

"They like to humiliate people—but subtly, so their target never knows. Lately they've taken to leading their victim through a conversation in alphabetical order. Very funny when the poor fool doesn't catch on."

They talked for an hour with great amiability and Piet

learned that Didier was the son of a Swiss chauffeur at Maarten Vermeulen-Sickerts' Amstel Hotel; that he had been a page there before Mr. Blok spotted him and promoted him to the house. "He got me a uniform with trousers so tight I could barely breathe when I first came. I had to get my mother to make me a new pair, for modesty's sake." Didier related the story of his seduction of Hilde and ended with the declaration that he and Piet should stick together in this swamp of sexual predators. It was a joke, of course, and both men laughed. "Careful!" Didier put his finger to his lips. "You don't want Blok to know we're awake or he'll join us. When I first arrived he used to come into my room, hoping to find me undressed. He'll do the same to you."

"Was he ever successful?"

"Once or twice before I learned."

"What about the other servants?"

"Naomi de Leeuw's a bitch, but she's a bloody good housekeeper. This place is run like the best hotel in Europe. The attic floor's raised so the family doesn't get woken when one of us lesser mortals goes for a piss in the night. *You* get the royal treatment too when you're with them."

"I'm looking forward to it."

Didier rose and bowed. " 'Bow, eye contact, smile, action, bow.' " He caught the housekeeper's joyless intonation perfectly. "You'll feel like the czar of bloody Russia. When I do it, remember it's *my* Chartreuse we were drinking up here tonight."

"I'm grateful, believe me."

"Don't be. It's a relief to have someone to talk to. The other tutors were hopeless, the chef never speaks to anyone, and otherwise there's only Blok."

"Who's in charge, him or Mrs. de Leeuw?"

"He's meant to be, but she really is. Keeps everyone *very*

firmly in line, and if you annoy her she'll find a way to have you dismissed. She loves Agneta Hemels and for some reason she puts up with Hilde. I think it's because she knows she can break her completely and rebuild her in her own image."

This intelligence was useful to Piet, who knew from watching certain undergraduates handle his father that getting on with petty tyrants is the key to a happy life. "What's the secret to Mrs. de Leeuw?"

"Keep very clean. Be prompt. Don't put on airs. She doesn't like it when tutors forget themselves and start behaving as if they aren't servants too."

"Cleanliness, punctuality, humility."

"Exactly. A little hard to do on two baths a week, but you can share my water if you want. In fact"—Didier grinned—"if we share each other's water we can both bathe every second day."

The prospect of bathing twice a week had until now seemed to Piet the height of luxe, but he was happy to raise his standards further. "Is there a lot of hot water?"

"Enough for one deep bath a night. Blok has Tuesdays, Fridays and Saturdays. We can split the others. You'll find a good bath a blessing after a day of tireless servility. It'll keep you in with Mrs. de Leeuw too."

"I'm game, then." Piet smiled. "Tell me about Egbert."

"You haven't met him? The strangest little boy I ever knew in my life. He used to drive us mad when he played the piano in this house. Same tune a hundred times over—I don't exaggerate. And this fear of going outside. It's not the kind of phobia poor children suffer from."

"I'm supposed to cure him of all that."

"Good luck to you. Many have fallen in the attempt." Didier shared the last of the Chartreuse between them.

"If Louisa never speaks in public, how do you know she and Constance gossip? Surely you don't listen at doors?"

"Certainly not. That's the sort of thing you get away with in other houses. Not here."

"How do you know then?"

"I'll show you. Come with me, but don't say a word or you'll wake Blok."

Didier opened the door and led Piet out into the darkened corridor. Gert Blok was dozing and heard the floorboards creak. He was instantly wide awake. One of the young men was going to the bathroom. Perhaps he should go too and stumble against him in the dark as if half asleep? But he hesitated too long and a door closed. It was the door to Didier's room, which was half the size of Piet's and much more plainly furnished.

Didier drew Piet towards the window. "Louisa's bedroom's just beneath mine. She smokes on her balcony because her parents wouldn't approve. When the door's open you can hear every word she and Constance are saying. That's how I know she's an atheist." He put his arm around Piet's shoulders. "They're probably talking about you tonight. Are you man enough to listen?"

The temptation to know precisely the impression he had made on two girls he so badly wished to charm was irresistible. Piet opened the window as quietly as possible. It was a narrow window and in order to get through it he had to lean across Didier, his shoulder resting against his new friend's back. They listened. The lights in the room below were on and they caught Constance in midsentence. ". . . most beautiful hands I've ever seen. And his manners are a vast improvement on the last one's."

"He's not as handsome as all that." Louisa spoke in the same noncommittal tone she had used to Piet at dinner.

"His mouth's too big for his face and there's something odd about his nose. We're just starved of men, sweet Constance. Our standards are slipping by the hour. Besides—"

But now she moved away, and the words were lost.

"She's unforgiving with everyone," whispered Didier, breathing warm, mint-scented breath against Piet's cheek.

The girls came back to the window. Both were laughing; but then Louisa said, in a much more serious voice: "There's something fishy about this Mr. Barol, Constance. Something false. You can see he has an astoundingly high opinion of himself."

"Well so do I, of myself," said Constance.

"Yes, but you're more straightforward than he is. I don't trust him. As I said: he's fishy."

It was a terrible end to a day of otherwise unblemished triumph for Piet. He pulled back into the room and smiled to suggest that he took all this in his stride. In fact he was deeply wounded.

"Don't worry." Didier squeezed his shoulder. "There's something fishy about me too."

Egbert Vermeulen-Sickerts woke the next morning a little after four o'clock while even Hilde Wilken—whose job it was to prepare the family's breakfast trays—was still fast asleep. He was a small child, with a high red complexion and very pale blond hair. The night before, lured by the sounds of merriment and music coming from the drawing room, he had forgotten the sore throat he had spent all day complaining of and crept to its open door. Through the hinges he had seen the man who was to be his new tutor. He was desperate not to embarrass himself before such an enviable figure.

He sat up and put his right foot onto the carpet, then his left, then he withdrew them both and repeated the proce-

dure six times. He went into his little bathroom and ran an
ice-cold bath, which he submerged himself in seven times.
He brushed his teeth seven times, until the iron taste of
blood filled his mouth, then, aware of passing time, he got
dressed. By a great effort of will—the kind only the fear
of shame can inspire—he disobeyed the impulse to get
undressed and dressed again a further six times. Spurred
by this small but meaningful achievement, he opened his
bedroom door.

The house was silent and dark. He preferred to move
through it unobserved, in case he should make an error that
required correction. This morning he was unusually alert
and made no mistakes. He went down the stairs, treading
with equal weight on a blessedly even number of red steps.
The marble floor of his own entrance hall, with its chaotic darts of black on gray, could be a violent sea; but this
morning it was calm and he crossed it with ease. He went
through the dining room and opened the door cut into the
wall. The grandfather clock struck the hour. It was five a.m.

Egbert never knew how the Number came to him. He
did not choose it. He had no idea Who was responsible for
its emphatic selection, but every morning as the door to
his great-aunt's house closed behind him, he heard it loud
and clear. This morning it was 495. He was relieved. On
days when it was above 1,200, he could not get to his piano
before lunch. Sometimes he was not able to reach it at all.
On these days he had to plead illness and return to bed. But
495 was manageable in three hours, even if he stumbled.

The forces to which Egbert Vermeulen-Sickerts paid his
obeisance every day were expressed in the tangible world
chiefly through the colors white and black, though they
lived in shades of light and darkness too. He called them
the Shadowers and they hated one another hysterically. If he
did not divide his attention equally between them, a vicious

mob-whispering broke out in his head and pronounced terrible punishments.

The Number governed the number of steps in the abasement he was obliged to perform each morning. The precise order of the colors derived from long memorized runs in the preludes and fugues of J. S. Bach, as played on his great-aunt's piano. They found literal expression in the black and white tiles of her entrance hall floor.

Egbert stepped across the tiles, swiftly touching four white ones in succession, then a black one, then another six whites. He moved rhythmically, backwards and forwards, up and down the entrance hall, his face tense with concentration. He heard the clock chime the quarter hour, then the half hour; then it was six a.m., and he heard unmistakable sounds of life coming from his own house.

On the 211th element of the sequence, he misjudged a leap and grazed a black tile when he had been aiming for a white one. Sweat broke out on his forehead. His mother had told him that Mr. Barol would be down at eight, and now he'd have to start all over again. He did so. This time he got to the 420th without error, but again he made a mistake and had to start at the beginning. By seven-thirty he was exhausted, going slowly for fear of a final error from which there would be no time to recover, but by a quarter to eight he had only reached the 193rd tile and was beginning to despair. A crazy recklessness seized him. He did not want to spend the day in bed, feigning illness, and couldn't possibly be found by his new tutor in this compromising position.

Like his father, Egbert was deeply private about his interior afflictions. He had never told anyone of the tyranny of the Shadowers and did his best to disguise his state of bondage from those who loved him. The infinite shades of light on the leafy street outside were so daunting, the possibility of navigating them so slim, that he had found it easier to face his father's wrath than rise up against his oppressors. He began to go faster and faster. Sometimes he spent all day like this. Sometimes he made seven mistakes: the maximum permitted, which required the taking of seven ice-cold baths in expiation. He had reached the middle of the volume of preludes and fugues when he heard voices in the dining room. His father had come down to breakfast. He was now trapped. Retreat was impossible until Maarten left for work, because he would neither credit nor sanction a convenient fever or sore throat. And by the time his papa had left, Mr. Barol would have found him.

Egbert began to dart across the tiles in a frenzy, faint with hunger and commitment. Fortune was smiling on him and detained Piet for several minutes with his employer in the breakfast room. He heard Mr. Barol's rich warm laugh and continued his leaping, ending the sequence on a white tile by the drawing room door. He went through it, panting, and threw himself into the final stage of his odyssey.

Piet Barol had not slept well. He was furious that Louisa Vermeulen-Sickerts should have seen through him, and said so for Didier Loubat to hear. As he washed his face he felt inclined to hate her. But it was the refuge of lesser men to hate and he refused to stoop to it. He resolved instead, as he knotted his tie, to make Louisa like him in spite of herself. *That* was the worthy challenge. But before it could be attempted there was the question of his new pupil, on whom a first impression remained to be made.

He heard Egbert as soon as he opened the door in the dining room wall. The boy was playing Bach with maniacal precision, and Piet stood in the entrance hall listening with admiration. It was clear that Egbert was already a far better pianist than Piet would ever be; there was nothing he could teach him on that score. He wished that Jacobina or Maarten were present to introduce them, but Maarten had instructed him to present himself alone. Piet hesitated. He did not much like Bach, and the boy's relentless repetition of the prelude did not inspire any new affection. He listened a few moments longer, then knocked at the drawing room door and opened it with his friendliest smile.

Egbert was at the piano, with his back to him. Piet coughed. Egbert did not stop or turn around: he was on his fifth repetition, and if he did not complete two more the strenuous efforts of the morning would be wasted.

"Good morning," said Piet. But still he was ignored. The music rattled on and on, came to an end and began again. Piet was nonplussed. His strategy, in so far as he had one, involved gaining his new pupil's trust and regard. He did not wish to begin their acquaintance with an undignified tussle for attention. At some point he will have to stop, he thought. And indeed, a few minutes later, Egbert did stop.

"Good morning," said Piet for the second time, "and bravo."

"Good morning, sir."

There was a table by the window. Egbert took his place at it with the slow indifference of an experienced criminal who intends to give nothing away under interrogation. He could not manufacture his sister Constance's warmth and unlike Louisa, who was also naturally taciturn, he had no boisterous sibling to shelter behind. He wished desperately to impress Mr. Barol, but the fear of not doing so made him behave with an hauteur learned from his elders, which was deeply unattractive in a ten-year-old boy who will one day be the possessor of a large fortune.

"We'll start with French grammar," said Piet, rather coldly. "Are you familiar with the subjunctive mood?"

"Yes, sir."

"Decline, then, if you please, the present, future and imperfect subjunctive forms of *avoir*."

Egbert did so, faultlessly. He also translated that morning's leader in the *Algemeen Handelsblad* into accurate, idiomatic French; and then into German of lesser but acceptable quality. They moved from this to still-life drawing, and here there was something Piet could teach him, for Egbert failed utterly to capture the supplications of a vase of tulips in the last stages of their glory. They worked for an hour or more on this challenge; then Piet said, with careful nonchalance, "It's very hot in here. Why don't we go outside and find another subject?"

But a stiffening of Egbert's posture and a stubborn glazing of his expression told Piet he was alive to such simple tricks. Piet's head was feeling delicate and he did not press the point. He rang for coffee. An urn of water was kept permanently at boiling point in the kitchen of Herengracht 605 and four minutes later Hilde Wilken knocked at the door and bowed, caught Piet's eye, and smiled and poured and bowed again—just as Didier had said she would. The impact was marvelous. He set Egbert one of Pliny's most rambling letters to translate into Dutch and removed himself to a comfortable armchair with the papers. The room was a trifle gaudy but there were worse places to spend a morning. As Egbert worked, Piet's good spirits reasserted themselves.

No one expected an immediate miracle. His charge was willful, certainly, but he moved from task to task without rebellion. It would not be so very hard to keep him occupied. And while Egbert was occupied, he, Piet Barol, could enjoy a handsome salary and the freedoms of the best-run domestic establishment in Amsterdam. It struck him as a very pretty bargain, and with the contentment it inspired came a whisper of inspiration. He would confound Egbert's expectations. He would never again suggest he leave the house. Forcing the child would not work; only the passage of time, and the avoidance of confrontation, might win his trust. It seemed an agreeable solution for them both, and when Egbert had finished Piet checked his translation and set him another and returned to the newspaper feeling rather jolly.

Piet Barol's first three months at Herengracht 605 passed swiftly, and in the main to his great satisfaction, because it was true what Didier had said: Maarten Vermeulen-Sickerts ran his house like the grandest of his hotels *du grand luxe*; and though time passed, the novelty of living in it did not fade for Piet Barol. Rather the reverse. He had a natural capacity for sensuous enjoyment, and no matter how often he sank into clean, pressed sheets at night, or emerged from a steaming bath to swap places with Didier Loubat, or ate *suprême de foie gras* from Meissen china, he savored each repetition to the full.

Sometimes he thought of the life he had left behind: the damp alcove in which he had slept, not six feet from his father's snoring head; the meals conducted in sullen silence; the claustrophobic impossibility of change or optimism that clung to Herman Barol like a stubborn mist. In the Vermeulen-Sickerts' household these recollections took on the quality of a fading nightmare.

Nina Barol had much regretted her impulsive decision to marry her handsome, taciturn second cousin, and for much of Piet's life she had not troubled herself to hide this regret. Having taught music to many fashionable people in Paris, she had learned the ways of the great world and taken care that her son should know them too. Her photograph, smiling from its leather frame beside his bed, offered him daily encouragement and reminded him of her maxims. Never lose your temper. Never appear to try too hard. Learn all you can.

The service at Herengracht 605 was prompt, lavish and invisible. Nothing that passed the lips of Maarten's family or his guests was purchased ready-made. A chef who had trained under Monsieur Escoffier in Paris oversaw the kitchen and produced meals of a quality that made Piet dread the necessity of having, ever again, to eat something made by anyone else. The family's bed linen was changed daily and sent to be dried in the fresh-smelling fields beyond the city's limits. Their clothes were cared for like works of art. And because Mr. Vermeulen-Sickerts deplored idleness and believed in the capacity of well-trained individuals of personal merit, all this was achieved by an indoor staff of only five servants. The chef, Monsieur la Chaume, was so well paid that he was able to keep his own house on the Egelantiersgracht.

The light chiming of the long case clock set the tempo and under orders from the magnificently efficient Mrs. de Leeuw, Didier Loubat, Agneta Hemels and Hilde Wilken laid and carried and cleared, polished and swept, bowed, smiled and poured in strict fidelity to its sweet tollings. To be served by one of them was to feel that one was at the center of a benignly ordered universe, and though Piet took care to avoid giving offense by asking for things on his own account (except, on occasion, from Hilde) he was so often with the family that he partook of their luxuries without giving the other servants any cause for resentment.

In this way, Piet was able to observe in detail the behavior of the very rich. In their steam-filled bathroom late at night, waiting to exchange places in the cooling tub, he and Didier discussed their observations with much hilarity; but while

Didier was often scornful of the family he served, Piet found something noble in their excesses. He did not judge them, because he intended to emulate them one day if he could.

As the winter faded, the house slowly surrendered its secrets. Piet became familiar with the large and small drawing rooms, the walnut-paneled library with its fine edition of the *Sertum Botanicum*; the parquet-floored ballroom; the stores of china and silver in the basement; and in his hours off he made drawings of the beautiful things he found in these beautiful rooms. He appreciated his surroundings with a wholeheartedness that was very flattering to Maarten Vermeulen-Sickerts, who had chosen all they contained. Only the bedrooms remained mysterious, and he sometimes watched Hilde returning from one, breakfast tray in hand, with an itching curiosity he knew he could never satisfy.

In the privacy of his cozy room, in the pleasant half hour before slipping between country-scented sheets, Piet congratulated himself on the expertise with which he had so far navigated the complexities of the household. It had helped, undoubtedly, to begin on favorable terms with the mistress of the house; but once he had negotiated his salary and received a substantial advance on it, he had not rushed to renew lingering eye contact with his master's wife. He knew that his reticence might cause Jacobina offense and permitted himself, occasionally, to convey to her in a glance that the effort required to resist her was monumental. Otherwise he treated her with superbly appropriate deference, and she never gave any hint of expecting anything more.

This was a relief, though sometimes he found himself thinking of her as he fell asleep and getting hard at the thought of subverting her morals. He put these ideas aside in daylight hours and was punctual and humble and amusing. He played the piano after dinner and avoided *Carmen* and retained everything Maarten told him about the objects in his collection and never once suggested that Egbert go outside. He was wise enough to treat Naomi de Leeuw and Gert Blok with the same *politesse* he accorded their employers, and in time this led to many small advantages: fresh flowers in his room; a daily newspaper of his own; the gift of certain suits and shirts, perfectly stored, that no longer fit his employer.

Agneta Hemels remained an enigma, but was not sufficiently corruptible to labor on unduly; and he handled Hilde Wilken, who was jealous of his intimacy with Didier, with a gentle disdain which reminded her that she was in no position to make life difficult for him.

Piet's greatest challenge in his first few months, just as Didier had predicted, was Constance Vermeulen-Sickerts, who was accustomed to being desired by young men and saw no reason why Piet Barol should be exempt from the general rule. She was shorter than her sister, radiantly blond, high spirited and popular, with (as Hilde told Didier, who told Piet) thick ankles she went to great lengths to keep secret.

Like her father, Constance was instinctively competitive and had devoted much effort to acquiring the power she wielded over her contemporaries. Her methods relied on the magnetism of her person and the impact she could make with it when she chose. Though she complained of living in a backwater, in fact Amsterdam's size suited Constance— because it is easier to rule unchallenged over a duchy than an empire. Her world was the city; her stage the salons and ballrooms of its canal houses; her subjects the privileged children who had been the playmates of her youth. Like Piet, she had developed over time a highly artificial naturalness that failed to charm only the least susceptible and allowed her to triumph through seduction rather than violence. Many women, despite themselves, formed intense friendships with Constance, for she was loyal and sympathetic and listened with attention. Those who did not feared her, and were wise to do so.

It was rare for a rival to challenge Constance directly. When one did they discovered that Louisa Vermeulen-Sickerts, generally so silent, was capable of devastating sarcasm and quite prepared to unleash it on her sister's behalf. Louisa's maxim was: "Those who laugh are always right." She was very good at ensuring that people laughed with the sisters, not against them.

Men grew sleepless and erratic over Constance, and she had already (so the newspapers said) received and rejected eighteen offers of marriage, as against three for the glacial Louisa. This discrepancy made no difference to the girls' friendship, which was devoted and tender. This was partly because Louisa discouraged all suitors, finding none to her taste, while her sister took satisfaction from quantity as well as quality.

Constance kept her paramours in the state of consuming desire that cannot long survive its fulfillment. She had no inclination to give up her sister's company and the freedoms of life beneath her parents' roof; and because Louisa felt the same, neither of them had ever seriously considered becoming any man's wife. The girls were unforgiving in the matter of masculine failings, and Constance in particular derived a cruel, self-regarding pleasure from observing how much young men minded when she dropped them.

Maarten Vermeulen-Sickerts knew that his girls—unlike the lesser daughters of lesser men—would remain highly eligible late into their twenties and was delighted to keep them at home as long as he could. He was amused by Constance's artifice, because beneath it she was warm and funny and family minded—as Piet learned from listening to the sisters through Didier Loubat's window.

Only with Louisa was Constance wholly herself, and this was partly because Louisa abhorred contrivance of any sort. In private, the listening young men half felt that Louisa was the dominant sister, which would not at all have been the verdict of someone who encountered the girls in public. On her balcony after dinner, Louisa dissected Constance's vanities so savagely that Constance screamed with laughter and threatened to wet herself.

Louisa was the schemer, the silent observer, the strategist behind the maintenance of Constance's position at the apex of the little world that was all she knew, or cared to know. Louisa designed Constance's clothes, adamantly refusing her requests for frills, stays and unnecessary adornments. She decided the set of her hair, forced her to brave the sun in August, and took charge of her care during the occasional bouts of hysterical darkness, succeeded by lethargy, that punctuated the shiny ebullience of her daily performances. Louisa teased her sister for toying with men but deftly assisted her in heightening their agonies. She relayed messages, engineered encounters, and betrayed confidences with amusing precision. She did not approve of Constance's efforts to ensnare their brother's tutor, and said so, and poked merciless fun at her sister's failure to provoke any response whatsoever from Piet.

"I tell you, he's a uranist," said Constance one evening, having leaned heavily on Piet's arm after dinner and received no answering pressure.

"Nonsense. He's just too ambitious to risk everything by entangling himself with a wildcat like you. He knows you could never marry. What does he have to gain?"

"My person," replied Constance, with dignity.

"You'd never give yourself to him in that way."

"Some girls do."

"Not you, my dear."

Constance knew that this was true but was nevertheless irked by Piet's relentless indifference to her charms. She decided that if he were not a uranist, he must fear rejection. She would have to make plain that his overtures would be well received and enlisted her sister's help—because she was beguiled by the quiet arrogance with which he wore her father's old clothes.

Louisa agreed to participate in the enterprise on the condition that its verdict was regarded as final. The sisters settled terms during a walk through the Vondelpark, to which neither Piet nor Didier was privy, and set their minds to the most advantageous way of getting Constance what she wanted. Constance understood that smiles and ravishing gestures were insufficient and secretly respected Piet for being so much more self-controlled than other men she knew. The thought of making a private declaration entered her head, but she dispatched it at once as far too rife with humiliating possibilities. How might she combine the advantages of directness with the imperatives of discretion? Louisa could not, on this occasion, act as go-between.

She was in her room, undressing and thinking of Piet's first night in the house, when the answer came to her, and she went through the connecting door to her sister's bedroom with only a silk kimono over her shoulders.

"It's not a bad idea," said Louisa, "but you'd better not do it when Papa's here."

So they waited until their father went to Paris, as he did every six weeks to inspect his hotels in that city, and after dinner they asked Mr. Barol to teach them about opera and opened the score of *Carmen* at her exchange with Le Dançaire.

Jacobina was by the fire, her embroidery in her lap. Louisa positioned herself to obscure the expression on her sister's face, should their mother happen to glance up. Then, taking the man's part, she began to read from the libretto and asked Constance why she so liked Don José.

"Parce qu'il est beau, et qu'il me plaît," said Constance, straight to Piet. Then in English, for emphasis: "Because he's handsome. Because he pleases me."

Piet Barol was aware of the dangers of even an innocent flirtation with his employer's daughters and had no intention of making this elemental mistake. He was also alive to the advantages of being seen to show impeccable restraint. Maarten would naturally be vigilant of Constance and Louisa. Good behavior with them would earn his trust more swiftly than other, more effortful stratagems.

Piet did not need Didier to tell him that Constance delighted in generating, and then spurning, male attention. In fact his vanity would have been injured had she made no attempt to seduce him. But what began as flattering and amusing became alarming as Constance's steeliness showed itself, and with it her absolute determination to prevail over those who resisted her.

In this determination, Constance Vermeulen-Sickerts and Piet Barol were well matched. As Constance's assaults on his equanimity became more adamant, Piet was able to decode her tactics with an expert's eye. She began, as he would have done, by subtle but significant increments in physical contact. She often took his arm on her way into and out of dinner, and occasionally her fingers touched his as they parted. He understood these fleeting invitations for what they were, but pretended not to notice them—with the result that Constance's dresses became a little more revealing and her conversation, when they met, significantly more animated.

She was a gifted storyteller, with the confidence to show herself at a disadvantage, and her tales of misadventures among the city's gilded youth were deft and funny.

Piet liked her enormously. For a time he hoped that her flirtatious interest would subside into friendship, but as the weeks passed he began to feel that a battle of wills was developing and that Constance would not rest until she had won it. This made her seem a little ridiculous and greatly eased the effort it cost to resist her. But he started to worry that Maarten would notice and act preemptively to avoid disaster by removing him from the house. This would have been so damaging to his plans that he began to wonder, just as Constance did, whether there might be some way to broach the topic euphemistically, but unequivocally, and lay it to rest.

"Only a fool would do that," said Didier. He was sitting on the radiator in the attic bathroom, in his dressing gown, while Piet lay submerged to his neck in the water Didier had just vacated. "You can't let her know that you know she's keen on you. Especially if you're going to reject her."

"But I can't let it go on this way forever. If her father suspects—"

"Suspicion's one thing. If you *say* anything, it'll go badly wrong."

Piet agreed with his friend, so he continued to feign obliviousness as Constance's attentions became more frequent and less subtle. When, one day, she fainted at tea and compelled him to lift her in his arms and deposit her on the sofa, a new and horrifying possibility occurred to him: that she might make an overt declaration that necessitated a plain response. What could he possibly say that would close forever the possibility of a liaison while sparing her the kind of embarrassment that so often demands vengeance? He did not wish to be her enemy. As the danger increased he began to prepare a little speech on the subject of his religious scruples, which would not permit him, etc. etc. But in the event this was not necessary, for two days later, as Didier Loubat and Hilde Wilken served the coffee and petits fours, Constance put him on the spot in a public yet deniable manner that demanded respect.

His first thought, as she told him he was handsome and that he pleased her, was relief that her father was not there to observe the interaction; but this was followed by the certainty that, if he did not make himself clear to her now, he might not have the opportunity to do so again without Maarten present. "Would you like to sing?" he asked, playing for time.

"I'd enjoy it much more if you would," said Constance.

Piet hesitated. The erotica of *Carmen* was not at all appropriate. It would be better to speak through music, but what could possibly serve? His choice should be moving, to avoid making light of Constance's feelings, but not melodramatic. Ideally it should end cheerfully but convey an emphatic rejection. What on earth . . . ?

And then, as inspiration so often did, it came as he needed it. He raised his eyes to Constance's and very, very gently played the first haunting chords of *La Traviata*.

Jacobina, who had observed the entire exchange, smiled and bent over her embroidery. Louisa was impressed too, though she also experienced a strange and contradictory desire to puncture Mr. Barol's improbable perfection, and see him fail. Hilde Wilken had left the room, and Didier, who never went to the opera, did not understand until Piet explained later. But Constance understood and as she listened to Piet play the overture to a story about disastrous liaisons between the classes and the tragedies they lead to, and as he looked at her firmly, making his meaning plain, she abruptly abandoned the effort of seducing him—because she preferred to renounce a challenge rather than fail at it. She picked up a copy of *La Mode Illustrée* and buried herself behind it and later submitted to Louisa's scalding mockery without much minding. For this was Constance Vermeulen-Sickerts' essential genius: that she was able to desist from desiring what she could not have—a trick that, had they emulated it, might have saved her male acquaintances much misery.

Piet was right: Maarten Vermeulen-Sickerts was watching his behavior closely, and when Maarten saw him resist Constance's assault he too wondered whether he was a uranist. But no. He was not like Mr. Blok. This made the young man's restraint all the more creditable and induced in Maarten a warm paternal regard he demonstrated in all sorts of touching ways. He explained to Piet how successful enterprises are run: with iron confidence, flexibility, and a willingness to innovate. He took him over every inch of the house, describing its contents with the delight of the self-made connoisseur, and lingered in particular over the cabinets in his office and the statues of Paris, Athena and Aphrodite that reigned over the staircase hall.

It was Paris' task, at the request of Zeus, king of the gods, to decide which of the goddesses was the most beautiful. "And that is why," said Maarten, pointing upwards, "I never take sides between my daughters and my wife. Paris' decision started the Trojan War."

It did not occur to Maarten, as he watched Constance lay unsuccessful siege to Piet Barol and steeled himself to intervene if necessary, that it was not his daughters' virtue the young man threatened but his wife's. Jacobina betrayed no indication of remembering Piet's first afternoon in the house, but she thought of it constantly and was not entirely relieved that Piet seemed to have forgotten it.

Jacobina was a woman who had lived her life correctly, even strictly, but this was because she had gradually lost the imagination to conceive of it otherwise and not the result of any great interior piety. Her youth's sole act of rebellion had been to accept the proposal of the cunning, boisterous Maarten Vermeulen, when she might have made a titled alliance. This had been rewarded by her husband's runaway success. But she had not been very impulsive since and Piet's arrival made her rather regret this.

Jacobina had gone to bed on his first night quietly proud that a handsome young man had stared so saucily at her. The next morning she was horrified by what had happened and resolved to censure any future impudence. At first she was relieved when no opportunity to do so arose. For several weeks she rehearsed the chilling speech she would deliver when Mr. Barol made protracted eye contact with her again. When he did not she grew rather indignant, and her contradictory emotions annoyed her. She began to embroider a great deal, which gave her something to do with her hands in the evening while Piet and Maarten sang duets at the piano. During these impromptu performances, she found herself noticing the young man's physique and contrasting her husband's unfavorably with it. After one evening of particular study, she began to imagine Piet naked, and then to do so with a frequency that alarmed her. She rejoiced when Constance set out to seduce him, because any incorrectness on Piet's part would get him dismissed and remove the temptation forever.

But Piet Barol did not behave incorrectly; and just once or twice she thought that it was at her, rather than her charming daughter, that he looked with the hunger she felt and tried not to show. She dreamed about him for the first time a month after his arrival, and in the dream he put his strong young body at her disposal. She woke from it aroused, and when Maarten had left she dismissed Agneta Hemels and spent the morning in bed, defying the prohibitions of her youth and pleasuring herself until the lunch bell sounded.

It was the custom of the household to attend church together and to sit in the same pew—for on Sundays all men are equal in the eyes of God. One Sunday near the end of May, Jacobina woke from a dream of wild abandon that chimed with the cheerful weather and made her wish, as Agneta did her hair, that no one, not even God, were watching her.

She found the servants waiting in the hall and Piet's smell provoked a spasm of longing. To have the fantasy companion of the night incarnated in all his earthly glory was an unfair temptation on the Sabbath morning. She turned from him and got into the Rolls-Royce, calling rather sharply for her daughters. Maarten was already in his seat and said "Good morning, my love" with a tenderness that painfully stimulated her conscience.

The clash of unsatisfied desire and self-reproach put Jacobina in a filthy temper. She said nothing during the short drive to the Nieuwe Kerk and once there hurried through the throng, bowing briefly to her friends, and sank to her knees in the Vermeulen-Sickerts' pew. But Jacobina was not praying. She was thinking about Piet Barol, and the sound of his deep, happy voice inquiring after Mrs. de Leeuw's rest made it hard to banish the image of him, bare chested and ready, that had followed her from her sleep.

The choir came in and the minister after them. During the first hymn she permitted herself the briefest glance in his direction and caught his profile, his dark brows and blue eyes, his full red lips parted in song. A wild, impulsive wish to touch him, if only for an instant, came over her. She redirected her attention to the hymnal but the thought persisted. Piet's resonant echoing of the prayers sustained it. She threw herself into atoning for her sinful flesh but this did not cleanse her—because a secret voice, from deep within, told her that she did not sincerely repent.

The sermon drew on the Beatitudes, as recounted in the Gospel of St. Matthew. Of the eleven people in the Vermeulen-Sickerts' pew, only Maarten and Piet listened to it with any attention, and both automatically evaluated themselves against the standards it outlined. Neither man considered himself poor in spirit, but only Maarten accepted that this might bar him from the kingdom of heaven. Piet was not sure he believed in the kingdom of heaven and wondered whether he was the only one in the congregation to harbor such doubts. *No.* According to Didier, Louisa Vermeulen-Sickerts was a passionate atheist.

He looked at her and understood from the quick movement of her head that she had been looking at him, too. He had not yet found a way into her affections. He had been too distracted by the dangers of Constance's infatuation to risk a full assault. Louisa was exquisitely dressed, in a tailored linen coat of her own design that made the dresses of the other women look ostentatious and foolish. Since his second day in the house, when he had resisted the impulse to hate her, he had been struck by the confidence of her taste. Louisa's small straw hat this morning shamed the millinery of the women around her, which was heavily burdened with flowers and dead birds. It was Constance whom the young bucks had watched as the party walked up the aisle; but the true beauty of the family was the grave, inscrutable Louisa.

His attention returned to the sermon. "Blessed are the meek, for they will inherit the earth," the minister was saying, and this was a point with which Piet emphatically disagreed. It seemed obvious to him that the strong took advantage of the meek and left them nothing. It was better to assert oneself against Fortune, as Machiavelli advised, and as he himself had done so profitably.

As she heard the words "Blessed are the pure in heart, for they will see God," Jacobina snapped to attention rather crossly. She had spent much of her life being pure and had not seen God yet. Her childhood nanny had been a devout Catholic, and from her she had absorbed the idea that sins are precisely quantifiable, with calibrated penances capable of removing their stain forever. As a little girl, she had secretly said a hundred Hail Marys every Saturday morning to atone for the gluttony she would display as soon as she received her pocket money, which she spent on hard, brightly colored sweets she did not share. Rising for the Eucharist, she wondered whether she might now make a similar bargain with God and win the right to think sordid thoughts without regret. *Nonsense, Jacobina,* she said to herself, but the censoriousness of her tone was undermined by the sight of Piet's buttocks as he waited to receive the Host.

When the service was finished she greeted the minister more absently than usual and was so flushed that Maarten asked if anything was wrong. "I'm perfectly well," she said; but in fact she felt afraid because she had decided to touch Piet Barol, come what may; just a little touch that no one would notice. The opportunity arose as they waited for the car, because Piet happened to be standing in front of its door as it drew up. She held out her hand to him quite naturally to be helped in. His grip was firm and dry. When she leaned against his arm, she saw his bicep swell as he took her weight. "Thank you, Mr. Barol," she said, and their eyes met, and in that meeting was the knowledge of what had gone before.

"Je vous en prie," said Piet.

It was insanely stupid—Piet knew this as he spoke the words, but spoke them anyway—to refer, however obliquely, to the hidden undercurrents of his first interview with Jacobina. As he followed the Rolls-Royce on foot with the other servants, he understood that he had acted dangerously, and yet . . . He watched Jacobina emerge from the vehicle and ascend the steps of the house.

She was undeniably an attractive woman.

He went into the hall feeling reckless. Fortunately he had Egbert's prayers to attend to, and he turned to this chore with relief because he knew it would calm him. Egbert's refusal to leave the house required Piet to take him through the morning service before Sunday lunch, except on the first Sunday of the month when the minister called in person to give him the sacraments. The boy was in his bedroom, his face so red Piet thought he might have a fever; but Egbert was perfectly well and red faced only because he had spent the morning in an ice-cold bath.

Between the child and the young man a wary ease had arisen, the result of Piet's scrupulous refusal to ask Egbert to explain himself or behave as other children did. This was convenient in many respects, but the persistent avoidance of frank discussion had prevented them from becoming friends. Piet knelt on the floor and asked Egbert to open his prayer book. Together they went through the service, and the boy sought the Holy Spirit's aid so fervently Piet felt sorry for him. He read him the Beatitudes, giving no hint of his own views, and when they had finished he sent him to his father's study to receive a homily.

He was on the landing outside Egbert's room, about to go to his own, when Jacobina emerged from her bedroom. Piet had loitered perhaps a little longer than he ought to have done, daring Fate; and Fate had not only called his bluff but doubled its money because Jacobina was wearing the dress of apple-green wool she had worn at their first encounter.

"Good afternoon, Mr. Barol. Will you be lunching with us?" Before changing, Jacobina had written a check for fifty guilders and asked Agneta to take it to the Civic Orphanage in the manner of a medieval merchant buying a papal indulgence. The money was drawn on her own account and had come from her father, not her husband.

"I should be delighted to, *mevrouw*."

Monsieur la Chaume had outdone himself. They ate turtle consommé and *corbeilles Polonaises*, followed by larks stuffed with pistachio and foie gras. The Château Neuf du Pape, of which Piet had three glasses, made the pursuit of pleasure seem obligatory. There was a wildness in the way Jacobina laughed at Constance's jokes that combined with the message of the dress she had chosen to tell him that he need only make a sign. The invitation, delivered so tracelessly, added a helping of flattered vanity to the assortment of delights offered by the elegant room, the fine food and the deference of the servants.

As Didier bowed, looked into his eyes, smiled, refilled his glass, and bowed again, Piet marveled at how far he had come from his father's dank and gloomy house, cleaned once a week by a woman with dandruff and chilblains. He thought contemptuously of the morning's sermon and of the poor fools who exchange their worldly ambitions for the vague promises of heaven.

A *gâteau de trois-frères* appeared and an exquisite champagne jelly, in which white elderflowers were magically suspended. Piet had watched the jelly being made, layer on fragile layer, the day before. He plunged his fork into it like a barbarian at the gates of Rome, destroying the labors of others for no better reason than this: he could.

"Some champagne, Monsieur Blok," said Maarten, who was in excellent spirits. He did no work on Sundays and was looking forward to a pleasantly drunken nap. "My dear, I insist you take some." He stroked his wife's hand. "You haven't been yourself all morning. It'll settle your digestion." He waved at the butler, in unconscious imitation of the rich men he had envied in the days before he could afford to be commanding with sommeliers. "Let us have the Moët Brut Impérial, 1900." He turned to Piet. "A superlative year, in my opinion."

Thus pressed, Jacobina did take a glass of champagne. When Louisa announced that she and Constance were out to tea with the van der Woudes, and might stay to dinner, she had another. Though her life was enviably luxurious by any objective standard, she nevertheless believed quite sincerely that she rarely did anything to please herself. Because the sight of her husband had the power to weaken her resolve, she rose and went to the window; and thus the party broke up.

Constance and Louisa went upstairs to change. Maarten summoned Egbert to read aloud to him. The servants cleared the table. As the household dispersed, Jacobina announced to no one in particular that she should see to the flowers in the schoolroom and went into the house next door with a thudding heart.

She had not been two minutes in the room when Piet knocked at its door. "I wondered if you needed me, *mevrouw*." He entered without her leave and came halfway across the carpet towards her. "If so, I am entirely at your disposal."

The similarity between this declaration and statements made by the Piet Barol of Jacobina's dreams was startling. "There is a very great deal you might do for me," she said.

"I had hoped there would be."

They looked at each other in silence. Now it was Jacobina who smiled, and when Piet did not look away, she felt embarrassed. But he was not, and his look conveyed this. She walked past him out of the room and climbed the stairs, wondering if he would follow. When he did, she took a key from a vase on the landing and let them both into her aunt's bedroom and locked the door behind them. But now the spur of her impulsiveness died, leaving her nonplussed and at a disadvantage. What if this young man has no idea? she thought.

But Piet Barol had every idea.

Two weeks before his seventeenth birthday, a similar exchange of bold glances had earned him his first invitation to the bed of a thirty-four-year-old mezzo-soprano whose husband was a visiting lecturer at Leiden. This lady had asked Madame Barol if she might hire her son to practice with her at home and had practiced with him at will, with no instrument but the human body, for the remaining nine months of the academic year. She had curbed Piet's uninventive, youthful exuberance and taught him the virtues of rhythm and pace while insisting on chivalric standards of discretion.

Jacobina's locking of the door was all the license Piet required. The blame would now be hers if pleasure were succeeded by recrimination. He had never before encountered a woman as tinderbox ready as Jacobina Vermeulen-Sickerts and was slightly unnerved by the suddenness of his success. He fell to his knees before her, as the mezzo-soprano had liked him to do, and lifted the hem of her apple-green dress. Jacobina neither objected nor looked at him. He kissed her ankle in its white silk stockings and this touch, too, was permitted. It was highly effective. Abruptly abandoning all consideration of the consequences, Jacobina sat, almost collapsed, on the chaise longue.

"Remove my shoes," she said. *"Lentement."*

With extreme delicacy, Piet liberated Jacobina's feet. *Very* slowly he ran his fingers up her calves, behind her knees, to the lace bands of her suspenders. This made her shake, as it had the mezzo-soprano. He loosed her stockings with studied reverence, but in truth he was uncertain. He had no idea what she would permit, and it seemed to him that she was not very clear on this point either. He hesitated, considering his repertoire. Then, with an animal growl that was indescribably pleasing to Jacobina, he pushed her skirts over her knees and put his head beneath them.

Jacobina's childhood nurse, Riejke Vedder, who had lived with the Sickertses until her death at the age of seventy-eight, had been far more beloved by the Sickerts children than either of their own parents. Jacobina had been the last of the brood and her favorite. For the first six years of her life, until a drizzly English governess challenged Riejke's exclusive rights to her attention, Jacobina had not spent a single waking moment beyond the range and sight of her nurse.

Riejke taught Jacobina to focus and crawl and speak and walk; and then to read and wash and count and go to the toilet by herself. She loved her with the unchallengeable enormity of the simpleminded and religious, and the responsibility she assumed over her was total. "Ugly language" was banned and included all but the most discreet euphemisms for any private place below the belly button. Faced with the occasional necessity of referring to these shameful regions, Riejke had devised a language that suited the needs of practical communication while remaining inoffensive. Thus, Jacobina's young vagina became her "little kitten," her bottom "the strawberry patch." Every evening before bed, Riejke told her charge to take her little kitten for a walk and Jacobina rose obediently and squatted over the chamber pot and peed and returned to her bed without fear of wetting it. On family picnics, when privacy was harder to achieve, Riejke would ask Jacobina whether she needed to "visit the strawberry patch" or could simply "walk her little kitten" (which, in extremis, could be done behind a bush).

As a consequence, Jacobina had grown up with a sense that the most intimate and rewarding part of her body was somehow independent of her, a little furry animal to be walked and cleaned and sometimes played with—but cautiously, because it might scratch or bite. She knew this was nonsense, and yet her nurse's prohibitions remained compelling and in her own mind she still remembered to walk her little kitten before taking a long journey and was revolted by the sight of strawberries on a chocolate cake. Her husband had once made a pet of this kitten, and on one mortifying occasion had put his tongue into it, and then withdrawn it, bright with embarrassment. But for ten years he had not touched her there or anywhere else, and nothing he had ever done compared with the sensations Piet Barol now produced.

Piet's mentor had taught him well and he was rewarded for finding his rhythm by a clenching of Jacobina's legs around his neck. This sign of favor removed the last of his doubts and he began to find the encounter as rewarding as she did—because there is nothing more flattering to a young man's vanity than the knowledge that he is capable of pleasing a woman.

Jacobina had no previous experience to prepare her for the currents of delight that radiated from Piet's tongue as it traced dwindling circles toward a place she knew existed, but for which she had no name. When she saw he was entirely lost in his devotions, a blissful serenity overpowered her; rose and fell away, to rise again as the light beyond the curtains faded and she forgot the discomfort of the chaise longue and the protestations of her conscience and the mediocrity of her aunt's pictures and everything else in the world except the smooth scratch of Piet's chin against her thighs and the warmth of his lips.

When Piet slid a thick finger into her, pressing upward with authority, her horsewoman's legs clenched around his neck so violently she thought she might choke him. He persisted, as every part of her tightened; and then she was twisting urgently and he knew that the end was near. It was announced by a shrill, high gasp and a gush of hot liquid over his face, which cooled as it ran down his chin. He remained on his knees as her convulsions subsided and when they had he wiped his face with his handkerchief and smiled—a respectful, happy smile that conveyed a becoming gratitude.

Jacobina rose shakily and put her stockings in a pocket and her feet into her shoes. She had almost lost the power of speech. At last she said, in the curt voice she used to mask awkwardness, "My compliments, Mr. Barol."

"Thank you, *mevrouw*."

"*Je vous en prie.*" She went to the door, but hesitated before unlocking it. "We should wait until you are presentable."

"Yes, *mevrouw*."

But erections are harder to suppress the harder one tries, and in the face of Jacobina's scrutiny Piet's stubbornly obeyed this law. This fact was tremendously gratifying to her. Eventually, with a laugh she had last given as a girl of twenty-two, she took from a bookcase a large, privately published history of the Amstel Hotel and handed it to Piet Barol. "It would be advisable for you to know something of

Mr. Vermeulen-Sickerts' business interests," she said briskly.
And with that she unlocked the door and stepped onto the
landing.

P iet followed her, the volume carefully positioned to hide
his embarrassment. By the time he reached the attic floor
of Herengracht 605 he no longer had need of its assistance
to preserve a modest silhouette. He closed his door and lay
on his bed, observed by the photograph of his mother. He
turned away from it. The heady exhilaration of three glasses
of wine and two of champagne had lifted and been replaced
by a dull, insistent throbbing at his temples. He was not a
man much given to bouts of conscience and had he not been
fond of Maarten Vermeulen-Sickerts he might have experienced none on this occasion. But as he stared at the ceiling,
the last embers of pleasure died and a chill horror crept over
him.

It was one thing to have flirted with Jacobina before
meeting her husband, quite another to insult him now that
he lived in his house and wore his clothes. Piet was accustomed to holding himself in high regard. He did not at all
enjoy feeling like a cad and thought—too late!—of Epicu-
rus' advice to consider the full consequences of a hedonistic
act before embarking on it. He could not deny the intensity
of the hedonism. Who would have thought that a woman so
universally well regarded was capable of sinning with such
abandon?

He got up and went to the mirror above the writing desk.
His lips were slightly swollen. "You are not to do that again,"
he told his reflection. But even as he spoke, he doubted his
resolve, because he knew that his conscience was insuf-
ficiently exercised to prevail over his pleasure impulse in
fullest sail. He repeated himself sternly, felt ridiculous and
considered praying for strength. But he did not. It seemed

foolish to draw attention to himself at a moment of such disadvantage, if indeed there was a God.

Instead he undressed and had a bath and was glad that Didier was not there to question him from the radiator. In the warm water his cock demanded satisfaction, and when this had been achieved he felt better. He got out and dried himself, rinsed the tub, and dressed. Then he told Mrs. de Leeuw he would not be dining in and spent half a guilder on roast beef and pickles, which he consumed meditatively on the terrace of a café on the Leidsegracht as the shimmering evening stole away and he wondered what on earth he was to do.

The decision Piet Barol reached was this: as soon as possible, while still in the grip of somber good intentions, he should perform for Jacobina the speech of the young believer, racked by religious scruple, that he had prepared for Constance but not had occasion to employ.

He went to see her at eleven the next morning, having set Egbert twenty lines from *Paradise Lost* to translate into Dutch. Jacobina was in the private salon, answering letters at a dainty escritoire that had once belonged to Madame de Montespan. She, too, had been wondering how best to behave after the wordless excesses of the previous afternoon, but she had reached a different conclusion from Piet Barol's.

"I would be grateful," she said coldly as he entered, "not to be disturbed. If you wish to be of service, you may present yourself at five o'clock in the same place in which you were so useful yesterday."

She returned to her letter, thrilled by her audacity. Jacobina did not at all wish to take a lover, and her conscience drew the line at verbal intimacies with a man who was not her husband. What she wanted was more, a great deal more, of the physical pleasure to which Piet had introduced her.

She did not deem it necessary to dismantle the social barriers between them in order to achieve this end; in fact, their inequality was useful to her.

Piet was rarely rendered speechless, but now his little soliloquy evaporated. "I have lived all my life in the shadow of a church, madam," he began, reaching after it clumsily. "God has been ever present to me. His will—"

"Your domestic arrangements do not interest me, Mr. Barol." Jacobina touched an electric bell on the wall and returned to her letter.

"*Mevrouw* . . ."

"I am a believer in actions over words." Jacobina continued to write. "If you are not at liberty this afternoon, I will quite understand. Though I confess"—and now she smiled at him—"that I should be a little disappointed."

Hilde Wilken knocked at the door, entered and curtsied.

"Please ask Monsieur la Chaume to come up and send some pear cordial with him. It's terribly hot today."

"Yes, madam."

"Thank you, Hilde. And thank you, Mr. Barol. You may both go."

As Piet went down the stairs, he found himself impressed and aroused by Jacobina's manner. He had never encountered patrician disdain from a conquest and it was highly stimulating. He waited until Egbert had finished his translation, then checked it and set him another, all the while valiantly supporting his conscience in its struggle against more animal instincts.

As they worked, Egbert's passivity and pampered helplessness began to exasperate him. He might have taken a normal boy to the Vondelpark and played chase with him until it was dark and the danger had passed. He understood that if he did not keep his rendezvous with Jacobina she would never again suggest one. But he could not leave the house and this left him in uncomfortable proximity to temptation.

The only available remedy was preemptive self-relief, but this had its dangers too. Piet knew well that desire peaks in the moments before it dies, and the dispassionate mood that succeeds a climax did not always last long with him. He feared it would not last long at all in this instance. He waited until a quarter to five. Then he sent his charge to have his supper, locked himself in the entrance hall cloakroom, and opened his flies. Images of Jacobina rose irresistibly. He took himself to the brink, but this state is the riskiest of all; and though he knew that he should, and wished earnestly that he would, he could not bring himself to abandon it.

His conscience, having done its best, abruptly gave up in the face of insuperable odds. He buttoned his flies and washed his hands and went upstairs.

Six weeks later, Constance Vermeulen-Sickerts turned twenty-two. The hospitality dispensed to celebrate this occasion was high and generous, and ostentation was not its chief motivation. Good nature was, because it pleased the Vermeulen-Sickertses to please others. That their guests would also be impressed was not the point of the enterprise, merely its inevitable by-product. A dance was given for two hundred, and for several days before it the house was full of workmen in the green-and-white overalls of the Amstel Hotel, hauling palm trees, polishing glasses and rails and door knobs and the parquet boards of the sprung floor in the ballroom. The wall that divided this apartment from the pale gray and gilt music room, though seemingly as solid as any other, could be lowered into the basement by a system of ingenious pulleys. Piet watched it disappear with unconcealed admiration.

He wanted desperately to be invited and would have been annoyed to know how strenuously Jacobina had opposed her husband's idea of including him. She did not at all relish the prospect of watching Piet flirt with her daughters' friends, and her objections were so strident that Maarten became indignant. "This is the twentieth century, Jacobina," he said one evening as, tight lipped, she brushed her hair before bed. "Piet Barol is an absolute gentleman. I will not have the snobberies of the past brought into my house."

So Piet was invited—not to the dinner, but to the dance that followed.

"You lucky bastard," was Didier's verdict. And the next day, when Piet received a check from Maarten "for shoes and a tailcoat; ask the women what you need," he felt very lucky indeed. He spent the money in a darkly paneled shop on the Kalverstraat and enjoyed the experience immensely, for it was the first time he had ever bought a brand-new suit of clothes.

On the night of the ball he dined on sandwiches in his room and listened to the sounds of merriment drifting from below in a state of mounting excitement. Maarten Vermeulen-Sickerts owned an interest in the Café Royal in London, and had brought that establishment's orchestra over in staterooms on the *Queen of Holland*. The music they played was modern and wildly glamorous. He went down, resolved to conquer, and the first person he countered was Louisa.

"Well, well, Mr. Barol."

"Good evening, Miss Vermeulen-Sickerts."

Louisa was dressed in aquamarine, with diamond pins in her hair. It was only when she moved that he saw silk trousers beneath her overskirt of metallic silver lace. The sight shocked him. "I like to move freely when I dance," she said sharply, as if he had challenged her on this point; and before he could make a compliment of it she had sauntered into the crush. He lacked the courage to follow her and went instead to get a glass of champagne from Didier.

"This is the night to find yourself a rich wife," his friend remarked, staring straight ahead.

This idea had occurred to Piet, but the thought of what Louisa Vermeulen-Sickerts would say if he pursued any of her friends made him desist. He believed, in any case, that he could earn large sums of money on his own and did not need to marry it. He drained the champagne so quickly it stung his throat, then followed the band's riotous summons to the dance floor.

Nina Barol had taught Piet to dance and he was good at it. Conscious that Jacobina was there to observe him he chose the ugliest of the four girls watching the revelers from a gilt sofa and asked whether she would give him the honor. The young lady was so astonished to be selected that for a moment she gaped at him, and his stomach tightened with fear that he had broken one of the invisible rules of the rich and would be refused. But he had not. They danced the waltz and then another; and then, seeing a young woman with fine dark down on her upper lip, to whom Jacobina could not possibly object, Piet extricated himself and asked if she would care to polka with him.

Observing Piet's selection of neglected partners, Maarten took his choices as further evidence of innate nobility. Jacobina watched him too and the prickings of jealousy that had made her laugh sound hollow all evening subsided. Constance's friend Myrthe Janssen said: "Who is that divine man who dances only with ugly women? Do you pay him, my dear?" To which Constance replied, after a moment's hesitation, "As it happens, yes. But not for the reason you suggest. He's Egbert's tutor."

"Adorable."

"I suppose. Rather a dry fish. He's terrifically sensible."

"Sensible men don't dance like that, darling." And Myrthe, who had a beautiful figure and a mass of natural blond curls and was used, like Constance, to getting her way with men, did her best to catch Piet's eye but did so in vain.

The band took a break a little after midnight. Piet broke free of his companion and went out into the velvet dark of the garden, in which the smell of the canals had been sweetened, if not quite obliterated, by banks of hothouse roses. He took with him a glass of champagne and drank it beneath a sky thickly spattered with stars. His shirt front was wet from dancing. As he stood in the cool air, a sense of superb well-being settled over him. With it came a surge of love—for the Vermeulen-Sickertses, who had given him a pass to this enchanting world; for life, and the splendors of standing alone in a rose-filled garden; for his mother and all she had taught him.

His conscience reminded him that his adventures with Jacobina were hardly consistent with affection for her husband; but in fact the contradiction troubled him less with each passing day, and two glasses of champagne were sufficient to still it entirely tonight. She did not, after all, permit him to take any but the essential liberties, and he approved of his self-restraint in not pressing the matter. He thought of her as she had been the afternoon before, almost unconscious with pleasure on her aunt's chaise longue, and grinned broadly. Then the orchestra struck up again and he turned towards the sound, resolved that this time he would not only dance, he would speak—as any equal would.

He entered the ballroom to find Constance and Louisa at the center of a crowd and loitered at its edges.

"When my grandfather went to New York in '42," a young man with straggling mustaches was saying, "it took three months to make the crossing. When I went on the *Celtic* in '03, it took eleven days."

"Took me six days on the *Kaiser Wilhelm der Grosse,*" said another, who had bright pink cheeks. "Steam triple-expansion engines geared to twin screw. But I must say I prefer the *Amerika*. First ship to have an elevator in first class."

"Damn elevators. What matters is the food. I went on the *Kronprinzessin Cecilie* last year. The restaurant has a fish tank so you can choose your dinner. I ate nothing but lobster for five days."

"Lobster!" cried Constance, with a significant glance at her sister. "I prefer apples."

"Bread and butter," said Louisa, "is all I need."

"Chocolate, my dears, for every meal," remarked Myrthe Janssen.

"Dreamlike, to have chocolate for every meal," said another young woman.

Only the faintest trace of a raised eyebrow from Didier, who was serving them drinks, alerted Piet to the commencement of the alphabet game. Lacking such coded assistance, the young stags rattled on boastfully. They discussed the charms of rival liners while their opinions were elicited on *English* engines, and *French* cooking, and *glamour*, and whether or not a suite on a Loire Lines Château of the Atlantic was a close approximation of *heaven*.

Now it was Constance's turn. She hesitated a moment and then said: "Investment. Who provides the investment for these ships?"

This was a topic on which the pink-cheeked gentleman, whose name was Norbert Breitner, and whose father was chairman of the Holland-America Line, had been eager to hold forth for some time. "The big competition's between the Germans and the English, of course," he explained with condescension. "No sooner has one country produced the biggest, fastest ship afloat, but the other must outdo it. When J. P. Morgan was trying to gain control of Cunard, the British government offered enormous subsidies if the company would remain independent and build the two biggest ships the world has ever known. The first one's called the *Lusitania*. She's well over thirty-one thousand gross tons. She'll be in service by the autumn."

"Of course," interjected his mustachioed friend, "the small print says they must be convertible for war use, in the event of a conflict."

"*J*. P. Morgan," said Louisa, stressing the first initial, "was in the box next to ours at Beyreuth last year."

"*King* of Wall Street, surely," added Myrthe.

"*Lusitania*'s going to be the world's grandest ship," said another young lady. "My parents have already booked passage on her—"

"*Maiden* voyage!" interrupted Louisa, in English and out of turn; and to the surprise of the two young men the girls around them burst into hysterical laughter.

Piet, who had been nerving himself to make an interjection, kept silent. But now another fellow stepped into the center of the group with the unstudied assurance of a handsome man who is also very rich. His face was thin and finely wrought, its expression disdainful. "You won't catch me on the *Lusitania*," he said. "The only ship worth the trouble is the *Eugénie*."

The appearance of this attractive oracle inspired an abrupt cessation of feminine hostilities. "And why is that, Mr. van Sigelen?" asked Constance, who assumed the right of first response.

"I don't care a fig for speed or size. Comfort and service are all I consider, and the French are best at both. Albert

Verignan's a genius. He built the Loire Lines Company from scratch and sees to every detail himself. She is the only ship to have a theater. The grill room is the most spectacular at sea. And the first-class suites rival those of your father's hotels, Miss Vermeulen-Sickerts. I recommend the Henri de Navarre, which has an enormous bath. Each is decorated for a figure from French history."

Piet listened as Mr. van Sigelen elaborated on the liner's charms. To disguise his awkwardness at lingering so long, he accepted another glass of champagne from Didier. He heard that the *Eugénie*'s first-class grill room, a miniature of the Hall of Mirrors at Versailles, with fourteen-foot windows running the length of one side, was located so high above the sundeck that only the horizon was visible. "It's like dining on a cloud," van Sigelen told them. "One half expects to see angels strumming harps."

This little joke provoked laughter of an altogether more sympathetic kind, and under cover of it Myrthe Janssen slipped her arm through Mr. van Sigelen's and led him to the dance floor.

"The *Eugénie*'s steam triple-expansion engines don't compare at all well with, say, the quadruple expansions of the *Kaiser Wilhelm II*," said Norbert Breitner, in an attempt to reassert his authority. "Forty thousand people came on board to inspect her the first time she docked at New York."

"No!" exclaimed Constance; and it seemed to Piet that her real objection was to Myrthe's deft removal of Mr. van Sigelen.

"Believe me, my dear Miss Vermeulen-Sickerts, that is absolutely true. I was there."

It was not clear to Piet that Constance, by employing a word that began with *n*, was resuming the alphabet game where Louisa's "maiden" had left it; but a third glass of champagne sanctioned daredevilry and in a clear, confident voice he said: "*Opium*. You must have smoked it to hallucinate such a crowd."

There was silence.

The young women turned to him, aghast to have their machinations exposed by a stranger. Louisa said nothing. But Constance, observing the intensifying pink of Norbert Breitner's cheeks and aware that she was looked to for leadership, said: "*Passion* is a wonderful quality. Don't tease, Mr. Barol."

F our hours later, having deposited an armful of birthday presents on her desk, Constance let her dress fall to the floor and crept into Louisa's bed in her shift. Her sister sat at the dressing table, taking the diamond clips from her hair. On the subject of Piet Barol she kept her silence until Agneta Hemels had brought in a tray of hot chocolate, removed Constance's dress, and congratulated them on a triumphant success. When the servant had gone, following her sister's train of thought with the precision that so unsettled their friends, she said: "I maintain, Constance, there's something false about him."

"You're so sullen and suspicious."

"You'll find I'm right."

"It's not because you think I'm in love with him any longer?"

"I never thought you were in love with him, darling. You wanted him to love you, which is something different entirely."

"Whatever it is, I'm done with it."

"I know."

"You'll agree it was funny."

"Suggesting that Norbert Breitner is an opium addict?"

"Being sharp enough to catch on and brave enough to play too. Norbert's such a pompous fool."

"With that I wholeheartedly agree. And I never suggested that our Mr. Barol was anything less than sharp."

"There, you said it. *'Our'* Mr. Barol."

" *'Your'* Mr. Barol, then."

Constance turned on her side. "Wouldn't it be fun to have a brother? Someone to go about with, and gossip with, and persuade our friends to marry?" She spoke wistfully to the wall. "Egbert's so hopeless."

"There's no use being friends with a person who doesn't tell the truth." Louisa climbed into bed next to her sister and yawned. "Piet Barol will always say what he thinks you want to hear."

"You're a miserable cynic."

They fought on as the sky lightened to indigo. Finally Louisa said: "Very well. Let's ask him to tea with Karina van Prinsterer. You mark my words: he'll tell us she charms him and the house is beautiful."

The next afternoon, Maarten Vermeulen-Sickerts left for New York to supervise the completion of his most ambitious undertaking yet, a hotel of unrivaled opulence at the corner of Fifth Avenue and the Central Park. The family saw him off at the docks and on their return to Herengracht 605 Constance asked Piet if he'd care to join them at tea with a friend.

"A *dear* friend," added Louisa. "With one of the loveliest houses in the city. Her mother's a lady-in-waiting to Queen Wilhelmina."

With difficulty, Piet disguised his excitement at the prospect of meeting a member of the royal household. He had only twenty minutes to change and chose the most elegant of the Charvet ties Maarten had given him. When he had knotted it five times he was more than satisfied with his reflection.

The van Prinsterers lived on the Keizersgracht. Piet escorted the girls on foot, wishing that a childhood enemy might cross his path and observe him with such a fashionable pair. Their destination proved to be a gloomy mansion, six windows across, with a coat of arms emblazoned in scarlet and gold above its doors. These opened before they could knock, as though someone were permanently on duty at them. In the vestibule were two very tall footmen in mustard-yellow livery. Piet gave his hat to one and looked about, prepared to be impressed.

But he was not impressed.

The hall was a strident blue, fussily embellished in shiny gold leaf. In the ornate wrought-iron balustrade of the staircase, the letters LVP (for Leopold van Prinsterer, the current occupants' grandfather) were pricked out in gilt. It struck Piet as overanxious to advertise oneself in this manner. He found it vulgar. Vulgar too was the cluttered drawing room full of heavily fringed furniture, its tables weighted with framed photographs of notable personages. Most vulgar of all was the presence on the mantelpiece of a large stuffed peacock, fanning its tail over the silver frames like a pagan deity in a graveyard.

He was examining a signed portrait of Crown Princess Marie of Romania when the van Prinsterer ladies appeared. They were absurdly overdressed. Miss van Prinsterer's skirt was tied tightly below her knees by a tasseled cord that swung wildly with every mincing step. Her lace sleeves hung almost to the floor and became fans whenever she raised her arms—which she often did to flaunt this effect. In her fuss of crinolines and tulles, her mother resembled a cream puff that has aged during its display at the baker's.

Nor did they compensate in charm for these sartorial deficiencies. Piet had looked forward to performing one of the anecdotes, as polished as the satinwood tea stand between them, with which he had delighted women of the better class before. He intended to make a deftly self-effacing impression and to bow to the demand that he continue his wonderful stories with becoming shyness. But he was first disconcerted and then annoyed to discover that he was not permitted to make any impression at all.

No one was.

The van Prinsterer ladies talked without ceasing and drew breath in relays. The result was that one or other was always speaking, and not even Piet Barol could find a way to insinuate himself into the conversation. He noticed that Constance and Louisa did not attempt to do so and were listening with gleeful attention.

The van Prinsterers had recently returned from Venice. They had found the heat unbearable and the gondoliers conceited and familiar. They swore never again to travel to a city in which Mr. Vermeulen-Sickerts had not yet opened a hotel. They repeated this refrain as they ate highly sugared cakes and complained of what they had endured at the hands of lesser hoteliers. Not once did they seek anything more substantive than a murmur of sympathy from their guests.

The room was very hot and held nothing in it to delight the eye. As one hour became two, Piet began to wish he might leave it. He could think of no way of doing so politely and sat on, astounded at his hostess' endurance. As they entered the third hour he felt that anything—the humiliation, even, of admitting to his station in life—would be worth the delirium of freedom. He was about to say that he should make sure Egbert had his bath on time when Constance looked at her watch and said "Goodness me! The hours have flown!" and so permitted them all to leave.

Outside, Piet filled his lungs gratefully with the stench of the canals.

"Adorable, aren't they?" Louisa unraveled her parasol.

The idea that anyone, least of all Louisa Vermeulen-Sickerts, found the van Prinsterer ladies adorable robbed Piet momentarily of the power of speech. At first he did not understand why Constance, observing his hesitation, broke into a fit of giggles so extreme she had to bend over double to contain them. "Go on, Mr. Barol," she said when they had turned the corner onto the Reguliersgracht. "Tell us what you really thought."

"I—" But Piet smelled a test, and this startled his higher functions from their stupor. "I thought two things," he said solemnly, resolving to pass it with panache. "Poor Queen Wilhelmina. . . . And poor peacock."

J acobina Vermeulen-Sickerts was an upstanding woman. Though she increasingly blamed her husband for his amatory neglect, she loved him dearly. She did not at all enjoy encountering him when floating in the aftermath of a tryst with Piet Barol and had looked forward to his absence—which she intended to use wisely.

Her nurse Riejke Vedder had had definite views on the delineation of masculine and feminine responsibilities, and Jacobina had never attempted to assert herself in questions of finance or sex. To taste the elixir of sexual authority in the fifth decade of life was marvelous.

So was Piet Barol.

He never made embarrassing declarations or asked for any reward save the knowledge that he had given good service. She addressed him with the polite formality she used with her household staff and set the time of their appointments as well as the limits of what took place. She did not permit Piet to undress or touch himself, or touch her with anything but his fingers, lips and tongue. This was the price her conscience demanded and it was a high one because she longed to see him naked. But the prohibitions were practical, too. She had dreaded the shame that settled on Maarten after spending and preferred to dismiss Piet fiercely and cheerfully aroused. The idea that he saw to himself later, and thought of her when he did so, pleased her greatly.

They did not speak to one another in her aunt's ugly bedroom, and as the weeks passed Piet's fluency in decoding the clenching of Jacobina's thighs and the meaning of certain half-suppressed sighs improved. But it was inevitably imperfect. The preferences of the mezzo-soprano were not, after all, quite Jacobina's, and Piet's unquestioning confidence in them diminished the impact of his labors.

The crucial distinction was that Jacobina Vermeulen-Sickerts was unpredictably ticklish. This meant that the mezzo-soprano's insistence on Piet's taking a meandering route upwards from her feet sometimes made Jacobina squirm in a way that was not at all pleasurable. Piet Barol interpreted this wriggling as a sign of the highest approbation and responded to it by going more slowly still, which made Jacobina yearn to tell him to hurry. She never did, because the idea of putting a base physical desire into words was mortifying; but her restraint was sorely tried when they met for the first time after Maarten's departure.

Piet's desire to make the encounter memorable inspired an exceptionally reverent start. When his lips brushed lightly against her ankles, Jacobina began to feel violently ticklish. As Piet's tongue made its too-gradual progress beyond her knees, she found the experience excruciating and started to writhe urgently. This made Piet slow down further and the sensation became so unbearable that from a place deep within her, potent and unstoppable, a loud voice cried, "Faster, Mr. Barol!"

This immediately had the desired effect. Jacobina's ticklishness subsided and was replaced by a heavenly sensation.

Now she saw the advantages in explicit communication, which yielded results of a precision that bucking limbs and fluttering sighs could not deliver. When Piet's index fingers began to prize her apart and his tongue to trace its way delicately between them, she wished he would push it into her as far as it would go; that he would lap greedily at her like a dog, wallow in her, force her open.

But what could she say? She could not ask him to do these things to a "little kitten." The word she had heard street boys use now came to her. It seemed much more accurately to convey her meaning, but the ghost of Riejke Vedder intervened and forbade it. Jacobina opened her eyes. Piet was entirely hidden by her bunched skirts. She hesitated, but the certainty that this was not an opportunity to squander rose up in her. She had come this far. Why should her transgression not have its rewards? She banished her nurse—but still she could not speak. The tickles worsened. She was shaking, and Piet's pace slackened. Oh, the agony of it!

At last, with a courage that made her proud for days, Jacobina Vermeulen-Sickerts spoke—and she did so in a crisp, commanding voice, in which there was not a trace of shame. "My cunt, Mr. Barol," she said firmly, gripping the arms of the chaise longue. "Be bolder with it!"

It was an indelibly erotic moment. Piet obeyed Jacobina's instruction with a brutal enthusiasm that kept her in a state of rolling orgasm until—several hours later—the knowledge that they should stop became insistent, and then absolute. It was a wrench. Finally Jacobina gathered all her self-control and closed her legs to Piet Barol. She dispatched him with a curt word of thanks, and once he had left the room it was almost fifteen minutes before she could stand. She made her way to her own house in a daze of euphoric tranquillity.

Piet went to his bedroom, volcanically aroused. There were no locks on the servants' quarters at Herengracht 605 and in order to secure his privacy he pulled the armchair in front of his door. He was undoing his flies when he heard a sharp knock. The door opened at once, hit against the chair and revealed Mr. Blok's white face.

Gert Blok knew at once what was up: the young man's flushed cheeks, the discreetly positioned furniture, the rich, sordid smell in the room told him all he needed to know. His eyes flicked to Piet's crotch and there—oh rapture!— was the unmistakable outline of an object to which he had devoted many hours of furtive imagining. This was too fine an opportunity to pass up. He insinuated himself into the room and began to talk.

Mr. Blok told Piet about the entertainment their employer arranged every year for his workers and complained of the extra responsibility the festivities placed on his shoulders. He described the ruined, ivy-clad country mansion Maarten Vermeulen-Sickerts had bought the year before, the tragic fire that had gutted the place a decade previously, the number of bathrooms Maarten intended to install once he found time to attend to its refurbishment. As he spoke, Piet Barol's excitement dwindled rapidly. He knew very well how pleased Blok was to have caught him, and the butler's persistence annoyed him.

Finally the dinner gong sounded. Now Blok had to leave, and when he had gone Piet washed his hands and face and went downstairs, his body painfully alert, his mind half crazed by the intoxications of the afternoon.

There were no guests, and the new friendliness of Constance and Louisa made the gathering intimate, almost cozy. Jacobina had taken a scented bath and was feeling wonderfully composed. She knew at once that Piet was not, and the jolt of power this sent through her banished all inclination to guilt. As Constance recounted the details of Myrthe Janssen's pursuit of Frederik van Sigelen, Jacobina thought that God would not have created human bodies as He did—in His own image, after all—if He disapproved of sexual pleasure. Consequently, what she had done was not the grievous sin the churchmen described. The minister of the Nieuwe Kerk came to her, a stupid, ugly man who could rail against carnality quite safely since no one was likely to engage in any with him. She knew that she had promised her body to Maarten twenty-eight years before, but surely his long failure to exercise his rights entitled her to reclaim a portion of his entitlements and bestow them on another?

Looking at Jacobina, Piet Barol could only see her on her aunt's chaise longue, her skirts pushed up to her waist. He was acutely sensitive to her. Every time she spoke or glanced in his direction, his cock throbbed like a risk-addicted being over whom he had no control. As the dessert was cleared he began to fear that he would not be able to rise from the table without embarrassment. He toyed with the *poires Carignon*, wondering desperately what he should do, which only increased his difficulties; and at last it was Virgil who rescued him with the speech Anchises makes to his descendants in the *Aeneid*. He had memorized it as a schoolboy and recited it silently, as a soothing incantation.

Classical poetry succeeded where all other distractions had not. By the time the ladies rose, he was presentable enough to rise with them, but he dared not risk an hour in the drawing room. He excused himself, complaining of a sore throat.

Jacobina was not deceived. The knowledge that a young man as desirable as Piet could not control himself in her presence made her soar with happiness. She said good night to him politely, and in the presence of her daughters told him that he might help her with some correspondence the following afternoon, at four o'clock.

Piet made his way to the attic floor, stumbling like a drunkard. It was hot and airless beneath the lead roofs. As he reached his bedroom, grateful to be alone, he heard Didier's voice and remembered it was a Thursday and his weekly evening off. Didier was in the bath. "Come and entertain me!" he called. "Himself's downstairs, doing the coffee."

Piet opened his own door, pretending he hadn't heard. But he did not go through it. He was a young man who had just sent a woman into ecstasy. The urge to boast about his achievement to another young man was invincible. He went into the bathroom, wondering how to do so discreetly, and found Didier stretched languidly in the tub. The windows were open; it was deliciously breezy after the stifling corridor. Piet took off his jacket and went to his place on the radiator.

Didier sank beneath the water and wet his hair. It fell sleek and blond over his eyes. "It's glorious in here. I'm not getting out for an hour."

"Selfish."

"You can get in if you like. There's plenty of space for two."

The young men were often undressed in each other's company and there was no awkwardness in this. They had some of their best conversations while one sat on the radiator, waiting for his turn in the water. But they had never shared the bath before. Tonight it seemed unusually long and full and white; especially inviting. Piet hesitated.

"Don't be so provincial."

This was a well-aimed barb. "All right, then. Thanks."

Piet took off his clothes and got into the bath at the opposite end from his friend. He lowered himself in slowly to avoid splashing the floor. The mass of his body brought the water to the brim.

"What've you been doing all afternoon?" Didier moved his feet to make space for Piet.

"Pleasing a woman."

"Not Hilde?"

"Of course not."

"Who then?"

"Can you keep a secret?"

"Certainly."

"Well—" And Piet told him a story, truthful in its essential elements, about a respectable married woman in her forties whom he had spent the afternoon, and others before it, pleasuring until she begged him to stop. He told Didier how the lady refused to let him undress or touch himself or speak; how she addressed him peremptorily, as one might a servant; and that this heightened his delight as he subdued her with his lips and tongue and fingers, reduced her to a moaning wreck who could barely stand when he was done. He told Didier that they had met in the Vondelpark, that her husband was often away, and that they had the run of her house when he was. By the time he was finished his cock had thrown off the anesthetic of the Virgil and was pulsing in the water.

So was Didier's. "D'you think she'd like two?" He smiled his crooked smile and watched Piet closely. When he saw his friend was not shocked, he told a story of his own. "My first year as a page at the Amstel, a guest asked me into his suite. His wife had noticed me. She was younger than him, Austrian, randy as hell. We spent the night gamuching her." He grinned. "Of course we didn't touch each other, him and me." As he spoke, his foot was bobbing lightly against Piet's thigh; he could feel the hair on Piet's leg against his toes. "It happened a lot after that."

Like Piet Barol, Didier Loubat was not telling the strict truth. He had, indeed, been invited to guests' rooms at the Amstel Hotel; it had happened on many occasions. But in each case the occupants of the rooms had been men—and their wives, if they had them, were not present. Now recklessness gripped him. He pulled the plug and let some water out of the bath, as though preparing to leave it; but when the level was sufficiently low to expose them both, he said, "We can't go in this state. Blok'll be up any minute. If he catches us . . ."

Piet's erection was almost painful. "Well, what then?"

"I won't look if you don't."

Both their cocks were now standing clear of the water. Didier's was long and thin, like his body. Piet's was squatter and fatter, rising from a dense clump of black hair. The memory of Blok's lascivious stares before dinner remained, and was highly unpleasant.

"All right, then," said Piet. "Eyes closed."

They leaned back and closed their eyes and began to rub themselves, making the water churn. At his end of the bath, Piet was loosening Jacobina's stays, pushing her dress roughly to the floor as she ripped the buttons on his shirt. He was proud of his body and longed to show it to her. He imagined her admiring him, sliding his undershorts down, taking his prick in her mouth. His legs spasmed and a foot jerked against Didier's buttock. In the instant he touched it, his friend's smooth skin became Jacobina's and this sent him hurtling towards the conclusion he sought.

Didier was listening carefully. When he judged that Piet was past caring, he opened his eyes. Piet's head was thrown back, his neck and shoulders magnificent. His right hand was thrashing in the water. For six hours Piet had been sub-

ject to the most demanding temptations, which first Jacobina, and later the obligations of dinner with her daughters,
had prevented him from satisfying.

Satisfaction, when it came, was bountiful.

Didier found the sight awe inspiring, and the impossibility of matching such profusion made him self-conscious. He
stood up and reached for a towel.

"Sorry." But Piet had no energy for embarrassment.

Didier finished drying and put on his dressing gown. "Do
ask your friend if she needs anyone else to lend a hand."

"Of course." Piet closed his eyes again. He was no longer
feeling loquacious and wanted Didier to leave.

"*Bonne nuit*, then."

"Good night, my friend."

D idier went to his room, pulled the table across the door,
hoarding the memory of what he had seen, opened the
window and lay on the bed. He understood the merits of
delay and did not touch himself for five long minutes while
he thought over what had just happened and improved
upon it—so that when he began his long, slow frig in the
hush of a summer's night, Piet Barol not only repeated his
performance in the bath but put his strong arms around
Didier's shoulders and stroked the back of his neck with his
fingers and looked deep into his eyes and kissed him.

Meanwhile Piet refilled the bath—*hot* this time—and
washed and went to bed, entertaining the tired protests
of his conscience and resolving to be better, without at all
intending to honor this promise.

A fter this, Piet Barol began to omit his daily ritual
of feigned regret. It seemed a pity to squander an
instant of that glorious summer on self-recrimination, so he
sedated his scruples and threw himself into sampling the

many pleasures available to him while Maarten Vermeulen-Sickerts was in America.

He thought less and less of his life in Leiden and grew bolder in his explorations, sometimes leaving Egbert with a translation for two hours at a stretch while he sketched in the shuttered ballroom the superb Louis XV furniture, or the silver table ornaments reserved for Christmas and baptisms. Every piece Maarten had bought was the product of masterly labor. The delicate butterflies and dancing bears engraved on a glass goblet of the sixteenth century had the power to move Piet to tears. So did the fact that Maarten owned seventy-eight such glasses and kept them in a cabinet, redolent of intrigue and secret treaties, that had once belonged to a doge of Venice.

Piet no longer felt embarrassed to be caught in contemplation of the family's possessions. At last he was at ease with the girls and immune from the disapproval of the servants thanks to the protection of Jacobina. Nevertheless, because it made him happy to be well liked, he continued to dispense his good nature without regard to rank or influence; and so became rather a favorite with Mrs. de Leeuw, who was not used to university men taking the trouble to inquire after her mother's health, still less to them remembering her ailments from week to week.

Egbert's docility in the matter of translation exercises was commendable. When Piet understood that his charge would not attempt to leave the schoolroom once he had reached it, he began to add other pursuits to his sketch making. It pleased him to volunteer his services to Jacobina in front of the other servants and to provoke the frown she always wore when setting the date and time of their next appointment. Though he imagined doing so often, he never undressed in front of her nor pretended to any further intimacy than that of a discreet and unusually obliging body servant. She, how-

ever, became a great deal more particular in her requirements, which she continued to articulate in the tone she
used when she outlined a menu to Monsieur la Chaume or
asked Hilde Wilken to clear the tea things. Permitted such
quantities of supervised experimentation, Piet began to see
that the way to sensual Nirvana is long, and that even an
inch of the journey, properly savored, can give two people
more pleasure than many enjoy in a lifetime.

As satisfying to him was the social intimacy he had
achieved with Constance and Louisa, who now included
him in the tête-à-têtes that took place in the summerhouse
at the end of the garden where Louisa kept her mannequins
and toiles and gave commands to seamstresses and milliners. She did not make any effort to contribute practically to
her creations, and Piet admired the way she took for granted
that others should labor to give life to her imaginings. She
knew her own mind well and was a severe critic. Twice,
while her sister and Piet played trictrac, she reduced to tears
a middle-aged embroiderer who had failed to catch a pattern
of ivy, clambering over a ruin, that she had designed for a
coat inspired by Arthurian legend.

Like her father, Louisa had no patience with incompe-
tents. The third time the embroiderer made a mistake, she
never appeared again. Once or twice Piet wondered what
had happened to her. Presumably she had a family to feed,
but such quotidian pressures were so far from life as it was
lived at Herengracht 605 that he never remembered to
inquire.

Didier remained hilarious on the subject of the girls'
extravagances and reported numerous instances of petu-
lance. But they were only rude to servants. Now that Piet
had graduated to the status of guest, he saw only their most
charming sides. He and Didier did not share a bath again or
refer in any way to the events of their first one together, but

they continued to use each other's water and exchange gossip from the vantage point of the radiator; and when Didier smiled into Piet's eyes as he served him coffee, or ice-cold lemonade, Piet smiled back.

On July 17th, Maarten Vermeulen-Sickerts returned from New York in low spirits. It was the first time he had gone into partnership with Americans and he had not enjoyed the experience. He had never met such uncontainable enthusiasm—for yet another story, another elevator shaft, another eighty thousand dollars spent on frescoes and gilt. More than a thousand crystal chandeliers had already been installed, and apparently a further six hundred were required. The project was likely to finish late and certain to cost much more than he had anticipated.

Maarten had well-established lines of credit, but just at the moment his finances were rather tighter than usual. His hotel on the shores of Lake Como was not doing well. The resort had fallen abruptly out of fashion a few months after it was finished. His establishments in London and Frankfurt had required new lead roofs and been closed for six months, since he could not have patrons in a building filled with banging workmen.

Unlike his wife and daughters, Maarten Vermeulen-Sickerts had a keen sense of the value of money. Because he was honest he was prepared to charge his guests the sums he did only for an experience that was, in every way, perfect. He personally supervised the selection of the telephonists. He turned every tap, stayed in every Suite Impériale, tried the butter in every breakfast room to make sure it was soft but solid. He would rather close for a season than offer accommodations that were less than first rate. But to have closed his two most profitable hotels for the same season left him inconveniently short of funds, since the new one in

New York, which his partner had decided to call the Plaza, was costing tens of thousands a week.

For some time, Maarten had been wondering whether God was punishing him for the venture's worldliness. He had sanctioned the architect's fancies from the other side of the Atlantic and visited to see the demolition of the existing building and the sinking of the new foundation's cornerstone. But the Americans had built very quickly and on his second visit he had been shocked by the grandiloquence he had financed. To have built a Renaissance French château thousands of miles from the Loire Valley was one thing. To have presumed to improve on the original by inserting nineteen floors beneath its turrets was another and seemed worryingly close to what others had done with the Tower of Babel. That enterprise had brought ruin and discord to its overreaching builders, and it seemed to Maarten that this one might do so, too.

His partner, an American named Lionel Dermont, whom he had met in the first-class dining room of the French liner *Provence*, appeared to have much less money now than he had seemed to have then. Indeed, Maarten was no longer sure Dermont had ever had the sums he claimed. Over his six weeks in the United States he had developed an energetic dislike for the man, who dressed so elegantly and told everybody what to do and contributed little of tangible worth to anything.

Lionel Dermont was a talker. Maarten Vermeulen-Sickerts, except with his closest associates, was not. Mr. Dermont's talk was generally the greatest rot and this did not make his monologues easier to endure. He had a thousand sincere ways of explaining the delay of a check, and though he had long ceased to contribute to the construction costs he was fiercely loyal to his vision of a hotel "fit for potentates" and determined to spend as much of Maarten's money as was necessary to achieve it. In this he was gleefully abetted by the architect and the gentleman responsible for the interiors. Through his acquaintance with these three men Maarten derived the inaccurate but unshakable impression that all Americans are brash and acquisitive and painfully dull dining companions besides.

Mr. Dermont's stylish postponement of his latest installment of capital had inspired Maarten to investigate how best to cope with future emergencies alone. He lunched with his bankers at the Knickerbocker Trust Company and sounded them out on the possibility of a further loan. But the shiny confidence expected of men who attempt to borrow large sums of money in New York was impossible for Maarten to emulate, since it would have been so unacceptable in Amsterdam. As he left their monumental offices on Fifth Avenue, he was aware that he had not done well.

This knowledge preoccupied him throughout his return voyage, during which he began to believe that God disapproved of his spending such sums and energies on a monument to human vanity. By the time his own door was opened to him he was feeling morose and apprehensive. Though he had not hesitated to spend $180 on an evening cloak for Louisa and only slightly less on gowns for Constance and Jacobina, he knew that he should not have bought them. It was a further challenge to the deity.

Jacobina was unusually solicitous when she came to chat in his dressing room before dinner. As he embraced her, he felt a tug of violent desire that horrified him and made him step backwards to avoid giving his Creator further offense. He could see that this annoyed his wife and did his best to be bright and amusing at dinner; but in fact the only thing that lifted his spirits was the way in which Constance and Louisa appeared to have dropped their guard with Piet Barol. Maarten was glad of that. He had often been cruelly cut by ladies like his daughters when he was a young man. He was pleased for Piet that it was 1907, not 1877, and that the world had moved on.

When dinner was over, Egbert was allowed to come down, having dined on sugared bread and milk in his room; and watched impassively by Didier Loubat the whole family unwrapped their gifts and exclaimed over them as the salon filled with tissue paper and ribbons.

Observing this happy scene, Piet saw that his father's presence disturbed Egbert and that he took care not to come into contact with any of the brightly colored paper; also that he shifted surreptitiously from foot to foot over the wreathed roses in the carpet, following a secret dance of his own.

Maarten had brought the boy a bright red fire engine and knew at once that Egbert did not care for it. He had no idea that the Shadowers were deeply suspicious of primary colors and that merely holding such an object required tremendous courage. This meant he was unmoved when Egbert carried it the whole way across the room to give to Hilde Wilken to take upstairs. Maarten saw only a sullen, pampered child, too fussed over by women, and this depressed him and reignited his anger over Mr. Dermont.

Jacobina knew her husband well and understood that Egbert was likely to be shouted at if his father's mood did not improve. Maarten's mounting impatience irked her and added insult to the injury he had done her in his dressing room. "Do sing us a duet, darling, with Mr. Barol," she said. Maarten had a decent voice and was always happier after using it. "Why not something by Bizet?" she added slyly, to punish him for his failures as a lover and a father.

Maarten, who had no appetite for conversation, was touched by his wife's suggestion. "Capital idea. What say you, Mr. Barol? Do you think we might manage it? We have *Carmen* somewhere."

But Piet had a better idea. He took out the *Pêcheurs de Perles* and suggested that they sing the duet commonly called "Au fond du temple saint." "Two old friends are reunited but fall in love with the same divine beauty. It nearly makes them enemies but in the end they swear eternal friendship."

"A splendid theme." Maarten took his glasses from their case and peered over the music. He remembered it was devilish tricky to fit the words to the notes.

Both men were baritones and the duet called for a tenor, so Piet took the higher part and sang it in falsetto. He had played the piano arrangement so often he had no need to look at his hands, and this left his eyes free to direct the meaning of the music as he wished. As he sang of the crowd falling to its knees, astonished at such loveliness, he stared fixedly over the piano lid and into the room beyond. Constance and Louisa were on the daybed, as usual. Egbert sat on a little stool at his mother's feet. Jacobina's chair was against the farthest wall, and her children could not see her face without turning round. This meant that when Piet sang "Look! There is the goddess!" no one saw that he did so straight into Jacobina's eyes; nor did anyone observe that she met his gaze unflinchingly.

Now Maarten joined him in rapt appreciation of the heavenly figure's beauty. But when he sang "O vision! O dream!" he was looking at Piet's hands to make sure his timing was accurate, and it struck Jacobina as significant that he should sing these words without even thinking of her. This made her bolder and she put down her embroidery. Now the male voices joined forces in rapturous major thirds, and though Maarten's pitch wobbled occasionally they made a fine sound. Singing straight to Jacobina, Piet declared that love had taken their hearts by storm and was turning them into enemies.

At this, Jacobina smiled.

But now the music was gaining control of them and Maarten was confident enough to look up from time to time, which meant that he was looking directly into Piet's eyes when he sang, "No, nothing will separate us!"

Piet Barol was genuinely moved. He had chosen the duet in order to communicate with Maarten's wife, but the passion of the music, the platonic fidelity of the male lines, drew him increasingly towards the man he had cuckolded. As they swore lustily to be friends forever, to treat each other as brothers, and promised that the goddess would unite them one day, Piet began to feel a mounting filial devotion. He *did* love Maarten, and the soaring declarations they made to each other dimmed his consciousness of all else. They sang the last chorus triumphantly, in a perfect unison of pitch and pace that left them feeling tender and inseparable, enormously refreshed, as though Bizet's rich harmonies had released the toxins from their souls.

Ten hours after closing his eyes, Maarten woke with the conviction that Piet Barol could be a useful ally. He had built his fortune on recognizing exceptional talent and did not consider that a man of Piet's gifts was best deployed teaching German verbs to a troubled little boy.

Maarten was a fearless realist. He did not pretend to himself that he had gained the confidence of his American bankers in their gaudy offices. As he lay propped up on his pillows, contemplating the soft-boiled egg Hilde Wilken had brought him, he was annoyed by this failure—but it did not induce panic. He knew many wealthy men in Holland and was confident he could persuade them to lend him large sums. In his own country he had a greater renown and surer touch than would ever be the case in America.

He got out of bed, knelt beside it and said his prayers,

in which he apologized sincerely for the waste of his American hotel. Then he opened his eyes and put this penitential mood aside. There was no retreating now, if he was to keep his wife and children in the luxury that was their natural atmosphere. The damned thing had cost more than ten million dollars already. It would probably cost another two million to finish, and then there would be staff salaries and interest to pay. . . . There was, perhaps, a further $500,000 to be borrowed from the Knickerbocker once his current credit was exhausted. This would be nowhere near enough.

Maarten had never had his collection valued, but it seemed to him that it would be wise to do so now, discreetly. He was too proud to introduce economies at Herengracht 605 and though he could postpone the building of his country place for another year, this would not release sufficient sums to cover his obligations. He had a great deal of furniture, far more than he needed, and he knew there were men across Europe who would pay high and confidential prices for the jewels of his collection. He needed someone he could trust to catalog and record them.

After his bath he rang for Mr. Blok and told him to ask Mr. Barol to wait on him at ten o'clock.

Piet Barol had already sketched several dozen objects in the house and chosen the finest pieces; and this was to Maarten Vermeulen-Sickerts a triumphant affirmation of his faith in the lad. As Piet showed him his drawings it seemed miraculous to Maarten that he should have anticipated his need, and fulfilled it in advance, without knowing anything of his difficulties.

Maarten's preoccupation with his own salvation had left him alert to the ways in which God communicates with Man, and he read great significance in what Piet had done.

It was vital no one should suspect him of valuing his treasures with an eye to raising money on them. His credit depended on the confidence of the public, which would be fatally undermined by the leaking of such news. Now there would be no need to hire a photographer whose loose talk might spoil everything. Turning the pages of Piet's sketchbook he could have kissed him. His execution was as precise as anything a machine might achieve, but so much more refined.

As he accepted the book to look over later, the memory of his son's behavior the night before recurred to him and seemed to complicate the message God had sent. "It is useful to me to have this little inventory," he went on, more briskly, "and I should be glad if you would devote some time each day to continuing it. However"—he grew sterner—"I have a serious matter to discuss with you. Please sit down."

To a conscience as tender as Piet Barol's, this was a disturbing instruction. The life he would return to if he lost this man's favor became vivid again, as it had not been in months. The shivering indignities of an outside toilet, his father's joyless gloom, the cold winter nights, the tepid entertainments of the university clerks, their petty hatreds and intrigues rose up and seemed to choke him.

"I am extremely distressed to discover that my son is no better," said Maarten. "We have greatly enjoyed having you in the house, but there has been no improvement in Egbert, and there must be improvement."

Maarten intended to sound peremptory, but Piet heard the hopelessness in his voice. He looked at his face. It was plain that his employer had no idea of his true transgression. He began to float with relief, but at the same time he wished that Maarten was not Jacobina's husband—because he longed to treat him worthily. It was no use pretending he would never touch his wife again. He had tried too many times to stop and never once succeeded. Here was an opportunity to atone for his repeated betrayals in another way.

"I will save Egbert for you, sir," he said fervently. "I know I can, and I will."

Piet Barol had never yet turned on Egbert Vermeulen-Sickerts the totality of attention he had so far devoted to every other member of his family. As he left Maarten's office he felt exhilarated by the challenge of getting to the bottom of his mysteries. Piet had great faith in his ability to make people love him. He was not daunted by the layers of calcified sediment that separated Egbert's humanity from the world beyond it.

Maarten had given him a green velvet box and asked him to sketch its contents; had told him, moreover, that he might ask to see anything in the house, whenever he had the inclination, so long as he undertook to draw it. To have the dread of the morning resolved so happily was wonderful. He passed beneath the statues of Paris, Aphrodite and Athena, taking the stairs two at a time and whistling. It was clear now that Jacobina would never confess. He was pleased that her reunion with her husband had not turned her into an hysterical penitent.

In the hall he encountered Mr. Blok and asked him breezily to fetch from the cabinet in the ballroom an object of such price he had never dared examine it: a jewel box, covered in golden vines and studded with pearls, that had been made for Catherine de Médicis.

"That would require Mr. Vermeulen-Sickerts' express permission."

"By all means seek it." Piet waited in the hall while the butler went upstairs. When he returned, Piet placed the jewel box on top of the green velvet case and went into the house next door, feeling full of the joys of life.

This mood was broken abruptly by the music coming from the schoolroom—a sad, lost music, in no discernible key.

At his Bösendorfer, Egbert was engaged in a negotiation of the utmost delicacy over his handling of the red fire engine the evening before. He had risen at 4:00 a.m. and lain submerged to his ears in iced water as the sky lightened. Faced with a keyboard of black and white, he sometimes found he could communicate with his tyrants more subtly than words alone permitted. He had abased himself and asked their forgiveness. This had been withheld. He had begged for it and been told that toying with primary colors was an offense that merited prolonged punishment.

By the time Piet Barol entered his aunt's house, Egbert was close to tears; and when his tutor opened the schoolroom door the Shadowers rebuked him for allowing their conference to be overheard. He broke at once into a frenetic rendition of the C Minor Prelude, taking care to play each note with identical force. The music's repeating patterns blocked his bid for freedom at every turn, and Bach's sly insinuation of a major note at the very end compelled him to begin again, and again, as Piet took a seat at the table and opened the velvet case.

Maarten had asked him to draw it because, of all his possessions, he cared for it the least. The box contained a set of Dresden figurines that had been childhood playthings of Catherine the Great, when she was plain little Sophia of Anhalt-Zerbst. The pirouetting maidens and courting couples did not please Piet Barol, but he set them in a line and began to draw, waiting for Egbert to stop.

Egbert did not stop. With each repetition of the prelude his shackles tightened, until he understood that his punishment was to be humiliated in front of his tutor. The impossibility of stopping made tears well in his pale blue eyes and spill down his cheeks, where they joined rivulets of sweat.

The day was turning into a scorcher. Piet had completed the figurines and was beginning the jewel box when exhaustion finally brought an end to his pupil's exertions. Egbert considered running from the room but lacked the energy even for that. Instead he slumped forward over the piano, wishing for oblivion.

Piet went to him. Egbert was prepared for anger and further punishment. To be met with kindness undid him and when Piet embraced him he burst into wrenching sobs. He cried and cried as his tutor carried him tenderly to the sofa, and when he was finished Piet asked in his gentlest voice the question he had been pondering all morning.

"Dear Egbert," he said. "Is music the solution or the problem?"

Six hours later, Hilde Wilken knocked on Egbert's door. When there was no answer, she opened it and went in and put the tray she was carrying on the writing desk. Egbert was fast asleep, his cheeks aflame. She looked at him nervously.

Hilde had a brother of her own, a year younger than Egbert, and at first she had looked forward to working in a house lived in by a ten-year-old boy. But Egbert Vermeulen-Sickerts frightened her. The music he made was so incomprehensible. He was so small and slender, and yet his hands were quite as large as a fifteen-year-old's, with long thin fingers that made her think of amphibians. He did not seem quite human. She gathered her courage and touched his arm. It was as cold as a corpse's. "M-Master Egbert," she whispered. He did not stir. She sat down in the comfortable armchair at the foot of his bed. She had spent all afternoon tidying his sisters' closets and worrying that no man would ever love her, and welcomed a moment to rest. She leaned back into the cushions, wondering if perhaps he had died. Death was no respecter of classes. It would serve this family right, she thought, thinking of the sharpness with which Louisa had just criticized her folding of a cashmere cloak. As if one was born knowing that cloaks must be hung, not folded! A cold violence settled on her, in which pain at the way Didier now smiled only at Piet Barol mingled with a hatred of her employer's daughters and effervesced into one bitter tear.

"Master Egbert!" she said, leaning forward and shaking his arm more vigorously, thinking how unjust it was that she, a fully grown woman, should call a ten-year-old imbecile "master."

Egbert opened his eyes.

Hilde stood hurriedly and curtsied. "I have brought your supper."

Egbert blinked, and the mortifying events of the afternoon returned with full force. "Thank you, Hilde." He copied his mother's cold formality. "Is everyone in to dinner?"

"Your sisters are out, I believe."

This meant that Piet Barol would be eating alone with his parents and might tell them what had happened. The look on Egbert's face prompted sympathy in Hilde, who was not as stony hearted as the Vermeulen-Sickertses often made her feel. "I'll bring you some jelly later," she said, and left him.

The next morning, Egbert found the courage to ask if his parents had been told about his crying. They had not, because Piet knew that nothing would be accomplished without the boy's trust and had not betrayed it. They spent a pleasant morning discussing the causes of the French

Revolution, but there was no repeat of the previous day's intimacy. The Shadowers demanded privacy and Egbert was too ashamed of his subjection to them to violate it. So when Piet asked again whether music was the solution or the problem, he turned on him the stubborn blankness that had defeated his other tutors and merely said he did not know.

Piet was wise enough not to show his exasperation, but as the hot summer weeks melted into one another it began to rise. Saving Egbert was the reparation his self-respect demanded, and each encounter with Jacobina heightened the urgency of making amends to her husband. He told the boy about his own mother's death, hoping that a confidence from him might inspire one in return. It did not. He complained of his father to show that he, too, had his troubles. But Egbert showed no curiosity about his private affairs. Piet Barol was not accustomed to encountering such implacable resistance, and it annoyed him. In their bathroom late at night, Didier Loubat mocked his efforts and told him that nothing, save the loss of his father's fortune, would ever save such a helpless brat. "No one's fixed him before, so they won't fire you" was his analysis. "Stay as long as you can put up with it, save the money for a new life, then let him drive someone else to lunacy."

But Piet did not intend to be vanquished; and one Saturday afternoon, coming across a handsomely bound edition of the Chopin ballades at a shop on the Kalverstraat, he bought it and went home whistling. He was up early the next morning and entered the house next door only a moment after Egbert had completed his crossing of the entrance hall floor. The boy was playing a martinet fugue and its claustrophobic precision convinced him he had found a tonic. Manic bouts of Bach were clearly doing Egbert no good; perhaps Romantic music would inspire some expression of inner feeling.

"I have a present for you," he said warmly, after the fugue's seventh rendition.

Egbert accepted the volume with a mumbled word of thanks; but when Piet suggested he play something from it the boy shook his head, left the piano, and opened his French dictionary.

Piet controlled his irritation with difficulty. He did not know that Egbert's masters insisted on white and black notes being played with equal weight, for precisely quantified periods, and that Chopin's time permissiveness, his infinite gradations of shade and meaning, were impossible; dangerous even to imagine.

He went to the piano himself and played haltingly through the first page of a ballade, hoping that his errors would tempt the boy to show him he could do better. They did not. Egbert remained at the table, apparently immersed in his dictionary; in fact in thrall to powerful and conflicting impulses he could not resolve. He had no friends, and no one outside his immediate family had ever bought him a gift. He yearned to show gratitude and seize the opportunity Piet offered, but fear of reprisals restrained him.

"Come and play this. It's too difficult for me," said Piet at last.

"No thanks," murmured Egbert, with maddening insouciance.

The following Sunday, the 11th of August, was Piet's day off. He did not even consider going to Leiden to visit his father but slept late and went downstairs to find Jacobina in her apple-green dress. She explained that she had missed church on account of a headache and asked whether he might perform a small service for her before the household returned. An hour later, they came back together

from the house next door and parted with careful formality. Jacobina went upstairs to bathe, but Piet rarely had the
house so completely to himself and did not wish to waste
the opportunity. There were still three rooms, besides the
maids' quarters, that he had not seen; and unsatisfied sensual desire made him foolhardy.

He checked the kitchen to make sure the other servants
had gone to church. They had. It was only 10:30. No one
would be back for at least another three-quarters of an hour.
He stood beside the icebox, weighing the risks, then climbed
the stairs to the second floor and opened Constance's bedroom door.

Hilde Wilken's devotions had prevented her from ordering the chaos Constance wreaked daily upon her possessions.
The girls had been at a dance the evening before, and Constance's dress of pink gauze stitched with silver was lying on
the floor where she had stepped out of it. The dressing table
was cluttered with combs and brushes and pots of rouge
(Constance overruled her sister's objections to maquillage)
and the air was laden with the scent of lily of the valley. Two
other dresses, discarded in favor of the pink, were thrown
carelessly over a chair. Piet touched one, wondering what
it cost, and opened a closet to find rows and rows of shoes,
many more than he had ever seen her wear.

In the corner by the window was a desk strewn with invitations. He opened a drawer, discovered a bundle of letters
tied with silk ribbon, untied it and read a passionate epistle
from a recent suitor whose adoration stretched to fifteen
pages. The young man's sentimentality made Piet smile
and remember with pride his own deft handling of Constance. He read a second gushing letter, retied the bundle
and returned it. He wanted desperately to see Louisa's room,
over which he had eavesdropped so often; but though the

temptation was powerful, it also frightened him, because he was still slightly scared of her.

He went boldly to a small paneled door and opened it. He was right: it led directly to Louisa's room, which stretched beyond him like a space glimpsed through a looking glass. It was quite unlike Constance's. There were no pinks, no flowers, no messy piles of clothes. The walls were a pale gray, the bed simple and restrained, with no draperies. The furniture had been made in France in the severe style of the Directory.

He stepped across the threshold. So this was where the girls discussed him. At one end of the room a pair of French windows gave onto the balcony, which overlooked the garden. There were no letters on the desk, or in either of the drawers he opened; no clutter of pillboxes and scent vials on the dressing table. He took a step toward the wardrobe, intent on examining its treasures. But as he moved a shadow loomed beyond the window, dark against the day's bright light, and before he could hide or retreat the glass door opened and Louisa Vermeulen-Sickerts came in.

The catastrophe was so sudden he marveled later at how deftly he managed it. "I thought you'd missed church," he said happily. "I've been calling for you. I'm desperate for a game of trictrac. Will you join me?"

"In a moment, Mr. Barol." Louisa went to her desk, with no trace of annoyance. "I'm just about to smoke a cigarette. Don't tell Papa, will you?" She was wearing jodhpurs and a riding habit that showed off her lean, athletic body.

"I'm an expert keeper of secrets."

"I'm sure of that." Louisa took an enameled cigarette case and a box of matches out of a drawer.

Piet lit the cigarette for her. "Do you like to ride?" He had the idea of introducing a compliment.

"Not as much as Mummy and Constance, but I do. Do you?"

"I adore it."

I t was an unwise boast. Piet regretted it the instant he had made it, because there was something dangerous in the way Louisa said: "In that case, we should all go riding one day." But he hid his nerves and chatted amiably while she smoked, and then they both went down to the summer-house and played trictrac until lunch.

In their bathroom later that night, when Piet sought counsel over the incident, Didier said: "You'll have to miss the workers' fête next week. Pity. The maids are willing and the food's good. But they keep their horses out there and they're monsters. Say you're ill."

Piet had never ridden a horse in his life but had no inten-tion of passing up the opportunity to inspect Willemshoven or to enjoy the annual *fête champêtre* Maarten put on for his Dutch workers. He thought of the docile horses owned by the farmers of Leiden. It could not be so very hard to man-age on one of them. "I'll be all right," he said.

On the floor below, Constance was saying, "Of course he can ride. I thought you liked him now."

"He's amusing company, but I tell you he's lying. I sus-pect he lies about many things."

"It's not fair to give him your horse, if that's what you really think. Aristotle's a beast."

Louisa smiled. "We'll give him Mummy's."

"I still maintain he's told the truth."

"We shall see."

P iet's judges did not have long to wait. The following Saturday, Didier's father appeared after breakfast in the white-and-green livery of the Amstel Hotel and drove Piet and the girls in the Vermeulen-Sickerts' second Rolls-Royce, while Mr. Blok took charge of the first. It was a perfect day for a party and as they left the city Piet's spirits soared. He had never been in an automobile before. It was a wonderful thing to be driven at twenty miles an hour, with two sought-after young ladies, to an entertainment given by a very rich man on his country estate. At every village, peasants left their fields to line the road, gawping at the handsome cars and elegant figures who rode in them. Maarten's workers had preceded them by horse-drawn omnibus. That Piet traveled with the family, as a matter of course, made him feel delightfully superior.

Their destination was achieved by a long, twisting drive through flower-filled woods. "Papa wanted somewhere he could rebuild entirely and make comfortable and modern," explained Constance, who was embarrassed to have a country place in such a poor state of repair. But Piet Barol was charmed by the ivy-covered façade and the charred, empty rooms behind it, in which wild herbs grew and owls nested. The gardens were laid out in the English style. Behind the house, on a wide smooth lawn that dipped in the distance towards a stream, a marquee and a bandstand had been erected, from which trombones glinted as the musicians tuned.

At the appearance of the Vermeulen-Sickertses, the band struck up the national anthem, and Piet emerged from the car with the dignity of visiting royalty. He was superbly dressed. He had paid an expensive and dexterous tailor to alter a light tweed suit of Maarten's and it fitted him as if he had been its first owner.

"Come and see the stables." Louisa slipped her arm through Constance's. "They're the only part of the house in working order."

They walked across the lawn into the shade of the trees. The knowledge that the hotel workers would take him for a guest pleased Piet enormously. He talked so naturally that Constance felt sure her sister was about to be confounded, and was glad. They reached a courtyard and crossed it, interrupted three grooms smoking cigarettes, who scrambled to their feet and bowed. Preceded by them, they moved beneath a great arch into a vast and gloomy barn; and now, for the first time, the enormity of Piet's boast struck him— because these horses were not at all like the friendly beasts that grazed the fields around Leiden.

"Saddle them for us after lunch," Louisa told the groom. "Mr. Barol shall have Sultan."

But Piet was ready for her. "Your father gave me this suit," he said regretfully. "He'd be offended if I ruined it."

"Oh, you can change." Louisa smiled. "Our cousin Jurgens left his riding things when he stayed last year, and we've never remembered to send them on. He's about your size. Bit fatter perhaps. I've brought them for you."

Jacobina Vermeulen-Sickerts, in a white dress by Poiret, did not address a word to her son's tutor all day. But as she entertained her husband's guests, aware that many eyes were on her, she found herself seeking him out and rejoicing in his beauty. She remembered last year's fête very well—it had rained; she had worn a wonderful Worth gown, now completely ruined—but already the woman she had been seemed a different, less vital creature.

Regular pleasure had restored the glow of Jacobina's youth more effectively than any of the painful treatments her friends endured in fashionable spa towns. She was aware, as she shook hands with her husband's staff, that she made him proud. This pleased her and made her go out of her way to charm the chambermaids and laundresses, the shriveled little wives of the porters, and to listen to their dull, awe-struck conversation as if she had never been more amused by anything in her life.

She had chosen Piet's suit carefully from among her hus-band's cast-offs and was entirely satisfied with the figure he cut. Her eyes kept flitting to him and her mind to the delights of the following Monday afternoon; but after lunch she found that he had disappeared, and this alarmed her. Had he sneaked off with a kitchen maid? The possibility was enraging and she began to roam restlessly between clus-ters of guests. She was at first relieved to see him walking with her daughters towards the stables, in jodhpurs and a smart riding coat. But when she saw Piet clamber onto her horse she faltered in midsentence. It was clear he had never ridden in his life.

This fact was also obvious to Constance and Louisa; and this time Constance did not at all feel like laughing at her sister's trap. "Perhaps it's unfriendly of us to make off like this," she said, as the color drained from Piet's cheeks. "Why don't we—"

"Nonsense, darling! It's perfect weather for a gallop. We mustn't waste it, especially since Mr. Barol enjoys riding so."

On the lawn far away, Jacobina saw at once what had happened, and understood that she alone could save Piet from laying his life on the altar of his pride. With a word of apology she left a group of waiters' wives and hurried towards the party on horseback. When it became clear that they were making for the woods she started to run as fast as her high-heeled shoes and constricting skirts permitted. Jacobina had been an athlete twenty years before and panic restored her powers. She reached them as the groom was opening the gate but was so out of breath she could barely speak. "Mr.—Barol— I— I'm worried about Egbert. I— would like you to return to—Amsterdam."

But Louisa, in her friendliest voice, said, "Let us have our half hour's pleasure, Mama. Egbert mustn't monopolize Mr. Barol." And with a wicked smile she spurred her horse into a trot, and there was nothing Piet could do to prevent his from following.

To the uninitiated human, the trot of a horse is a profoundly unnatural movement. Piet made the error of leaning forward as he had seen jockeys do, but this revelation of inexperience only confirmed Sultan's suspicion that a novice had mounted him. Sultan was part Friesian, part Arab, and had an extremely high opinion of himself. He felt for Jacobina Vermeulen-Sickerts a devotion so total he would gladly have died for her in a cavalry charge, as his ancestors had been bred to do. What he would not stomach was the insult of an untrained rider, and he determined to make this plain.

Beside the graceful, straight-backed Vermeulen-Sickerts girls, Piet Barol felt like a fool and knew that he looked like one. He was not often at such a disadvantage and found it irksome. To be asked pleasantly by Louisa how he liked his horse was almost as shaming as the look of anxious sympathy on Constance's face. He made a valiant effort but could not agree on a rhythm with the beast beneath him; and when Piet whispered Sultan's name, hoping to soothe him, this presumption of intimacy caused further offense.

As they passed beyond sight of the house, his testicles slamming against the saddle with every step Sultan took, a pain worse than embarrassment began to rise through Piet Barol. Its severity clarified his priorities, and he was on the verge of admitting his lie and apologizing for it when Louisa began to canter.

A hundred years before, a wide avenue had been cut through the ancient woods, but the estate had been derelict before Maarten's purchase and the forest had seized its chance to recolonize lost ground. Straplings already four feet high were spreading their roots through the gravel and established trees stretched across the clearing for lost friends.

Piet was liable to be decapitated by branches his mistress' daughters missed by a foot, and Sultan decreed that this should be his fate. He began to go at a tremendous pace. Now terror combined with physical agony to silence Piet emphatically. He had strong thighs and gripped with them for his life, crouching low over the brute's neck. Several times Sultan swerved abruptly and almost threw him. Piet had never known such fear. As they leaped a narrow stream, the knowledge that he might die rose in his throat. It made him furious—with himself, but more directly with Louisa Vermeulen-Sickerts, because it was clear she would not stop until she had seen him fail.

When they reached the stables, having galloped through the wood and come back over the fields, Piet Barol was aching and bruised and incandescent with rage. He got off his horse, his inner thighs in agony, and without a word strode off towards the house. The fête was ending. The speeches had been made and the band was playing its last march. If he had had a match and a barrel of gasoline he would have torched the place. The idea of going back to the city in the company of the women who had orchestrated his humiliation was insupportable. He tried for a place on the workers' omnibus—but every seat was taken. I'll walk then, he decided; but the walk would take the better part of the afternoon and night, and with each step the pain in his groin and buttocks grew worse.

In the end there was nothing for it and he took his place in the Rolls in thundering silence. Constance was the first to follow him. The tenderness in her glance annoyed him enormously. He did not reply when she ventured that it had been a lovely day. Louisa got in. In painful silence they endured the journey to the city, the girls responding to Monsieur Loubat's cheery queries from the driver's seat while Piet sat in the furnace of his own thoughts.

Outside Herengracht 605 a crowd had gathered. Servants were unpacking china and glasses from a goods cart; street urchins had congregated, hoping for tips and a glimpse of the ladies in their finery. Piet knew that Didier would laugh when told his story; also that he was not ready to be laughed at. The Rolls-Royce stopped at the foot of the stairs. Monsieur Loubat got out, opened the passenger door on Piet's side, and bowed.

Louisa had been steadfastly ignoring her sister's wordless hints ever since entering the vehicle, but now she steeled herself to do what must be done. She leaned towards Piet and touched his knee. "Mr. Barol. Forgive me."

This was the final provocation.

Piet would have shouted, had Monsieur Loubat not been present to hear. "Are you satisfied now?" The words came out in a strangled compromise between fury and discretion. "I am not as rich as you and I don't mind admitting it. I have not had so many advantages." Without waiting for a reply, he jumped to the ground and went up the stairs and into the house. Maarten was in the entrance hall with the manager of the Amstel Hotel. Piet allowed himself to be introduced and agreed that it had, indeed, been a marvelous day. Then he excused himself and went to see to Egbert.

In the house next door, his charge was locked in the depths of the C Minor Prelude. He was just finishing his ninth repetition when Piet entered the room. Because the Shadowers had demanded twenty-one and the presto run towards the end was fiendish, he ignored his tutor as best he could to preserve his concentration.

Egbert played the prelude twice while Piet watched him, fuming. But his next repetition, compounding the day's earlier indignities, pushed his tutor beyond the limits of his self-control.

Piet picked up the child and slung him over his shoulder. At first Egbert was too astonished to protest but when Piet opened the drawing room door, he began to whimper "No, Mr. Barol. Please, no!" to no avail. At the moment Piet entered the hall, he had no fear of any consequence; was consumed only by a determination to take a stand against this pampered family.

He saw that Jacobina had joined her husband and the manager of his hotel. He did not care. He carried the child through the front door, down the steps and into the crowd. In an act of defiance directed at the whole order of things, he set Egbert down on the cobblestones.

E gbert's screech made even Agneta Hemels put her hands over her ears. The boy began to hop from one foot to another, as if the street were made of molten steel. He wailed and ripped his hair out in clumps. The servants stood back, aghast. Only Monsieur Loubat took action. He approached, making the solicitous *click-click* sound he used to calm nervous horses, but at his touch Egbert lunged at him, kicking and biting with the strength of a man twice his age.

It took three adults, including Maarten Vermeulen-Sickerts, to subdue Egbert and carry him into the house, away from the prying glances of the street. All Piet heard as he followed them was Jacobina's shrill instruction: "To his bedroom! At once!"

He went there too, overcome by a contrition as sincere as it was practical; but Mr. Blok was playing sentry and would not let him pass. When he reached his own room he was thoroughly frightened. Perhaps he had sabotaged his future irreparably. How unbelievably maladroit. He rarely lost control, and as his anger drained it exposed the knowledge that his own vanity had brought about his downfall. His mother watched him from the bedside table. She had never shouted at him but expressed her displeasure with a regretful silence that now seemed to fill the room. He saw himself sent back to Leiden with no references, no hope of alternative employment in Amsterdam—for he could not bear the shame of encountering Constance and Louisa in another house, where he was another family's servant. It would be better to leave the country altogether—but with what funds?

He ignored Didier's knock and was relieved to be spared the embarrassment of consolation, but it took him a long time to fall asleep; and when he did, his dreams were full of taunting young women in elegant dresses.

Egbert did not calm down until he had submerged himself sixty-three times in a bath full of water and crushed ice. His mother held his hand while he did this and ordered more ice when he demanded it. Jacobina had helped Egbert through similar ordeals before and understood that intervention made things worse. She had never shared the details of these scenes with Maarten. Nor did she tonight when she placed their child's freezing body in the soft sheets of their own bed, kissed him tenderly, and told him that he was safe and should sleep. Maarten Vermeulen-Sickerts had too much experience of rising to an occasion to look leniently on prolonged lapses of will. The knowledge that every one of the day's guests would spend the next in rapt discussion of his family's eccentricities inspired a searing shame, closely succeeded by the terror of the righteous man who knows he has offended his god.

The entertainment at Willemshoven had gone off so well that for several hours Maarten's self-confidence had regained its customary solidity. Now he was reminded that life is full of unexpected humiliations. This knowledge, cut with a sympathy he did not think he should feel for the boy, much less display, ensured that the rising sun found him in an explosive temper.

So did the fact that Egbert, beset by writhing dreams, kicked like a mule all night.

Gert Blok opened Piet's door the next morning, immediately after knocking, and was gratified to find his quarry still dressing for church. It was the first time he had seen Piet's naked chest and he drank in every detail to enjoy at his leisure. He had not imagined that the young man's arms bulged in quite the way they did when he reached for his shirt. He informed Piet, with extreme frostiness, that his presence was required in the study.

"Is he angry?"

"Beside himself." As Gert Blok spoke, it came to him that this might be his last opportunity to catch Piet Barol half naked; indeed, it might be the last time he spoke to him at all. He knew his master in this mood. Blok's desire for the young man disturbed him, almost made him hate him. But the prospect of never seeing Piet again was insupportable. "The important thing," he said, "is that you should not attempt to justify yourself. I've known him more than twenty years. You acted very wrongly yesterday. Don't pretend otherwise. It's your only chance."

For the next forty-five minutes, Piet followed the butler's advice. He made no attempt to justify his actions, showed only the most passionate and rueful contrition, and endured Maarten's torrent of damning accusation with the commitment of a flagellant. It worked. He left Maarten's office, cheeks flaming but still employed; and as he climbed the stairs he reminded himself that he was not yet an equal of the family he served.

He had been barred from church and told to say his prayers with Egbert. He knocked at the boy's door but received no answer. He closed his eyes, gathered himself, and went in. Egbert was sitting in his pajamas by the window. At his tutor's appearance he assumed the expression Louisa reserved for errant milliners. Piet knew the boy deserved an apology; also that his own future in the household depended on winning his forgiveness—because Jacobina would never side with him against her son. Nevertheless, he found the prospect galling.

"Good morning, Egbert."

"Good morning, Mr. Barol."

"Would you like to say your prayers with me?"

Egbert went to the center of the room and knelt. He brought his hands together, closed his eyes, and set his mouth in an expression of unshakable severity. "I am ready."

"Let us begin, then."

The hour Piet spent with Egbert on a Sunday was usually the dullest of his week, because the reiteration of a service he had just sat through was tiresome. He found the events outlined in the Creed highly improbable and the defiant certainty of its register irritating. At least today he had been excused church and need only say the prayers once.

The boy's expensive bedroom reminded Piet how inadequate his savings were to the requirements of a happy life in New York and emphasized the disadvantages of starting out as a *plongeur* or errand boy, living in slums full of Poles and Greeks and Irish. He turned from this thought and took the prayer book from the desk. "Would you like to read the Commandments?"

Egbert did not reply, so Piet read them himself. He usually took their devotions at a brisk pace but today he proceeded solemnly. At the injunction to honor your father and mother he remembered that he had only written twice to Herman Barol since his arrival in Amsterdam; then, with irritation, that neither of these letters had been answered. He pressed on. "You shall not commit adultery." His conscience began to smart. "You shall not covet your neighbor's house; you shall not covet your neighbor's wife."

When the Commandments were over, he turned to the psalm with relief, but its first verse was disquietingly relevant: "Truly God is good to the upright, to those who are pure in heart. But as for me, my feet had stumbled, my steps had well nigh slipped." He felt watched and the reading from the Book of Job did little to ease his discomfort: "Let the day perish wherein I was born, and the night which said, 'There is a man-child conceived.'"

By the time Piet Barol had finished the service, he felt more thoroughly chastised than he ever had in his life and his conscience stung with the knowledge that he deserved it. The sensation was extremely unpleasant. It meant, however, that his apology when it came was heartfelt. "I had no right to take you outside, Egbert," he said meekly. "Perhaps I deserve to lose my place. I certainly will if you don't forgive me." He took the boy's cold hand. "Please let me help you and make amends."

Egbert had spent the day planning the banishment of Piet Barol. He had imagined Piet packing his possessions, carrying his suitcase down the stairs, returning to the hovel from which he had come. Egbert had the invalid child's authority over his parents and knew he could have his tutor dismissed if he chose.

He had expected an apology and said nothing when it was made, because the prospect of punishing Piet was deeply soothing. But towards evening, as his temper subsided, so did the protection it provided against his wounded pride. He sat in his room, staring at the wall as though chained to it. Slowly a newer feeling began to twist through the ropes that bound him. Perhaps what Piet had done had been good for him. He had been outside now and proved empty the threats of the Shadowers.

His mother brought him his supper and was surprised by the mood she found him in. She had spent the afternoon feeling treacherous for not dismissing Piet Barol at once and was pleased to see her son looking so much better. Her heart was easier when she left him; and when Maarten said "I suppose I should go up and see him," she advised him to leave it a day and called Constance to the drawing room to tell them amusing stories.

Eight hours after saying his prayers with Piet, Egbert did something defiant. He took a *warm* bath. He had not had one since he was eight years old and the experience was wonderful. He had grown used to fearing water. To take pleasure from it was transformative. He lay in the bath until his fingers shriveled, and when it cooled he added more hot water. The well-being this inspired made him admit that none of his other tutors would have dared to do what Piet had done: they had all been too scared of him. Very gradually, he started to be glad that he had not brought about Mr. Barol's removal from the house; and when he got out of the bath he was shivering—not with cold, but with the audacity of the idea that had come to him.

Perhaps Piet Barol *could* save him.

Egbert Vermeulen-Sickerts wished desperately to be free of his family's claustrophobic, demanding house, from which he glimpsed nothing of the outside world beyond what his sisters told him of their impossibly brilliant lives. As he dried, he examined every inch of his body and found no trace of injury. This confirmed the creeping realization that the Shadowers were powerless without him to do their bidding. He went to bed and said his prayers but did not sleep. Tantalizing possibilities were shining in his head. For three hours he gathered his courage, then as the entrance hall clock chimed midnight he asked his masters for permission to tell Piet everything.

The very suggestion provoked a menacing chatter in the shadows of the room, in the shards of white light sent through the chink in the curtains by the moon. But Egbert bargained with a new confidence and insisted with a metal inherited from his father. By dawn a deal had been reached: Piet Barol could be brought into the secret, but only if he passed the Test of the Entrance Hall Floor.

Three weeks later, Maarten and Jacobina left for England to join the *Lusitania* on her maiden voyage to New York, seen off from the quayside at Liverpool by 200,000 sightseers. September had already begun. If the hotel was to open as planned on the first day of October, Maarten knew he would have to see to its completion himself. Mr. Dermont had proved ominously hard to reach by telephone or cable. The only information easily available was that contained in the decorator's bills, which had reached new heights of absurdity. In the six weeks since Maarten's departure from America, two hundred further gold-plated taps had been ordered, eighteen hundred gilt-edged plates (for which no discount had been sought or achieved!). And although the Knickerbocker Trust Company had agreed to extend his credit by $150,000, this was far from sufficient.

Three days before he sailed, Maarten had sent thirty of Piet's drawings to a Zurich dealer whose discretion was total. He did not intend to sell the pieces but needed accurate valuations as collateral for the loans he would be obliged to seek from his Amsterdam friends.

Father and son parted stiffly, each daunted by crises they did not confide. When the servants had dispersed, Egbert followed Piet into the dining room and said, "I will answer your question, Mr. Barol, about the music. But only if you pass a test. Please select a number between one hundred and twelve hundred."

It was the first time Egbert had initiated a conversation since the episode on the cobblestones. Piet was relieved. "One hundred and seventy-eight."

The boy looked pleased. He considered any choice beneath two hundred achievable for a novice. "You mustn't ask me anything. I can only explain if you succeed. It is important you step on the tiles in the order I give you and don't make a mistake, or you shall have to start again from the beginning."

"I'm ready for you."

"Start with white, please."

The tiles on the entrance hall floor were small and Piet Barol's feet were large. As Egbert called the colors he stepped from one to the next, smiling at first at this childish game but then finding, as the boy's tempo increased, that it was harder than he thought to obey him accurately. Piet's forty-first step grazed the tile beside the one he had aimed for. "Begin again," Egbert commanded. "You may only start six more times."

"Otherwise what?"

"Otherwise you shall never know the secret."

There was such calm certainty in the boy's voice that Piet understood his future rested on his ability to hop from one foot to another, in a precise yet mysterious order, on the instructions of a child. It was absurd but he did not intend to fail. He tried harder, and the better he did the faster Egbert went—because the Shadowers were driving him on, willing Piet to stumble. He did, and was obliged to begin once more. Now he was sweating and wished he could remove his jacket; but any lapse in concentration led to error.

Piet made five mistakes, but on his sixth attempt he reached the 177th tile, a white one, and balanced on it at some distance from the schoolroom door.

"Now I'll come to you." Egbert too began to hop. The neatness of his footwork was impressive. He reached Piet and went five tiles farther on. "You need to step on black one more time and then immediately into the room. Aim for that one there."

The tile the boy indicated was a foot away from the door but a stride and a half from where Piet was. Egbert stretched towards him. "Lean on me and jump! You'll make it."

Maarten had looked forward to spending two months alone with his wife in New York. He felt sure Jacobina would know how to handle Lionel Dermont and her presence would certainly enliven the meals he was obliged to consume with his associates. But his hopes of a rejuvenating, contented voyage foundered on the second day out. Complaining that the vibrations of the engines made her ill, Jacobina took to her cabin; and in the countless ways by which couples of long-standing communicate with each other, she made it plain to her husband that he had offended her.

Jacobina had had no contact with Piet Barol since the afternoon before the workers' fête, and her body, accustomed to regular pleasure, did not take kindly to the abstinence imposed on it by Maarten. She had imagined that they would have a suite as usual and had relied on the refuge of a private sitting room. To be cooped up instead in a small compartment with a man who showed no inclination to touch her was maddening. It inspired an uncharacteristic small-mindedness, whose chief victim was Agneta Hemels—who found that there was no way she could dress her mistress's hair satisfactorily or press her clothes to the standard required.

Maarten knew his wife was a good sailor and her insistence on permanent nausea first troubled and then annoyed him. He took to spending large parts of each day in the first-class smoking room, in the company of other men who wished to complain of their wives over a whiskey and soda. This offered temporary relief but it did not make him happy. Neither did the spectacle that awaited him at the southeastern end of Central Park: a hotel in name only; in fact a chaotic and costly building site where the curtains had been hung before the cornice work was complete; where there was no hot water beyond the fourth floor and no functioning kitchen in which to train the brigades of busboys and waiters whom Mr. Dermont had already engaged and was now paying to loiter and chew gum and set practical jokes.

One of these preceded Maarten's arrival by minutes. On finding that a bucket of water had been balanced over the ballroom doors and had drenched the plasterer who dislodged it as well as the newly laid parquet floor, Maarten gave vent to his feelings by firing every one of the twenty laughing bystanders. This sobered even Mr. Dermont, who conducted his Dutch partner and his wife to the Hotel Metropole across the street and took the afternoon train for Philadelphia, with his 50 percent share certificate in a black pigskin bag. He had no desire to be present when the decorator presented his latest bill, particularly since he had nothing to contribute toward it. He was rather sick of the whole business and already coming to see himself as the situation's victim—the man who had bravely shouldered the practical burden and received nothing in return but queries and suspicion and demands for money. He rehearsed this narrative so spiritedly that by the time he reached his destination he entirely believed it. This enabled him to send a brief and unapologetic cable to Maarten—"Relative unwell STOP See you Opening October 1st STOP"—without the faintest twinge of contrition.

On receiving this communication, Maarten locked himself in the marble bathroom of his suite, ripped the telegram into tiny pieces, stamped on them, flushed them down the toilet and spat into the bowl after them. Then he prayed. It was not a happy prayer, and he opened his eyes convinced that the deity had declined to rescue him.

He went into the salon and found his wife with the hotel's manicurist. The bill presented by this lady depressed him further. He paid it and left the building and took a cup of coffee at Walker's Café; and when he had paid for this also and left a large tip, he walked slowly toward the Plaza. It is dangerous for a man to peer too closely at the workings of God, he told himself, and took courage from the optimistic blue of the sky.

Above him loomed the vast façade he had called into being. For the first time he saw something marvelous in it and not merely monumental. It was a building that might survive a hundred years and it made him remember what his father had taught him: that there is nobility in anything that endures.

By the time he reached it, he felt better, and before its elaborate doors he made a solemn vow: that he would not let these Americans break him.

The day Maarten Vermeulen-Sickerts fired the Plaza's decorator, the head of construction, the chief plumber, and a further fifteen, mischief-filled bellboys, Egbert honored his promise to Piet Barol. At the end of the morning's translation exercise he took from a kid purse his grandfather's signet ring and put it on his middle finger, which was the only one thick enough to secure it. He had been given this ring at his confirmation and through injudicious experimentation had unlocked with it marvels over which he had no control. Now it frightened him, but he knew he could explain nothing without it.

An alertness to sequence and order was deeply buried in Egbert's nature, but the tyranny of the Shadowers had not been inevitable. He stood up and went to the piano. Piet was sketching a small table carried down from Jacobina's sitting room and did not look up. The boy coughed self-consciously and rapped six times with the ring on the piano's lid. "Listen," he whispered. "You can hear them."

Piet raised his head and listened. The ringing strings made a sound like the small talk of ghosts. Egbert knocked again, requesting entry to an invisible universe. It seemed to Piet he caught snatches of waltzes and gavottes and the fast movements of concerti, and that these were all that remained of the people who had played them; who had once been as vigorous as he was and were now dead and forgotten.

Quite abruptly, the young man understood that he would one day lie in the earth and be eaten by wild things. So would the child who stood before him, looking so brave. Piet had met Death early, when it snatched his mother from him; but until this moment he had felt removed from it, as though extinction awaited other people.

"What does this whispering mean?" he asked.

And Egbert told him.

As his son's demons were growing weaker, Maarten's were threatening to overwhelm him. He kept this fact secret, especially from his wife, and to the outside world presented a façade of implacable calm that was exhausting to maintain. He dismissed the most important men Mr. Dermont had hired, engaged new builders, watched over them closely, and summoned from Lucerne the maître d'hôtel of his establishment there who took the training of the staff in hand.

A spirit of terrified industry took hold of the site at the bottom of the Central Park, but each small triumph was succeeded by a greater disaster. Ten days before the scheduled opening a fire destroyed a third of the kitchen. Forty-eight hours later, a cistern in the maids' bedrooms on the top floor exploded, leaving seventeen rooms uninhabitable.

Maarten cabled to Amsterdam for money. He promised favorable terms and deposited $500,000 in the vaults of the Knickerbocker Trust Company, from which he hoped to elicit a further million dollars in credit. His own deposits were sufficient to keep the project afloat while the trust company deliberated, but he would soon need more. He kept on doggedly, determined to win; but though he spent eighteen hours of every day at work, the end of September found him facing a brutal choice: to open as planned, while there were workmen in the building, or delay the project until they had finished.

He decided to open, against all precedent. At once the New York Stock Exchange, which had lost a quarter of its value since the commencement of his hotel, dipped further. He was alerted to this by a screeching newspaper boy, and as he read the headlines he understood that God was willing to break thousands in order to chastise him.

He walked through the Plaza's lobby and stood beneath the stained-glass ceiling of its Palm Court, thinking of Babylon's fate. The light outside was fierce and cold and fairies of colored light flitted across the furniture, which smelled of new upholstery and glue. It was a splendid room, but its opulence demanded the presence of patrons with money. If these did not come in their hundreds he would be ruined.

He sat with this thought for some time. Then he went to find his wife. She was in the sitting room of their suite at the Metropole, surrounded by boxes from which Agneta Hemels was removing shoes and cuffs and scarves and gowns, each more ravishing than the next. Finding no way to articulate her dissatisfactions, Jacobina had punished her husband by spending a provocatively large sum of money. She had bought presents for herself and the children and a painting for her aunt at Baden-Baden. As Maarten entered, Agneta was removing from tissue paper a pair of ankle boots in dark blue leather, fastened with nine pink pearls and lined in scarlet. The sight made him angry, then sad. "If you please, Miss Hemels," he muttered, and when the maid had curtsied and left he said, "I have annoyed you on this trip, my dear."

"Not at all."

"I am sorry for it. It was not my intention to displease you."

"Why ever should I be displeased?"

"I have absolutely no idea, and I cannot make amends until you tell me."

Jacobina put down the sapphire choker she had taken, on approval, for Constance and looked at her husband. She was very fond of him and in the past he had been an attentive recipient of her few, pathetic secrets. It appalled her to possess a secret she could not share with him. But the recollection of Piet Barol prohibited truthfulness, and instead of saying "You never touch me," which was what she wanted to say, she smiled and said, "I'm just anxious, darling. I want the hotel to be a success, as you deserve. I promise to be more cheerful."

In this way, neither husband nor wife communicated anything of substance. All Jacobina did to show Maarten she was sorry for a crime to which she would never confess was exert herself at the Plaza's opening and ensure by the deft bestowing of an empty suite that the first name in the visitors' register was "Vanderbilt."

Piet Barol did not insult Egbert Vermeulen-Sickerts by telling him that the Shadowers were not real. To the child they were very real indeed, and that was the only useful truth. He addressed him on the subject, therefore, as one general to another on the eve of a great battle.

First he ascertained the enemies' methods and territory. He observed Egbert crossing the entrance hall floor and inquired what the punishment was for seven missteps. When he learned of the ice-cold baths he almost cried. He saw to it that a warm one was run for Egbert every morning and evening and that at other times the cistern in his private bathroom was drained and inoperable. This innovation produced a gradual but unmistakable improvement. So did jovial admiration. When he told the boy he looked braver and stronger every day, Egbert began to feel brave and strong. It was his first encounter with these emotions and he enjoyed it wildly. He began to dare other audacities for the pleasure of recounting them to his tutor, who listened with absolute attention.

For the first time a genuine affection blossomed between them, nourished by a sincere unity of purpose. On the seventeenth day of joint operations Egbert did not accept the first number announced to him and crossed his aunt's entrance hall floor in 70 steps rather than 821. In celebration of this triumph Piet asked Mrs. de Leeuw to make one of her excellent apple cakes. They shared it while conducting an optimistic review of their progress.

Egbert sat on the midnight-blue sofa in his great-aunt's drawing room, his feet on the cushions and crumbs on his lap. Piet had never sworn in his presence and did so now to reinforce their comrade bond. "We're ready for a stand against these bastards, Egbert. We must defy them." He offered the child his hand. "If I lead, will you follow?"

Two weeks later, Agneta Hemels gave way to the temptations that had besieged her since her first sight of New York. Standing on the *Lusitania's* deck as she steamed into the harbor, the city's glinting towers had struck her like a land in a fairy tale. The chaos of porters and automobiles on the quay had given this paradise an earthly dimension. But in the seething swirls of humanity she had glimpsed a treasure that cozy little Amsterdam could never offer: anonymity.

Agneta had spent her life in the company of people who knew her. She had never strayed three streets beyond her home without encountering an acquaintance, and this had required her to spend thirty-two years on guard.

She was a private woman, with a dread of gossip. New York's utter indifference excited her as much as it frustrated Maarten. As Jacobina's maid she had traveled extensively through Europe and seen much to admire; but nothing— not Versailles nor the Coliseum, not even the soaring cathedral at Köln—had inspired the rush of love New York did.

She had accompanied her mistress on shopping trips that left her wide eyed with wonder. Crossing town in a hansom cab as the avenues swung out to left and right, she had been unable to contain her enthusiasm or understand Jacobina's lack of it. The joylessness with which Mevrouw Vermeulen-Sickerts acquired expensive clothes and trinkets disgusted her. It seemed grossly unfair to Agneta that a woman so free from financial constraint should derive so little pleasure from it, and this thought began to undermine her ability to refrain from judging her betters.

From her little room on the top floor of the Metropole, Agneta stared out over the city's lush park and sparkling rooftops, her heart aflame. She was allowed an afternoon off once a fortnight. Though the first of these was delirious, her second solitary promenade was spoiled by her simple Dutch clothes, which did not at all complement the triumphant splendor of the city.

It was on her return from this unsatisfactory expedition that Agneta was beset by the most seductive temptation of her life. As she put away Jacobina's latest purchases and added them to the inventory of her clothes, the desire to wear one of them, and to wander down Fifth Avenue like a fine lady, took hold of her. It became imperative when she removed from a box an afternoon gown of peacock-blue satin with a jacket trimmed in ermine. She held it up to the glass. She was not as tall as Jacobina, but she knew that in the closet was a pair of very high-heeled shoes that would solve this problem. She went to the door and locked it, though she knew her mistress was at a fitting. It was four o'clock in the afternoon. She was not on duty again until six. Might she not . . . ?

She did.

She took off her own dress and hung it in the wardrobe. Then she sat at the dressing table and arranged her hair. When that was done to her satisfaction she put on the peacock-blue satin, which did wonders for her eyes. Bravely she stepped into the high-heeled shoes and contemplated herself in the mirror. The transformation was dazzling. She went to the safe and removed Jacobina's jewel box. From this she took the sapphire choker that had been bought for Constance and a pair of pearl earrings.

Agneta was at heart a modest woman, but the city's

immodesty had infected her. Now she laughed to see how magnificent she looked. She left the Vermeulen-Sickerts' suite and entered the elevator. Although the operator saw her every day he did not recognize her and bowed. Two gentlemen entered the lift and bowed also.

"May I order a carriage for you, miss?" asked the doorman, as though he could think of no greater honor.

"No, thank you. I prefer to walk." And Agneta swept past him to find that the crowds on Fifth Avenue parted for her and every gentleman among them doffed his hat.

That same afternoon, October 21st, an unforeseen catastrophe occurred that provided Maarten with conclusive proof of God's directed wrath. He had an appointment with the chairman of the Knickerbocker Trust Company and had spent the morning honing what he intended to be a brilliant performance. If he could obtain a further million dollars in America, he felt confident of making up any further shortfall with European capital and thus prevailing against the odds. He was aware, however, that nothing repels credit like desperation; and because he was desperate he had taken the step of ordering a cocktail at luncheon.

He emerged from his cab ten minutes early, feeling cavalier. He was disconcerted to find a line outside the company's offices and annoyed when the doorman refused to let him step past it.

"But I have an appointment with Mr. Barney."

"Mr. Barney is seeing no one today."

Over this individual's shoulder, Maarten could see into the green marble banking room. It took him a moment to decode the chaos at the tellers' windows. Every person in the long line was withdrawing money, apparently as much as they could. The doorman pushed him roughly aside, and when Maarten said, "I will report this insolence to Mr.

Barney himself!" the man shrugged and said, "Mr. Barney's resigned. Join the line like everyone else."

To be treated in this peremptory fashion reminded Maarten of slights he had endured in his youth and over-come. Seeing that nothing more was to be gained by com-plaining, he joined the line, noting with alarm that among the ranks of messenger boys were persons of quality, evi-dently unwilling to rely on subordinates to retrieve their funds for them. From a lady in green serge and fox fur he learned that Mr. Barney had been implicated in a failed attempt to corner the stock of the United Copper Com-pany; that this had exposed a web of risky commitments between the banks he had an interest in; and that it was rumored the Knickerbocker Trust Company did not have sufficient reserves to honor the claims of its depositors.

"But, madam," said Maarten. "No bank has sufficient reserves to satisfy all its depositors at once. If everybody would simply calm down . . ."

But it seemed that no one was prepared to calm down. As 34th Street filled with anxious clients, the panic of the crowd began to take hold of Maarten too. Not only did he require a further million dollars in credit; the $500,000 he had raised in Amsterdam was in the trust company's vaults and its loss would precipitate a crisis he might not survive.

The Knickerbocker closed its immense bronze doors promptly at five o'clock, while there remained dozens of people ahead of Maarten in the queue. Were it not for the lady in fox fur he might have abandoned his stoicism and begun to shout, as others were doing. Instead he said good-bye calmly and walked through eddying crowds to his hotel. From the newspapers he learned that J. P. Morgan had gathered the city's leading financiers in his library to find a way of preventing a full-scale run on the banks; also that the National Bank of Commerce had refused to clear the Knickerbocker's checks.

It annoyed Maarten profoundly to be a nonentity in this tangled city. In Amsterdam he would have been in Morgan's library, taking decisions. In New York he was just another fellow in a fix.

He found his wife having hysterics in front of the hotel's manager. A sapphire choker was missing and her pearl earrings. (She had not yet discovered the loss of the peacock-blue dress.) "My maid never forgets to lock the safe. It must have been forced," she was shouting, her voice high and distracted.

The Metropole's manager was used to defending his staff from the accusations of absent-minded patrons. He pointed out most respectfully that no violence had been done to the safe. "Could you, perhaps, have taken the jewels off elsewhere, madam?" he asked gently, and when Jacobina insisted that she had not, and that her maid would have found them if she had, he put on his gravest face and said: "Is your own servant wholly to be trusted?"

"Of course," snapped Jacobina.

B ut she was wrong.

Agneta Hemels had lived her life scrupulously. She had cared for her parents, both now dead, and worked very hard to pay her older brother's gambling debts. She had never stolen anything in her life. But as she stepped daintily down Fifth Avenue in Jacobina's gown and Constance's jewels, she found the experience addictively delightful.

She went into a shop and was fussed over by the attendants. It was a jeweler's, and she asked to see several diamond bracelets. For a happy fifteen minutes she behaved as if she might buy one. No one had ever bowed and scraped before Agneta Hemels, nor told her that wrists as graceful as hers deserved the best. She pretended to consider an emerald ring, but in fact she was weighing another possibility that had opened before her, as glittering as the stone on her finger.

If she chose to disappear in this vast country of adventurers, she was sure she could. "I shall return tomorrow," she told the tail-suited salesman, deceitfully. "Keep the ring and those two bracelets aside for me."

She left the shop trembling. It was almost six o'clock. She walked back towards the Metropole, wondering if there was a God and, if so, what He would do to her if she did what she was contemplating. (If He existed, she was sure He was a "He.") Agneta had sat through hundreds of church services but could never decide if she truly believed. As she reached the hotel she set the Deity a test: she would enter like a guest and ride the lift in her finery. If she was seen and apprehended she would face the consequences. If not, she would claim her reward for the years she had spent anticipating other people's whims.

The doorman bowed low to her. So did the elevator attendant. Neither Maarten nor Jacobina was in the lobby, and she gained her own room without incident. Once in it she undressed quickly, put on a dress of her own, packed the peacock-blue satin in her valise with all the underwear she possessed, placed the sapphire choker and pearls between its folds, called a bellboy and instructed him to take the case downstairs and to order a cab for her. Next she went to the Vermeulen-Sickerts' suite, which the hotel's manager had just left, and expressed the greatest outrage that someone should have profited by her absence to steal from her beloved mistress.

She helped Jacobina undress and advised her to lie down before dinner. She ordered some bouillon for Maarten, whose ashen face irritated her. How easily he could bear the loss of a few precious stones! She left him trying to place a telephone call to Philadelphia and went into his wife's dressing room. There she selected five gowns, two cloaks, seven pairs of shoes and a muff and packed them in a trunk, into which she also placed the contents of Jacobina's jewel box and a quantity of cash. She put on a double-breasted traveling dress with a velvet collar and a chic hat. The dressing room had its own door to the corridor and she summoned a footman to take her luggage downstairs.

Again the elevator attendant bowed to her. As the doorman lifted her into her hired carriage, she pressed a dollar bill into his hand. It was all the spending money Jacobina had given her and it gave her pleasure to leave it behind. "Grand Central Station," she told the driver; and when they had turned the corner and no one had run after her, she began to cry with happiness.

The revelation of Agneta Hemels' perfidy shook Maarten profoundly and contributed to his conviction that old certainties were crumbling. He discovered that the maid had bolted when she failed to wake them the next morning, and the trauma of the missing jewels delayed him so long that by the time he reached the Knickerbocker Trust Company, the line to its door stretched halfway round the block.

The rumor was that J. P. Morgan and his associates were prepared to let the Knickerbocker fail. Many in line—men and women—were fighting back tears. Others were angry. Maarten took his place burdened by an awful resignation. He knew he had lost his money.

It was the will of God.

And so it proved. Soon after midday, the great bronze doors were closed to screams of protest. In three hours that morning, more than $8 million had been paid out in cash—$500,000 of it was Maarten's own and lost for good. He could hardly believe it and yet, now that the disaster had occurred, he saw that he had been expecting it.

He went to other banks but he knew it was hopeless and it was. The call money rate on the New York Stock Exchange was nearing 100 percent and no one was lending. "We must go home, my dear," he told Jacobina. "I can barely pay the hotel bill as it is." And that evening they took the midnight sailing to Liverpool and for the first time since her girlhood Jacobina packed her own clothes.

The ship's extravagance reproached Maarten and he spent the first three days of the voyage in bed. On the morning of the fourth he woke early and crept from their darkened cabin to a stretch of isolated deck and thought. It was no use trying to save himself if God was against him. Nothing he attempted would work; the Almighty had made that clear by bringing the entire banking system of the United States to its knees, merely to punish him. Before he took any practical steps it was vital to regain the affections of his Creator—unless, of course, he was predestined to damnation, in which case . . . He knelt heavily, not caring that a steward had appeared to lay out the deck chairs, and threw himself on the mercy of his Maker. He was used to dreading the flames of hell, but earthly success had so far shielded him from more immediate manifestations of divine disfavor. He prayed until the steward asked him if he would care for some coffee; and this interruption broke his concentration, leaving him answerless and afraid.

Naomi de Leeuw received the telegram announcing her employer's unexpected return and sent Hilde Wilken to the schoolroom to convey the good news to Egbert. Opening the door in the dining room wall, the maid was confronted by an odd tableau: Piet Barol was balancing precariously on one leg in the middle of the entrance hall while his pupil watched him, shivering. She curtsied. "If you please, Master Egbert, your parents will be home tomorrow."

Piet had counted on having weeks more to defeat Egbert's foes. "Thank you, Hilde," he said sharply, and once she had gone, with a greater sense of urgency, "Call again, old fellow."

"Black."

Piet swung his left foot away from his body in a balletic movement and very slowly brought it down on a white tile. "Call again."

"White."

Now Piet lifted his right leg and placed it very gently over the intersection of four tiles. He waited. The room was silent. He could hear the boy's rough breathing and the gurgle of a filling radiator. "Call again," he said, but Egbert did not speak.

The Vermeulen-Sickerts arrived the next morning, after spending an anxious night in a hotel at Liverpool. Mr. Blok was extremely annoyed to see that Agneta Hemels was not of the party. He assumed she had been let go in New York and regretted the lost opportunity to dismiss her himself. He enjoyed such scenes, which Mrs. de Leeuw's stable management of the household rarely afforded him.

The news of her protégée's wickedness shocked the housekeeper to her core. Informed of it by Jacobina, she took the unprecedented step of sitting down in her mistress' presence, and the first thing she said was: "We must keep this from the lower servants."

"I quite agree," said Mr. Blok. "It would set a most unfortunate example."

And so the fiction that Agneta Hemels had met a man in

America, and been proposed to, and departed for Chicago with her employers' blessing was devised; and when Hilde heard it she went up to the attic and sobbed among the boxes and old trunks and descended in a mood as black as Maarten's.

Since his unsatisfactory plea for guidance and compassion on the deck of the *Lusitania*, Maarten Vermeulen-Sickerts had resorted to extreme self-denial. He had consumed nothing but coffee and bread for the remainder of the voyage, which meant that he endured this interview with his butler and housekeeper in a state of detached despair. It was Monday, October 28th, and the newspapers contained apocalyptic news: on both the previous Thursday and Friday, the New York Stock Exchange had barely made it to the closing bell and call money rates were at 150 percent.

Constance saw at once that something very serious was wrong. She kissed her father tenderly, resolving not to pry, but her curiosity did not long go unsatisfied. Before lunch she and Louisa were summoned to the study.

In his bath it had come to Maarten that only total humiliation, consciously self-inflicted, might cleanse the sin of overreaching. It was necessary to tell his family of their changed situation without subterfuge or excuse, and he did not delay. He did not invite Egbert to the conference, though he wished he could include his tutor—because a man of Piet Barol's merits might have shared the burden of masculine responsibility. But this was impossible. Methodically, in a voice calmed by hunger, he told his wife and daughters what had happened—the snake-tongued Mr. Dermont and his vision of a potentate's hotel; his own quiescence in the architect's sinful grandeur; the disappearance of his partner at the crucial hour; his attempts to struggle on; and the Lord's final, incontrovertible sanction: the loss of half a million dollars and the abrupt expiry of his credit. "I have asked my friends to come after dinner and will throw myself on their mercy," he said, bleakly. "Without their help, I will go under."

Listening to him, Louisa longed to shake her father free of his superstitions and was appalled by the totality of his subjection to them. The protective instincts of which Constance was the usual focus surged within her. How she wished she were a man! She would sail to America; track down this Lionel Dermont in Philadelphia; speak to Mr. J. P. Morgan himself, if necessary; demand and secure the restoration of her family's money. But all she said was, "We'll manage, Papa. Of course we will," and hoped that the interview would end before the delivery of her morning's purchases. It did not. While the family sat in bewildered silence, Hilde Wilken knocked on the door and staggered into the room beneath a bale of oyster cashmere, the card on which read *Urgent Delivery—Paid In Full.* Louisa had intended to have matching habits made for herself and her sister, but now the idea embarrassed her. "You may take it upstairs, Hilde," she said. And to her father, once the maid had left them: "I will return it, Papa. It's the least I can do."

Maarten was touched by this offer, but it underlined how little experience his daughters had of the real world and how poorly they would navigate it without his money to protect them. "Keep it, my dear," he replied forlornly. "It will not be the making or the breaking of us."

Piet had a hint of the crisis that night, leaning out of Didier Loubat's window, but the young men could not make sense of what they heard.

The girls were engaged in collecting their disposable

assets. "I suppose you did always want to open a shop," said Constance doubtfully, surveying the pile of clothes Louisa had decided they could do without.

"I won't let you starve, darling. You can be my chief vendeuse." Once the shock of her father's news had subsided, Louisa had seen possibilities in her family's sudden misfortune. "Poor girls go out to work." She opened her jewel case and removed the ruby bracelet her godmother had left her. "Haven't you always rather envied them?"

"No."

"That's because you lack imagination, my dear." Louisa sat on the bed. "Think of having a little shop on the Kalverstraat. Very chic, of course, inside. Mirrors and good lighting and soft carpets. All our friends would buy from us."

"And take pleasure in our downfall." Constance spoke bitterly. She was thinking of Myrthe Janssen, whose engagement to Frederik van Sigelen had just been announced. Perhaps she had been unwise not to marry when she could. "Do you think anyone will have us now?" she asked, contemplating her reflection in the mirror and deriving some comfort from it.

"What a silly question. Think of the love letters in your desk."

"They were written to a girl who had a dowry."

"No, Constance, they were written to you."

There was silence. Louisa began taking shoes from her closet.

"I wouldn't marry for money in any case," said Constance at last, following her own train of thought.

"If you worked with me, you wouldn't have to."

"You're not serious, Louisa."

"Why ever not?" Until an hour before, Louisa Vermeulen-Sickerts had not been at all serious about opening a shop.

She had been content to daydream about what never could be. Now it seemed that her father's right to oppose her had dwindled dramatically, and her sister's skepticism provoked a rush of conviction. "If we sold our jewels, we could rent a place and hire Mevrouw Wunder and Babette to work for us. Babette's an excellent cutter. You could be the model. I'll design everything and make sure people don't swindle us."

"Don't look so happy about all of this."

"I'm not." Louisa adjusted her expression. "But one of us has to be practical."

"Not tonight, darling." And Constance went to the window and closed it, because she felt afraid of the future and did not wish her sister to see cowardice in her face.

The servants' ignorance was shattered the next afternoon by a raspy-voiced newspaper boy hawking a special edition of *De Amsterdamsche Lantaren*, a scandal sheet whose front page proclaimed LIKELY RUIN OF LEADING BURGHER. Piet was drawn to the schoolroom's window in time to see Mrs. de Leeuw buy up the entire edition. He set Egbert an exercise in geometry and went into the kitchen, which was in a state of uproar.

Monsieur la Chaume had abandoned his sauce on the stove and snatched a copy from the housekeeper before she could incinerate her haul. The article mentioned no names, but its hints were broad, and in the leaking of the story its horrors had expanded. "Several millions of dollars" had been lost by one of the "city's first citizens." His "extensive collection of *objets d'art*" was "likely to be sold at conducive rates."

It was true that Maarten had been closeted in his study with various grave-faced gentlemen ever since his return from America. Hilde reported that the conversation had ceased whenever she appeared, which was not at all the usual manner of the house.

"I had better take this libelous publication upstairs," said Mr. Blok.

Maarten Vermeulen-Sickerts, like Piet Barol, inspired instinctive jealousy in a significant proportion of other men. As he contemplated the newspaper ten minutes later, he understood that one of the friends in whom he had trusted everything had betrayed him. He did his best to manufacture a becoming Christian forgiveness. He failed and flung his Venetian-glass paperweight to the floor. Beside him, on the table it always occupied, was the silver miniature of the man on a tightrope—balancing so precariously, yet permanently preserved from disaster.

It did not comfort him.

Maarten had consumed nothing all day but three cups of coffee and two slices of rye bread; and between appointments had prayed fervently. "I can do nothing without you," he said aloud, looking heavenwards. For the first time in many weeks he felt the stirrings of the Holy Spirit. He picked up the Bible on his desk and opened it at random, convinced that he would learn his fate, and what he read brought tears to his eyes because it was the repeating assurance of the 136th Psalm: "His steadfast love endures forever."

Maarten took this as an indication that his relationship with the Almighty was on the mend. He felt immediately easier and made a solemn vow that if the Plaza ever turned a profit he would give a third of it away. This allowed him to believe that the Plaza *might* make money one day, since good would come of it. Surely the Americans would recover their delight in spending. It was so instinctive in them.

It had shamed Maarten to ask his friends for money, but since God required his humiliation, he had endured it without complaint. At an extravagant rate of interest, payable a year hence, with his entire silver collection as collateral, he had been loaned enough to keep afloat for six weeks. He was aware that his own recovery depended on that of the American financial system—but since God had caused that cataclysm in order to humble him, might He not resolve it now that His purpose had been accomplished?

He rang for food. He was very hungry, and the feast sent up by Monsieur la Chaume fortified his spirits. When he had finished, he wrote a stern and litigious letter to the editor of *De Amsterdamsche Lantaren* and sent Didier Loubat to deliver it. He did not imagine that this action would be taken by his servants as confirmation of the article's contents, but when Didier returned he found Hilde in tears and Monsieur la Chaume halving the quantity of champagne he was adding to the evening's dessert.

In the *sous-terrain* of the house, the day proceeded methodically. But by teatime it was clear to Mr. Blok that he should take a stand. He had worked for Maarten Vermeulen-Sickerts for twenty-five years and consumed a great deal of chivalric fiction in that time. He had often imagined following his knight into battle when all was lost, and his courage now was reinforced by having enough put by to fund a modest retirement in Amersfoort. This limitation of personal vulnerability allowed him to inhabit the role of doomed retainer with total conviction.

He called the staff together after dinner had been served and cleared. Though Agneta Hemels had refrained absolutely from intimacy with anyone, her absence was felt. It was as though she had already been seized by the debt collectors and would be followed in due course by the furniture and the sculpture and the contents of the wine cellar.

Gert Blok sat at the head of the table and opened with

a calming address. He reminded his audience that it was their duty to refrain from below-stairs gossip, since Mr. Vermeulen-Sickerts' rivals would seek information from their own servants. He exhorted them to present a confident front to the world.

"Have they really lost all their money?" asked Hilde, who did not have Mr. Blok's savings and was nauseous with worry.

Gert Blok hesitated. To deny this would be to diminish the gravity of the crisis, and hence his own importance in mitigating it. To agree would be disloyal and might encourage Hilde and Didier to look for places elsewhere. In the end he told the truth, which was that he did not know. "What I do know is that—"

But Mrs. de Leeuw interrupted him. "This family will never be poor, Hilde. They may lose a painting, perhaps all their paintings, perhaps the china that takes you two days to polish and is never used. But they will not know cold, or hunger, or the misery of unwashed clothes all through a hot summer. It is we who will suffer." The housekeeper was not much given to public speaking, and the sudden intensity of her feelings produced two patches of deep burgundy on either side of her narrow nose.

Mr. Blok coughed. "I object to that. Mr. Vermeulen-Sickerts will provide us each with a pension, should the worst occur. The family has always paid us well. They—"

But Naomi de Leeuw had lost all composure. "Oh yes, Mr. Blok, they have paid more than their friends pay. Twice as much." She arranged her lips in the smile of perfect concern she wore when a guest felt unwell. "But it is so *little* when you think of all we do, and all they have."

Didier caught Piet's eye and for an instant they swayed on the precipice of laughter. But they did not laugh because tears began to well in Mrs. de Leeuw's fierce brown eyes and in a very different voice she said: "I know you all think me cold and mean-spirited."

There was silence. As often happens after a statement of accurate fact, those present were briefly unable to contradict it.

Piet recovered first, perhaps because, knowing her mother's ailments as closely as he did, he was most able to feel sympathy for her. "Of course we don't. Today has simply been—"

But she raised her hand to stop him. "You are very generous, Mr. Barol, and an expert flatterer. But I know you whisper about me behind my back. You and Mr. Loubat and Hilde. You think because I do not show all I see that I am blind. I am not!" She dabbed her eyes with the edge of the tablecloth. "You think me cold because I do not smile. But that is because I have smiled so much, at so many people who have no concern for me, that my smile has lost its meaning. In my youth I was a cheerful person. I wished often to tell you, Hilde, not to fear me. But I never could because I can no longer smile. And that is why, Mr. Blok, Maarten Vermeulen-Sickerts owes each of us far more than a pension."

"Nevertheless," said Hilde, less timidly than before, "I would rather have a pension than nothing at all."

Naomi de Leeuw had made a lifelong habit of suppressing her resentments. She could not otherwise have been the flawless housekeeper she was. But the dam once breached could not be refortified, and though Mr. Blok brought the servants' discussion to an abrupt end the patches of red on her cheeks did not subside.

She went to her room directly after dinner. It was the largest of the servants' bedrooms, but it had no windows, having once been a coal cellar, and she longed for starlight and fresh breezes. As soon as she heard Hilde close her door, she changed into slippers and went out into the corridor. The house was dark but she knew every inch of it. At the foot of the servants' stairs she stopped and listened. No one was abroad. She went up them and into the dining room. From a cabinet with a smooth-swinging door she took a liqueur glass and exchanged it, after a moment's hesitation, for a larger vessel. She filled this to the brim from the first decanter on the drinks tray, pinched her nose, and drank it all down.

It was port wine—very sweet, and it made her splutter. She was not an experienced drinker. She put the glass on the sideboard, where Hilde would think she had missed it when laying for breakfast, and went down the passage to the octagonal parlor. In her precisely ordered brain were stored the needs of every piece she passed—which chairs were to be waxed twice a year, which never; which tapestries must be moved in the summer months. These details mattered much more to her than the objects' provenance or value. Her allegiance to each was total.

The octagonal room was draped in a light like silver organza. She closed the door, opened the French windows to the garden, and sat on the gilt sofa that had been made for the palace of St. Cloud. It upset her to think of all this beautiful furniture being sold to people with indifferent housekeepers.

The air was cold and stimulating. She brought her hands together but did not pray. Naomi de Leeuw had long since stopped bothering herself with God. In the mystical half-light Maarten Vermeulen came to her, bounding and energetic as he had been on the day of their first meeting, thirty-one years before.

He had just bought a share in the Amstel Hotel. She was

a senior chambermaid, barred from advancement by a jealous superior. Maarten had recognized her talent and made her housekeeper of the mansion he had purchased on the Herengracht. He was unsophisticated in those days, still acquiring possessions and polish. It was she who had trained the servants and arranged the flowers and furniture. How she had helped him! Jacobina Sickerts would never have married him had she not spent three years teaching him to take deference for granted.

She looked up at the chandelier of gilded griffins above her: one of a pair bought by Maarten in the days of his bachelorhood for the salon on the first floor. In that time the drawing room had been a masculine, Gothic preserve. Miss Sickerts had objected to its gloom and Maarten had redecorated and banished its fittings as soon as they were engaged. One griffin chandelier had been relegated here; the other had been given to her—an impetuous, thoughtless gift that caused her much anguish.

Naomi de Leeuw had not known her father and was well into her teens before she understood that the strange men she passed on the stairs helped her mother pay the bills. It was her sister Annetjie, thirteen years older, who was her protectress, the fount of all affection and knowledge, a warm, sweet body to cling to at night when snow fell through the broken tiles of the roof.

When Annetjie met Gerhardt Moritz, she was twenty-four and Naomi eleven. Naomi never imagined her handsome brother-in-law might steal her sister away; it had never occurred to her that anyone could. But a year later, Mr. Moritz announced the couple's departure for the Orange Free State, where there were farms aplenty and no white woman need do her own washing. Only then did she grasp the reality of his theft.

Gerhardt took Annetjie away one week after Naomi's twelfth birthday, and on that day Naomi made a vow: that she would earn the money to visit her sister at the outer reaches of the world. She went into service at fourteen, and though the fantasy remained ungraspable she did not abandon it; held it, instead, as a talisman against the wretchedness of cleaning other people's floors.

The Vermeulen-Sickerts' gift of the griffin chandelier had seemed miraculous—because Naomi knew what her employer had paid for it, and this was more than sufficient for a passage to South Africa.

Throughout the wet winter of 1879 she had done her best to sell it; had spent her savings on the carriages required to transport it to dealers who took one look at her clothes and offered a fraction of its value; or accused her of theft. She obtained from Maarten a letter certifying her ownership, but this made the dealers less skeptical, not more generous. She began to wish that Maarten had sold it himself and given her the money, but she was too proud to ask this favor.

It was at this period that Naomi, without ever saying so aloud, jettisoned her faith in God. She continued to set an excellent example of church attendance to the lower servants but never again believed the assurances she heard that God would not abandon His children or test them more severely than they could withstand.

Three decades later, she unclasped her hands, and the anger of the evening flowed through her fingers and cooled. It left behind a polished pebble of truth: that the Vermeulen-Sickertses were not wicked. They simply did not care to imagine what life was like for other people.

It had taken the squandering of half Naomi's savings to suffocate her long-nourished dream. With the last of her money she sent the chandelier as a wedding gift to Annetjie's daughter, Gertruida, who was marrying a man named van Vuuren. For years, until middle age deadened such fancies, she imagined a link between the winged lions in Amsterdam and their siblings in Bloemfontein and polished their dragonscale shades herself, talking as she did so to her sister as though they were sitting side by side.

Annetjie had been dead for fifteen years, but the griffins observed her with an encouraging sternness that reminded Naomi of her sister when she wished to scold her. She rose and stood very straight. "As long as I can walk and speak," she said to the moon-drenched garden, "I will make my own luck."

And she went to bed and behaved the next day as though her outburst had never taken place.

In answer to Maarten's plea, the banking system of the United States began an abrupt and emphatic recovery. On October 23rd, while he lay in despair in his cabin on the *Lusitania*, J. P. Morgan succeeded in persuading New York's leading financiers to provide loans of $8.25 million to prevent a second trust company from following the Knickerbocker into oblivion. The next day, Thursday 24th, Secretary Cortelyou of the Treasury deposited $25 million of government money in the New York banks and J. D. Rockefeller pledged half his fortune to maintain America's credit. The New York Stock Exchange almost suspended trading that day and the next, and the markets only made it to Friday's closing bell thanks to Morgan's raising of $33.3 million in forty-eight hours.

When Maarten later pieced together these events and compared them with the trajectory of his own drama, he was not surprised to discover that none of these measures had worked. None of them could have done while God remained intent on punishing him. Only over the weekend of October 26th and 27th, when through fasting he had begun to see clearly, did the panic ebb. And only on Monday 28th, after Maarten had confessed to his family and begun the grueling admission of his downfall to his friends (one of whom would play Iscariot) was $100 million in loan certificates issued by the New York Clearing House.

In the absence of a central bank these loan certificates functioned as de facto currency. With each confession Maarten made, more banks agreed to accept them in settlement of loans and advances. This enabled other institutions to retain reserves of real greenbacks to honor the demands of frightened depositors. By Tuesday 29th, when Maarten, having abandoned all pride, threw himself wholly on his Creator's mercy, proof of God's steadfast love was provided by the restoration of calm in New York.

The news reached Amsterdam on Wednesday 30th and confirmed to Maarten the centrality of his position in the Almighty's plans. He resumed his fast as a precaution against resurgent pride and consumed nothing but coffee and rye bread for a further two weeks—because the stock market continued its fall and the situation remained delicate. Having secured six weeks of funding, he did not waste time in courting moneylenders. He threw himself into punishing bouts of prayer, refusing to rise from his knees until the ache in them was agony and his body, like Christ's, was paying a physical price for the sins of the world.

In the end, further self-sacrifice was required. It took a promise to give to the poor three-quarters of the Plaza's profits, after interest on its loans was paid, to save the Exchange. Maarten made this pledge in all solemnity on November 14th. The following day, the Dow Jones Industrial Average touched a low of fifty-three, then started to climb; and the

confidence this unleashed filled the Plaza's bar to overflow-
ing, and then its palatial suites, and thus God preserved
Maarten from the necessity of requesting more money from
his friends.

The banks were quite prepared to lend again, and
delighted to serve a client who owned New York's most
fashionable hotel.

Shortly after her father received confirmation that a credit
facility of $2 million had been placed at his disposal at
the National City Bank of New York, Louisa Vermeulen-
Sickerts pulled the silk bellpull outside his office door. She
had spent the days of his prayer-filled sequestration energet-
ically and tasted a happiness that her former life of wasteful
leisure had never offered her. Overruling Constance, she had
sought and discovered an empty shop just off the Kalverstraat on which a year's lease might be obtained for rather
less than the value of her ruby bracelet. She had sold this
bauble without embarrassment to Frederik van Sigelen, who
had paid a full and generous price, and disposed of a rope of
pearls and a pair of diamond earrings similarly. This left her
with the funds to pay two cutters and an embroiderer for a
year, and her own extensive collection of fabrics would see
her through a first season. Though her palms were wet with
perspiration, she told her father all this with aplomb.

Maarten, so narrowly rescued from ruin, was in tremendous spirits. "What a kind and generous step to have taken,
my darling. I'm sure you would have saved us all from
penury."

This was not at all the response Louisa had expected. Her
shoulders relaxed. She sat down. "I have so much to learn
from you, Papa, but be assured I will be an attentive and
diligent student. If only you will show me how to do the

first few months' accounts, I promise I'll manage thereafter. Constance has agreed to help in the shop and model the collection. I am certain—"

"But there is no longer any need, my precious." Maarten squeezed her shoulder. "You must buy back your jewels at once. The world has come to its senses. The Plaza is full. This very morning I have had word that sufficient credit has been extended to see me through, and the refurbishments in London and Frankfurt will soon be finished. You may carry on living gaily amongst your friends."

"But that is not how I wish to live."

"Nonsense, my treasure."

"It is not nonsense, I assure you."

"You are right." Maarten grew penitent. "Your motives are generous and thoughtful. I do not mean to disparage your efforts, only to tell you that the crisis has passed."

"I am glad of that, but I mean to do this, Father."

"Do what?"

"Open a shop. Make my own money."

"Whatever do you mean?"

Louisa began at the beginning and repeated her plan in detail. This time she was not nervous but angry.

"It is quite impossible," said Maarten when she had finished.

"On the contrary. It is quite possible, Papa."

"Then it is not advisable."

"On what grounds?"

"On the grounds of decency and common sense, Louisa."

"Where is the shame in hard work? In making one's own way, as you yourself—"

"You are not at all in the situation I faced when I was your age. Believe me, you should be glad of that."

"I am grateful for the start you have given me. But I wish, I wish—"

"What do you wish, my child?"

"To make my own way in the world."

"Then you must marry a man with talent and ambition, whose interests you may serve as your mother has served mine. That is the way in which a woman may succeed."

"I am capable of succeeding on my own, Papa."

"I do not doubt it. But that is not the way of the world."

Constance Vermeulen-Sickerts had not at all looked forward to fawning over her former rivals in an effort to sell them clothes. She had not been a wholly benevolent ruler of Amsterdam's *jeunesse dorée* and she knew she had enemies who would pay large sums to have her kneel at their feet as they tried on shoes. She felt a moment's disloyal relief to learn of the enterprise's doom. "My sweet—"

But Louisa stalked past her, closed her door in her face, and dragged the dressing table against it. I will defy them, she thought. I will open my shop whatever they say. But she knew, even as she made these promises, that she would break them. The knowledge inspired a wish to break other things. She flung open her closet and pulled from it all the presents her mother had brought her from New York. She was about to take her scissors to them when a more pointed vengeance occurred to her. She rang for Hilde.

Hilde Wilken was not often summoned by Louisa Vermeulen-Sickerts, except to be told off. When she saw the pile of clothes on the floor and the fury on Louisa's face, she started to cry.

"No time for tears, Hilde." Louisa intended to act before her passion cooled, in case she thought better of challenging her parents in this manner. She picked up the dresses. "These are for you."

"Pardon, miss?"

"These are a gift for you." Louisa attempted to inject

warmth into her voice. She was not over fond of Hilde, whose timidity and lack of initiative annoyed her. She would much rather have given her clothes to Agneta Hemels, who had been an active collaborator in several memorable coiffures. "I wish you to have them," she repeated, and in her tone was a note of command.

"Yes, miss." Hilde stopped crying.

Louisa smiled. "You have been a good and loyal servant, and this is your reward. Come, let us find some shoes to match them."

L ike Piet Barol, Egbert had dreamed of conquering his captors before his parents' return from New York. Their sudden arrival was inhibiting. But the anxiety they brought with them was not. Egbert was used to being the failed member of a high-achieving family; for the first time it seemed that his parents and sisters had troubles of their own, and this gave him strength. So did Piet Barol's deliberate provocation of the Shadowers, who retaliated only by instructing Egbert not to speak to him—and this was the first commandment he broke. The second was their punishment for this betrayal, which he refused to implement.

He took two warm baths a day as a point of honor, and with each his determination grew. But he did not take the decisive step, and as the household's confidence seeped back he began to worry that his captors would recover as his family was doing. Piet Barol, after all, was an outsider and a grown-up; perhaps he *could* flout the Shadowers' decrees with impunity.

Lying awake one morning, fretting in the dark, Egbert made up his mind to act. He got out of bed. He did not return to it a further six times. Neither did he dress and undress repeatedly. He splashed water on his face, put on his clothes, and bit his lip till he tasted blood. Then he went to his door and opened it. He ran down the stairs and arrived in the entrance hall just as the clock was striking five. The lamps by the front door were burning low and gave an encouraging glow. He paused, but he knew delay would undo him. Like a fugitive evading a distracted guard he ran down the hall, through the dining room, and opened the secret door.

His great-aunt's entrance hall floor loomed before him. He switched on a light. He had spent hundreds of hours navigating this treacherous terrain and remembered the shame of such journeys; then Piet Barol's calm courage and his masters' inability to punish it.

He held his breath and ran.

Hilde Wilken was aware that Louisa Vermeulen-Sickerts had no great affection for her, and she did not trust her motives. Her first thought, on receiving Louisa's gifts, was that she should spirit them from the house before they were countermanded. But where could she store such clothes? They would test the honesty of the truest friend and Hilde did not have any friends in Amsterdam. An afternoon off every fortnight did not leave her much time to make them. She decided, finally, to put her faith in the Baggage Store of the Central Station.

The morning of Egbert's bid for freedom, Hilde rose early too. As he was dressing, she was folding his sister's clothes as tightly as she could and putting them into a sack. She could not carry a trunk unaided and had no money for a hired carriage. When she had laid the table for Maarten's breakfast and set fires in his office, the kitchen, the drawing room and the dining room, she told Mr. Blok that Mrs. de Leeuw had an errand for her, and Mrs. de Leeuw that Mr. Blok had one; and in order to escape the prying eyes of the servants she left Herengracht 605 by the front door.

Hilde was not used to sudden good fortune. She ran the whole way to the station, possessed by a superstitious certainty that something or someone would snatch it away. But nothing and no one did. She hired a locker and deposited her haul in it. She obtained a ticket and a receipt. If Mrs. Vermeulen-Sickerts demanded the return of her daughter's possessions, she could now say she had sold them. She walked back to the Herengracht. Mist was rising from the canals and the cold inhibited their stench. It was a sparkling winter's day. You may have found a husband, Agneta Hemels, she thought, but you've missed the chance of all this.

E gbert reached the schoolroom. From the shadows came hysterical hissing. He silenced it by switching on the lights. He went to the piano. On the music stand was the edition of Chopin Piet had bought him, which opened like an invitation at the fourth ballade.

The boy sat on the stool, resolved to play it come what may. His aunt's piano had known less tedious masters than Egbert. As his hands stretched in the opening octaves, its strings quivered in recognition and joy. He had never heard the ballade before, but its opening soothed his fear and beckoned him from the Bach-like maze in which he had wandered for so long. The tune prepared him for adventure. When it slipped away only to return, embroidered as finely as any garment of Louisa's, he had to search in the mass of notes to find it.

Once grasped he did not let it go. His fingers went faster or slowed down as the music led him; he obeyed no regimenting discipline but began to delight in his skill. As the page filled with notes, he was astonished by what he could do—for the sound his hands and feet produced was one of transcendent beauty.

When he had finished, he knew for the first time that there is value even in the darkest sorrow. He stood up. He went to the drawer in which his aunt's front-door key was kept and removed it. Then he took his grandfather's signet ring from its box and picked up his collected Bach. Without hesitation, he crossed the hall and let himself out onto the street.

So many unusual things had happened to Hilde Wilken since the previous afternoon that the sight of Egbert Vermeulen-Sickerts throwing a music book and a gold ring into the water from the Utrechtsestraat was almost unremarkable. At first she barely registered what she was seeing. When she did, she hurried closer. The boy was standing on the bridge, his face shining in the morning light. Was he a ghost? She crossed herself and crept closer.

"Good morning, Hilde."

"Good morning, Master Egbert." Hilde was too astonished to curtsy. For the first time she was not afraid of this little boy.

"It is a very pleasant morning, is it not?"

"Indeed it is." Hilde could not help herself; she leaned forward to touch him.

"I am quite real, I assure you."

And this was confirmed by the warmth of Egbert's skin.

Hilde ran into the drawing room without knocking and spoke without curtsying. "Oh, madam! Master Egbert is outside!"

"Whatever can you mean, Hilde?"

"I have spoken to him."

"Are you sure?"

"I am certain, madam."

"Call my husband at once." Jacobina went to fetch a cloak; then thought better of it and ran down the stairs.

Maarten was in his office. It was now his habit to spend

three hours each morning in prayer. At the tinkling of the silver bell he rose painfully. Hilde's breathlessness annoyed him, but as he listened he saw that proof of his salvation had come at last. Finally he understood the purpose of his recent sufferings. By forcing him to renounce vanity, God had prepared him for a gift greater than riches returned: the glory of a son like other sons.

He too ran down the stairs and into the street.

Piet Barol had been searching halfheartedly for his pupil for an hour, and it was Didier Loubat who conveyed the extraordinary news. By now the entire household had learned it. This meant that when Egbert turned the corner of the Herengracht, the nine people who had witnessed his years of failure and confinement were there to celebrate his triumph.

It was Mr. Blok who sounded the first cheer, and Monsieur la Chaume who lustily seconded it. Maarten Vermeulen-Sickerts began to run. He had not run for many years and it was fortunate that his son was not very far away. He reached him a moment after Jacobina did and picked him up and embraced him. Then he burst into tears, not caring a damn who saw.

Egbert completed the journey to his home smiling shyly, but inside he felt like a hero. He was ravenous with hunger and consumed an enormous breakfast. When it was finished a delicious heaviness stole over him, quite unlike the exhaustion that had succeeded his journeys across his great-aunt's entrance hall floor. With his head against his father's shoulder he fell into a deep doze at the dining room table.

"Let him sleep as long as he likes," said Piet, with the authority of a *staretz*. "When he wakes, he will be cured."

Egbert did not wake until midmorning of the following day, and when he did his father took him out and bought him half the contents of a toy shop. They returned from this expedition in great good humor and had an excellent lunch. As soon as it was over, Maarten went to his office and called for Piet Barol.

"Mr. Barol!" He leaped to his feet and embraced him. He had not been so excited since the day of Egbert's birth. "You have achieved what I had begun to fear was impossible. How ever did you manage it?"

"The credit is Egbert's alone, sir."

"Don't be so devilish modest. Sit down and tell me all about it."

Piet sat, but he had already decided to preserve his pupil's confidence. "All that was wanted was patience and sympathy and"—with sudden inspiration—"prayer." He inclined his head. "The Lord God Almighty has intervened here."

This was exactly the right thing to say. In a locked drawer of his desk Maarten had a large gift of money for Piet Barol, but the young fellow's piety demanded greater recognition. He glanced around his office and his eye fell on the miniature of the man on a tightrope. He hesitated. It was the jewel of his silver collection, worth twice what he had paid for it to say nothing of the luck it had brought him over twenty years. "My dear man." He pressed it into Piet's open hand. "You have given me back my son. I should like you to have this. And this." He unlocked the drawer and took out an envelope promisingly swollen with cash. "Let me say that should you wish to work for me in a more dignified, better remunerated position than the one you currently occupy, you need only say the word."

Piet had expected a bonus. He had not imagined it would be accompanied by a life-changing offer. He looked at the money and the miniature in his lap. They represented freedom, the capital to make his own way. They were what he had come to Amsterdam to seek. A job with Maarten would mean more of a life he had already glimpsed. And then there was the question of Jacobina . . . It seemed that the opportunity had arisen to exit with honor from the Vermeulen-Sickerts' lives and he was minded to take it.

"I am grateful for this gift and for your confidence, sir," he said, finally. "But for the moment I am very happy as Egbert's tutor, and after that I wish to work for myself, and no other man."

Maarten clapped him on the back. "If that is your answer, I shall not dissuade you from it. The best strike out on their own. When the moment comes, you must go into the world and make your fortune as I did."

"That is my intention."

"And an admirable one. Keep that man on a tightrope ever beside you. He will protect you from harm."

"I shall treasure him."

The next day was a Saturday. Didier had one good suit of his own and Piet loaned him an Hermès tie and a set of studs and squeezed his large feet into a pair of Maarten's discarded shoes. He was not superstitious and had no intention of keeping the miniature Maarten had given him, but he knew that guile—and a guileful accomplice—would be required to realize its full value.

They left the house looking like gentlemen of good family and ample means and exploited this impression at three of the city's leading silver galleries. Piet had watched many young men in Leiden liquidate their possessions and knew better than to appear at all anxious for money. He also knew that good prices are paid only to those with the confidence to decline bad ones. He had no idea what the thing was worth so he decided that no sum would tempt him to sell to the first two buyers. This allowed him to bluster convincingly with the third.

He and Didier presented themselves as cousins and the object as an unwanted gift from Didier's father. They elicited promises of absolute discretion.

"I shall wait, naturally, a dignified interval before offering it for sale," said the gentleman to whom Piet finally sold it. "And I will not put it in the shop window. We would not like to cause your uncle any offense."

"No indeed." Didier frowned. "I'm afraid my father would be extremely displeased."

"And his father is extremely alarming when displeased," added Piet.

The dealer smiled. He had paid an approximately fair price, much against his usual custom, but he had also been prepared to offer more. Now he disparaged his purchase to make the young gentlemen feel they had done well out of him. "You may rest easy, dear sirs. Though charming and undoubtedly finished by hand, this miniature is made from a mold. There are others in existence. Even if your uncle were, by chance, to encounter it, he would not be able to tell that it was the one he gave you."

The young men left the shop, arm in arm. Didier was thrilled by Piet's bravado and proud to be walking beside him. He was also proud of himself because he was not jealous of Piet's sudden luck. He cared for him enough to rejoice in his blessings. "What will you do with all this money?"

"Buy passage to New York on a wonderful ship. I don't mean to go steerage, either." Piet's impersonation of a gentleman of means had worked its magic on him and his imagination had polished his future to a high sheen. He did not intend to sleep on planks with hordes of snoring immigrants now that he could avoid it.

Didier put his arm around Piet's shoulder, to show that he did not resent his good fortune, and ruffled his thick, sweet-smelling hair. "Why leave Holland? Everything for a happy life is here."

"There's no adventure in staying in the same place and I mean to have adventures. If you'd come with me to buy my ticket, we can celebrate with wild drunkenness and a fine dinner. The expense will be mine."

Didier Loubat had long since given up hoping for a drunken night with Piet Barol and the sudden granting of one made him feel that the day was glorious for him, too. "It's the least you can do, you lucky bastard," he said gruffly, and made a show of pushing his friend into the gutter.

They went to the offices of the Loire Lines, an ornate building on the Damrak. As they passed beneath the crossed gilt *L*s set in a marble shell above its door, the doorman bowed so low that Piet was briefly ashamed to join the throng at the third-class window. His hesitation confirmed the doorman's first assessment. He pressed a discreetly placed bell, which summoned a deferential official. This gentleman escorted Piet and Didier to a private office and assured them of his very best attention at all times.

"May I ask your destination, my dear sirs?" Karel Huysman took his seat beneath a framed oil painting of the liner *Eugénie.*

The picture reminded Piet of Constance's handsome, unpleasant friend, who had refused to travel on any other ship. "I'm inclining towards New York." He spoke languidly, still acting the part he had reprised for the silver dealers. "I'll be traveling alone but I insist on the *Eugénie.*" It gave him great pleasure to mimic an aristocrat's prejudices before a credulous audience and Didier. He decided to bluff here as long as it amused him and buy his ticket elsewhere.

Mr. Huysman's face fell. "A most judicious choice, may

I say. But the *Eugénie* is full in first class for the next four years. Now the *Joséphine* is—"

"But I insist on the *Eugénie.*"

Mr. Huysman inclined his head. "And very wise you are to do so. Many notable Americans reserve their favorite cabins for every crossing, merely to keep them permanently at their disposal. It is, of course, their right, but so inconvenient for others." He looked down at the ledger before him. "Tourist class to New York is also full until the middle of 1909, I regret to say."

"No matter." Piet stood up. "I'm told Cunard's *Mauretania* is very comfortable."

But Karel Huysman's competitive instincts were aroused. "You will find that Cunarders fall regrettably short of our standards, sir. I should not forgive myself if you had an uncomfortable voyage." He had correctly assessed his young client as an adventurous type. "Perhaps I might suggest an alternative. Will you be traveling for business or leisure?"

"Leisure, naturally."

"There is a berth in tourist class. Just one, in a shared cabin. Departing January 18th."

"My cousin only travels first class." Didier also rose.

"Quite so." Mr. Huysman smiled. "But tourist class on the *Eugénie* is in every way superior to first class on every other ship. Besides, her January voyage will be an event to describe to your grandchildren." He lowered his voice. "She is christening the company's new service to South Africa. En route she will call at the island of St. Helena. How many can boast of having seen it? A ball is being given there in aid of orphaned infants. It will be talked of for years to come—though unfortunately all the tickets have long since been sold." He drew breath and smiled. "Would you at all consider Cape Town? It is a city full of opportunities for enterprise and pleasure."

"My cousin doesn't——" began Didier.

"It would be remiss of me not to mention," Mr. Huysman continued, "that though the voyage will last seventeen days, it will cost only a trifle more than the six-day crossing to New York." He pointed to a number on a list in front of him and slid the paper towards Piet. "This represents a superb compromise between quality and value."

The figure was so confidently astronomical that Piet was gripped by the idea of paying it, since for the first time in his life he could. His vague plans of New York shimmered a moment, then disintegrated. He was sure to be a success wherever he went. Besides, Africa was cheap, and life with so much native labor was bound to be comfortable. To sail to his future on a ship as luxurious as the *Eugénie* struck him as wholly appropriate. With his savings and the money Maarten had given him, he could afford a one-way passage and still have money left over to start his new life. It would not be as much as he had intended, but the South African War was over and calm restored; men had made fortunes in diamonds and gold. He was sure he could find a way to divert some of that free-flowing cash into his own pocket.

Observing the look on his client's face, Mr. Huysman pressed home his advantage. "Every cabin in tourist class has hot running water, salt and fresh," he murmured, "and taps plated in the latest white metals. The food is equal to that of the best restaurants in Paris."

"A moment with my cousin, if you please," said Didier.

"Of course, sir."

As soon as the agent had withdrawn, Didier said, "That's most of your money."

"Cape Town will be less expensive than New York. I wouldn't need so much."

"But you'll need some. You've had a stroke of luck. That's not the same as being rich."

But Piet was already imagining himself in a mahogany deck chair, being fawned over by obliging stewards; and the vision's foolhardiness was part of its appeal. "I'd have enough to get by for a few months. And, more important, to buy us dinner tonight. I'll find some way of prospering once I'm there. Think of the fun of a seventeen-day voyage! You never know who you might meet."

"Don't be a fool."

But this only fortified Piet's resolve. With a young man's delight in showing off to a friend he called the agent back and paid for the cabin then and there and emerged into the dwindling light aware that he had made a wager with Fortune and confident of winning it.

They went to the Karseboom, a music hall and tavern frequented by a boisterous crowd. As he pushed his way to the bar behind Piet, Didier did not miss the chance to press heavily against him or to lean so close to make himself heard that their cheeks touched. Piet's immediate proximity eased the looming wrench of his departure.

"When will you tell your father?" he shouted as their beers were set before them.

"At Christmas. He won't mind."

"Won't he miss you?"

"He's not sentimental."

"Mine would have a fit if I went off to the other side of the world."

Piet thought of the genial Monsieur Loubat, and for the first time all day a trickle of sorrow contaminated his triumph. "My father's not like yours," he said briefly. "Let's play billiards."

The game of Wilhelmina billiards was taken seriously at the Karseboom. Piet and Didier secured one of the twenty-four tables but they were soon challenged for it; and their joint defense was so successful they drew a large crowd. Didier was an indifferent player, but Piet's presence combined with just the right amount of alcohol unleashed a long run of luck. The watching women sided with the handsome "cousins" and their cheers prompted them to accept ever greater bets, which they won as if claiming a natural right. At eleven they adjourned for supper with fistfuls of coins and a pewter flask pledged in lieu of cash. They selected two of the most forward spectators to join them at it. These ladies made it clear, as they ate beef and oysters, that they were prepared to lower their prices considerably for the pleasure of entertaining their hosts for the night.

The one with her hand on Didier's thigh was called Greetje. "Two is better than one, and four is better than two," she whispered, brushing her lips against his ear. She had had a long run of foul-smelling, middle-aged men. Since she had to be where she was, she did not want to pass up the chance of Didier Loubat and Piet Barol. Neither did her colleague Klara, who at that moment was sliding her finger under the waistband of Piet's trousers.

The thought of sharing these women in naked abandon with Piet Barol made Didier do some calculations of his own. His yearly bottle of Chartreuse aside, he permitted himself few luxuries. He had many uses for his half of the winnings, and yet— He would never have the chance again. He considered the practicalities. "Have you a place?"

"Not a minute's walk from here."

"I'll put it to my friend."

But Piet would not. He had a horror of venereal disease, gained from the nasty pustules exhibited by certain university acquaintances, and was quite imaginative enough to know that many had preceded him with Klara and paid for the honor (not always very well). As her vulgar polished nails clawed the tender flesh of his backside, he was seized by an urgent longing for the chaste, patrician Jacobina.

They had had no contact since the day he carried Egbert out onto the street. Both had shunned the indecency of the idea. But Piet had now cured Jacobina's son. He had honored his conscience's debt to Maarten and showed her that she had no reason to chastise him. He was slightly appalled that Didier should wish to cavort with two women of the night and told him sternly that a man like him did not have to pay for pleasure.

Didier took this as a terrific compliment and was consoled. They walked home through the chilly air, arms about each other's shoulders, uncoordinated from drinking. Didier was half a head taller and their hold was not wholly comfortable; but neither let go. As they turned onto the Leidsegracht, Piet stopped. Above the unlit street the night sky was bright with starlight. The waters of the canal reflected the houses faintly; they were entirely alone. "I'll be sorry to leave all this," he said contemplatively. "And you, of course."

What would happen if I kissed him now? Didier wondered. But he did not dare. Piet had never shown any inclination that way, and yet— *He is standing with his arm around me, in a beautiful place, late at night.* Didier had slept with men encountered in far less tender circumstances. Testing the possibilities, he leaned heavily against his friend's unyielding body and said, "I can barely stand, I'm so drunk." He knew that a few feet farther on, beneath the bridge, was a small quay sheltered from wind and prying eyes. It was a place he went to alone; it held no illicit memories. "I know somewhere we can sit." He lurched forward, drawing Piet with him.

They climbed down the slippery steps and sat on Didier's

coat with their legs dangling over the water. Their knees knocked, but their descent had loosened their grip on each other. Piet opened the pewter flask they had won, which was half full of decent brandy. They passed it between them, cold fingers touching, and relived their exploits in the silver galleries. They praised each other extravagantly and agreed that it was marvelous to be grown-up. Didier stared at Piet's profile, hoarding its memory.

"I bet those tarts are missing us," he said. "How's your married lady?"

"She's been away."

"Frustrating for you."

"Unimaginably."

They sat in silence, each thinking of sex. Didier broke it. "Have you cuckolded many husbands?"

"Hers is the second."

"Whose was the first?"

Told of the mezzo-soprano at Leiden, Didier pretended to be less impressed than he was and produced some stories of his own—each lewder than the next, the genders of the participants carefully reversed. An atmosphere of bawdy candor grew up between the young men. Didier coarsened his language and considered provoking a friendly brawl. It would get their arms around each other again. "I should beat you for leaving me at Blok's mercy," he growled, laying the ground for provocation later.

But Piet had stood up and did not hear. He retreated to the dark space beneath the bridge. Didier hesitated, but a sixth sense told him not to follow. The silence lasted so long he almost thought himself mistaken until a thunder of urine confirmed that this was a call of nature and not an invitation. When Piet returned he was paler.

"Regretting the brandy?"

"Beginning to."

Didier considered. It would be easier to initiate a play fight during the walk home, but there were also possibilities in the view and the moonlight. He decided in favor of tenderness. "You'll be sick if you move at once. Stay here a bit."

Piet obeyed. It was obvious from the way he sat down that he was considerably drunker than Didier, who took heart from this advantage. Nina Barol had liked to play with her son's hair. When Didier ran his fingers through it—very calmly, with no trace of nerves—Piet did not resist. He was not troubled by physical affection. On many occasions he had spent an hour or two lying in another boy's arms and had often profited from the willingness of certain school friends to perform relieving favors for him. Tonight his thoughts were running in a wholly different direction. As Didier stroked his curls he imagined Jacobina Vermeulen-Sickerts in a slip of rippable muslin and began to wish for morning. Finally he shook his friend's hand from his head and stood up. "Come on. Have to sleep."

They walked home together, not touching. Didier let them into the kitchen, and when he had locked the door he bent down and undid Piet's laces. He pushed him against the range, lifted his feet one by one and pulled his boots off. "They'll squeak on the tiles." He leaned very close as he whispered. "If we wake the witch she'll turn us to stone."

"Mustn't wake the witch."

"Indeed not."

"What I need . . ."

"Is some help getting to bed."

"No. Witch's apple cake. Must have some of the witch's apple cake."

Didier took his hand and led him to the stairs. "You go up before you break something. I'll bring it in a minute."

As Gert Blok readied himself for bed on the deserted attic floor of Herengracht 605, he knew instinctively that the young men were out together. The knowledge lurked on the edges of his consciousness: a heavy, gray mass of bitterness. It was not the first time Gert Blok had been left out. As he brushed his teeth he felt like the seven-year-old he had once been, forced by the popular boys to play in the woods alone. The intervening fifty years had not made this misery easier to bear; they had fossilized it into rage.

He went into his bedroom and closed the door, resisting a mounting, savage lust. Unexpressed, unsatisfied, sincerely repented; capable, nevertheless, of overthrowing his reason. He hesitated before taking off his dressing gown. He was sure the boys would not be back for hours. A devilish voice suggested he profit by their absence, since the opportunity might not recur for months. He stood still, paralyzed by a familiar and unequal struggle; then he lost it and went into the corridor and opened Didier's door.

Gert Blok remembered very well his first glimpse of Didier Loubat: holding a silver-plate cake stand on the terrace of the Amstel Hotel, bending slightly toward the gentleman he was serving, his trousers hugging the curve of his spectacular arse. He had seconded him at once to the house and trained him personally. Since that day, on two occasions, he had seen his buttocks wrapped in a tightly stretched towel. Once, by creeping to his door and throwing it open the instant he knocked, he had caught him with nothing on at all. He went into his bedroom and buried his nose in Didier's pillow. Though the linen was changed regularly, it was incontrovertibly *his* pillow. This was where his cheek rested; here was a fine blond hair.

Mr. Blok put the hair into his dressing gown pocket and began to touch himself. For a moment he was handsome and vigorous and carousing with the young men. The vision made him bold. He replaced Didier's pillow and rifled his laundry bag, where the smells were stronger and less decorous. Next he went to Piet's room, but found to his irritation that his sheets were clean and held no trace of him. His laundry bag was empty. All he had were the memories of summoning him to Maarten's office or barging in before dinner and catching him half dressed.

He took these images back to his own bed and opened the Pandora's box in which he kept other guilty treasures: snatched glimpses of a foot or a strong bare arm; the ripple of youthful muscle beneath a starched shirt. He started to sweat as he rubbed himself faster and to dread the end even as he neared it. It was announced by a spurt of warm slime, and at once the customary revulsion settled over him and cooled into a sarcophagus of shame. He remembered the prohibitions of Leviticus and St. Paul; he thought of them constantly and did his best to abide by them and always failed. He was accustomed to self-loathing, but tonight it mixed with the ache of abandonment and coagulated into hatred.

He lay in the dark as he had lain on many nights, listening to Piet and Didier laugh in the echoing bathroom across the hall. With a slow, deliberate cruelty he tortured himself by imagining them together—maybe with women, certainly drunk and happy. So real were these visions that when he heard a floorboard creak he thought he had imagined it. But he had not. Piet was climbing the stairs. Where was Didier? He felt in the dark for his pocket handkerchief and dried his sticky fingers. Then he switched on the light. The evening's agonies demanded expression, and the only expression was vengeance. He felt sure that Didier was doing something for which he might punish him; with any luck, something so grave that the punishment might be permanent. He owed the lad nothing. If he could not have him he would not protect him.

When he had washed his hands and arranged himself he put on his dressing gown, parted his hair carefully, and went downstairs. He found Didier in the kitchen stealing two slices of the Vermeulen-Sickerts' apple cake and dismissed him on the spot. "You may stay the night since it is so late," he said with splendid *froideur.* "But I will not tolerate thieving. Make sure you are gone before lunch tomorrow."

And when Didier had stumbled up the stairs, his apologies refused, Gert Blok sat down at the kitchen table, and ate both slices of cake, and felt better.

Didier went straight to Piet's room. He was horny enough not to mind much about the future. Piet was lying on his bed, shirt and trousers on the floor, head back, mouth open. He was fast asleep. The moon's light caught his profile and shadowed the indentations of his powerful body. He was snoring lightly and twitching as he dreamed. A longing to kiss him stole over Didier, but again he resisted it.

He sat down on the bed, suddenly tired. Piet muttered in his sleep and turned on his side, pulled his thick, hairy legs under him. The movement struck Didier as an invitation, as though Piet half sensed his presence and was making space for him. He took off his shirt and lay down beside him. He pressed his shoulder against Piet's back. He could feel the warmth of Piet's body and smell the cigar smoke in his hair; see the pimple on the back of his neck, the imperfection that made him perfect. And though the darkness had begun to spin he fell into a deep and easeful sleep.

The sound of the bell ringing to summon the household to church infiltrated Piet's dreams as fiery, crashing cymbals. He did not often drink and was not at all accustomed to the inconveniences of a hangover. He was desperately thirsty and at the same time unable to move his body in search of water. He opened his eyes. Church was impossible. He closed them again, but then his door was knocked on and opened.

"Cheer up, chum." Didier had risen at dawn to enjoy his final bath and pack his trunk. "You've got my hot water to yourself now. I was just saying good-bye."

"Good-bye?"

"Blok caught me last night getting our cake. I have to be out of the house before they get back from their prayers."

Piet sat up. "Again . . . slower."

Didier repeated himself. When Piet understood what had happened, he subsided onto his pillows and told Didier to stop packing. "Mrs. Vermeulen-Sickerts trusts me. I'll make sure of everything."

"Cocky, aren't you?"

"It's only cake. She'll see that."

"She can't countermand her own butler. That's not how these things work."

Piet got out of bed and pulled his trousers on. "I'll see to it. There's no need to pack."

"I don't much fancy being here when you're gone, as it happens. Blok's only prey. Get me a reference if you've got so much influence."

"That's easily done." But Piet's conscience was troubled. He did not think Didier should pay the penalty for the purloined apple cake alone. "Are you sure you don't want to stay?"

"Not if you're not."

"All right, then." He stepped by him, went to the desk, and opened the steel box he kept in it. He had a small bundle of notes left and counted out ten of them. "I always earned more than you, though I hardly deserved to. Take your share and have the winnings from last night, too."

"I couldn't."

"Of course you could."

"I won't."

Piet made as if to put the money back, but at the last moment he grabbed Didier's arms and pinned them behind him. He put the notes forcibly into his trouser pocket. "And now you have. I feel sure we will meet again. God bless, and good speed."

Piet slept for four hours, and as he drifted towards consciousness Jacobina appeared to him, aloof but available. He woke with the idea that he should not delay and got out of bed. As he washed and dressed he almost brought himself to believe that Maarten *owed* him the freedom to pleasure his wife.

He had saved his son, after all.

The house was Sunday-quiet. He went to Jacobina's private sitting room and found her in her reading chair, beside the window that looked onto the canal. On her lap was an open book that had rested there for half an hour.

"Good afternoon, Mr. Barol," she said coolly.

"Good afternoon, mevrouw."

"You missed church."

"I was unwell. I said my devotions in private."

"I trust you are better now?"

"I am, thank you. I have come about Didier Loubat."

Jacobina's face tightened. "There can be no leniency for thieves. I would never have thought it of him."

"I asked him to get the cake. I did not know it was forbidden."

"You woke him at three in the morning to send him on an errand?"

"No, mevrouw. We were out together."

Jacobina's older brothers had been merry carousers, and she had often heard them defend themselves to her parents. She approved of boys sticking up for one another. "Why did he not come to me to explain?"

"He did not wish to place you in the awkward position of going against Mr. Blok."

"I see."

"He is an upstanding fellow. I come to ask you to give him the reference he deserves."

Jacobina did not intend to gratify Piet's request too readily. "I will consult my husband. The last word on the matter is his."

"Thank you, mevrouw."

"Is there anything else?"

"I should like to give my notice."

"May I ask why?"

"Now that Master Egbert is well, he should go to school. He will have no need of a tutor after Christmas."

"On the contrary, Mr. Barol. He may need your assistance to make up lost ground."

"He is far ahead of his peers in anything I can teach him."

"What if he relapses?"

"He will not. Be firm with him if he stumbles."

Jacobina was not in the habit of begging servants to stay on, and she did not intend to do so now. Nevertheless, she had imagined having the time to subdue her conscience and enjoy Piet again. The knowledge that this was not so made her petulant. "Have you not been happy with us, Mr. Barol?"

"It has been an honor to be of service to your family."

Piet paused. "And especially to you. I have never had such rewarding employment."

"You have done fine work."

"Perhaps I might be useful in some small way before I leave?"

Jacobina rang the bell. "Tomorrow afternoon at three o'clock." She spoke without emotion. "I have some letters you might address."

"With pleasure."

And when Piet had bowed and left her, Jacobina ordered hot chocolate from Hilde and found fault with the china she had selected, and the composition of the tray, and told her that if she did not improve she would have to get rid of her.

Then she sat down and wrote Didier Loubat an excellent reference.

Almost twenty-four hours separated this brief conversation from the time Jacobina had named. Piet passed them in a state of trying anticipation. There was no Didier to hurry the minutes along with, and weeks without touching a woman made the wait unendurable. His suspense was heightened the next morning when Maarten proposed a visit to Willemshoven to show Egbert the place for the first time. The boy accepted excitedly; so did Constance; but Jacobina said she had too much to do to go frolicking about the countryside. She was wearing her apple-green dress and looked at her plate when Piet excused himself too, on the grounds that it should be a family outing. Louisa also refused, because she was angry with her father and wished to make this plain to him.

"We shall spend the night in an inn in the village and return tomorrow," said Maarten merrily.

"Don't hesitate to spend two if you're enjoying yourselves." Jacobina had spent much of the previous day, and all this morning, adjudicating a fierce debate between her conscience and her inclination. She had decided at last on a rendezvous with Piet Barol; now the question remained what its business might be.

The party left after lunch. As she waved them off she reached a compromise she found acceptable and climbed the stairs to her aunt's bedroom, feeling fearful but alive. She *would* see Piet naked, but this would be their last encounter. She would never repeat such wickedness with him or anyone else.

He knocked ten minutes later and had had the good taste to change into the suit of English wool he had worn to their first interview. He was wearing nothing that had once been her husband's.

"Good afternoon, Mr. Barol."

"Good afternoon, Mevrouw Vermeulen-Sickerts."

At the foot of the bed was a round carpet, which had been the setting for certain fantastical scenes Jacobina now intended to act out. "Please stand in the center of the circle and remove your jacket," she said.

Piet did as he was told.

"And your waistcoat."

He complied again.

"Your tie, if you please." She spoke in exactly the tone she had used to Hilde that morning, when instructing her on the correct way to lay out her clothes. "Your shirt."

Now Piet understood her intentions. He had long wished to show her his body, but his hands as they undid his buttons were shaking.

"You may drop it at your feet."

He did so.

"Now your shoes and socks."

He bent down before her and removed them.

"Your trousers," said Jacobina.

Piet took his trousers off. In the cheval glass on the wardrobe door he could see his reflection: his pale, muscular body; the patch of dark hair on his chest; the trail of it that led over his stomach and thickened at the waistband of his drawers, which were unequal to restraining their contents. He was proud of his cock, which had aroused admiring attention before. And the clipped, disinterested voice in which Jacobina said, "You may remove your undershorts," satisfied the last demands of ego.

He obeyed her. The spectacle of his nakedness exceeded Jacobina's expectations by some measure. She had lived this scene many times before but had never pursued it beyond this climactic point. Now she saw that Piet would honor further direction, and the desire to touch him took hold of her. This was not part of the bargain she had made with her conscience. However, having come so far she could not resist the urge to continue. I will never do this again, she thought, and made up her mind to do as she pleased.

But where should she touch him? Where first?

She walked the circumference of the carpet twice, inspecting Piet carefully. She chose his shoulder blades and ran her hand across them. Goose pimples rippled over his back. She circled him again. His cock was throbbing in time to the pulsing artery on his neck. She put her left hand to the place where his buttocks began their hairy outward curve, then her right in the middle of his chest, on the cushion of soft black curls between his pectorals. His body was wonderfully solid and warm. She put her arms around his neck and leaned back, watching his sinews tighten as he took her weight. Piet shivered, but he was not cold. When she had touched his thighs and his calves and the hard roundness of his upper arms, the idea of handling his cock began to mesmerize her. She stood in front of him. It was pointing straight up at her from a thicket of coarse black hair. She put her index finger to it and provoked a violent spasm. Piet grinned. Now she looked at his face, and his excitement made her brave.

She gripped it with her right hand and squeezed.

This action sent an instruction to Piet Barol's brain that no human effort could override. His eyelids snapped shut. His knees buckled. His overfull balls discharged their cargo with thundering conviction. But the anesthetic of ecstasy did not last long. He opened his eyes to find the front of Jacobina's apple-green dress thickly adorned with white matter. He was appalled to have lost control in this schoolboy fashion. For a moment he wanted to cry.

"Forgive me, mevrouw."

Jacobina was also horrified, but horror was not the only emotion she felt. The simultaneous crumpling of Piet's body and spirit inspired an unexpected tenderness. She could hardly blame him for finding her presence stimulating beyond endurance. Neither did she intend to terminate this encounter until she, too, had achieved the release Piet's body had so abruptly claimed. Her dress was ruined, but the presence of this divine young man, so delectably cowed, overcame the promptings of mortification. A daredevil spirit alighted on her shoulder. Obliging its whispered instruction, she turned her back on him and said, "Unfasten my buttons, Mr. Barol."

Piet put his undershorts on and complied. Jacobina's buttons were tiny and covered in slippery apple-green silk. There were twenty-seven between neck and bustle, and his large fingers handled them clumsily. He did not know what he should expect. Certainly he did not imagine that Jacobina, having stepped out of her dress, would instruct him to unlace her corset and remove her petticoat, her stockings and silk knickers, and would cross to the chaise longue and recline on it in the position she had so often assumed when fully clothed. But she did all these things. He followed her meekly and knelt on one knee before her.

This afternoon there were no tickles. Jacobina could not silence a low protest of delight. She raised herself on her elbows, the better to see him. "I did not ask you to dress again."

"No, mevrouw."

Piet removed his drawers to reveal an emphatic recovery. Its rapidity was exceedingly flattering. Jacobina arched her back and pushed her cunt against his face, pulling his curly head closer with both hands.

The sensation was electrifying. Piet's cock jolted taut. He had often thought of having this haughty, still-beautiful woman and sensed that the day was one of unprecedented permissions. He looked up. So did she, and neither looked away. He straightened his back, brought his face closer to hers. There was wantonness in her eyes, and it decided him. He held her legs apart, raised himself from the floor, and plunged his cock into her.

It was much wider than Maarten's.

Jacobina cried out. The effrontery of it! But she had imagined this impudent act too often to resist sincerely at the final hour. The room began to swim. Piet was fucking her with quick, violating thrusts. It was stupendous, but he was shaking so severely she feared a repeat of his former punctuality.

"*Lentement*, Mr. Barol."

Piet slowed down. As he found his rhythm and kept to it, Jacobina closed her eyes. She had never in her life experienced such a thing, and the longer it lasted the more complex and wonder-filled it became. The pleasure was so consuming it left no space in her head for any consciousness of wrongdoing. She floated upwards, until she could clearly see the shining muscles of Piet's back, then herself on the chaise longue and the room and the house and the city, the fields around her childhood home, Riejke Vedder's blue-veined breasts, her children's births. As she soared over her life she felt *free*—and in that freedom was the knowledge that Egbert was free too, that she need no longer blame herself for his suffering, and that the young man who had saved him was now leading her towards this blissful extinction of the self.

On an impulse, she kissed him.

Then nothing mattered any longer. They threw themselves into one another, kissing and clutching and fucking. A wild delirium took hold of them; lifted them up, caressed them, goaded them. Jacobina's climax unfurled and billowed, hurtled her into the air, only to catch her again on a zephyr breeze. She was conscious much later of the spurts of Piet's semen; felt the death throes of his body, a pre-echo of its end at this moment of heightened life. They clung to each other, two naked human animals in a true state of innocence—unconscious of their nakedness and of everything else.

Then it was over. As the pleasure lifted so did its protections against reality. Jacobina was the first to regain her senses and pushed Piet from her.

He got up at once and dressed.

Now she could see herself in the cheval glass, naked and sweaty. She did not inspect the reflection closely. As the practicalities of the situation crowded in on her, she rose and arranged her disordered underwear. How was she to get back to her room? Her own dress was in no state to be worn. She considered sending Piet for a clean one, but what if he were caught rifling her closet? There was no one in the house she could trust.

Without looking at him, she went to her aunt's wardrobe and selected a mauve tea gown. It was three seasons old and far too big for her, but it had a sash and would have to do. She put her own dress in a drawer and put her aunt's on. "My buttons, please, Mr. Barol." She turned her back to him.

As Piet fastened them, Jacobina's self-possession returned. She had not scrutinized her body in the mirror for fear of the signs of aging and decay she might detect, but these did not seem to have mattered to her heroic young slave, and that made them matter much less to her. When Piet had finished, she pinned her hair and went to the door.

"Thank you," she said, and stalked down the stairs without a backward glance.

When Jacobina had gone, Piet collapsed in an armchair and closed his eyes. What an afternoon! He was wholly satisfied with life. He had come to the Vermeulen-Sickerts' resolved to live in opulence. He had done so. He'd intended to make the money for a new start; he had done this too, in less than a year. He had cured the little boy in his charge and given his mother a first-class fuck. In the drawer of his dressing table was a tourist-class ticket on the world's most luxurious ship, beside a bundle of cash. These facts combined to induce a sensation of tranquil and total self-approval.

He dozed for ten minutes, then straightened the cushions on the chaise longue and checked that he was presentable. He was. He locked the door behind him, put the key in its vase, and went down the stairs.

Louisa was in the hall at Herengracht 605. "Have you seen my mother?"

"Not since lunch."

"She's marching about in a ghastly old frock."

Piet smiled. "Perhaps you should dress her."

"She is beyond my assistance."

"No one is."

But Louisa did not reach for this pretty compliment. Instead she said, "What's that smell of dead flowers?"

Piet stepped away from her, careful not to blush. "I've no idea," he replied, and went upstairs to wash.

When informed of Piet Barol's imminent departure, Maarten Vermeulen-Sickerts was delighted by the young man's vim. He thought Jacobina might be angry with him for giving Piet the means to leave so soon—but it seemed, as December began, that there was nothing he could do to try his wife's patience. Jacobina was as attentive and amusing and tender as she had been in their first year of marriage. It was marvelous. As he contemplated Christmas, Maarten felt profoundly at peace. His hotels in London and Frankfurt had reopened triumphantly and the Plaza's Presidential Suite was booked until the middle of 1908. His debts remained burdensome, but he had again the means to service them without anxiety. Now that God was formally on his side, he did not doubt his ability to repay the capital when required.

Egbert's remarkable recovery made him feel like Abraham: sorely tried but amply rewarded. The joy of showing his son over the properties he would one day own made Maarten giddy. To be blessed, besides this, with a thoughtful wife, two charming daughters, a house still full of fine things and a chef as gifted as Monsieur la Chaume further stoked the high spirits of the season. He was aware that Louisa was cross with him but refused to be provoked; and to each slight or cold word he responded with humor, which he considered the best medicine for her fanciful afflictions. Rising from his knees each morning, rejoicing in the ache of his body after three hours of prayer, he felt quietly secure among the Elect. For the first time in his life he was certain of salvation.

Piet Barol was also having a splendid time. Egbert was so often out with his father that he had many hours to while away in studied leisure. The secondment of three chambermaids and a footman from the Amstel Hotel allowed him to ask for things he would never have troubled Agneta Hemels for. Their acceptance of his authority showed him how much he had learned from the Vermeulen-Sickertses, and this made him sentimental. He completed his sketches of the most arresting pieces of furniture and presented twelve of the best to Maarten. He sang for the guests who came four nights of every seven and went skating with the girls and their friends on the lake in the Vondelpark and enjoyed Egbert's enthusiastic devotion. With deepening affection he took him over the house and taught him to appreciate the treasures that would be his.

By mutual and wordless consent neither he nor Jacobina alluded to their indiscretions or made any attempt to resume them. They had had their fill of one another. Neither wished to blur by repetition the perfections of their last encounter.

Piet's final day was set for December 20th. He would spend the holidays with his father in Leiden and sail for Cape Town in January. To his great satisfaction, Maarten proposed a farewell dinner and Constance threw herself into organizing it. The guests were invited for Wednesday 18th. That afternoon Piet was sitting on the first-floor landing, sketching the statues beneath the dome, when Louisa Vermeulen-Sickerts sat down beside him.

"There should be four, of course," she remarked.

"Four what?"

"Figures. That's Paris in the center, but there are only

two goddesses when there should be three. The myth says
Aphrodite, Athena *and* Hera competed for his golden apple."

"A dangerous contest."

Louisa kept her hands still; she was nervous and tempted
to play with her fingers. "He gave it to Aphrodite, who
bribed him with the love of Helen of Troy. He would have
done better to take the riches Hera offered him, or Athena's
wisdom."

"I didn't know you were a classical scholar."

"There's a good deal you don't know about me, Mr. Barol."
Louisa had promised herself to meet his eyes, but when the
moment came she could not. "We will lose our very own
Paris when you go."

"In me?"

"Of course. The only young man in a household of
women." She smiled. "It fits beautifully, does it not? Constance is the prettiest. Aphrodite, if you will. I'm the wisest,
like Athena."

"And Hilde is Hera, queen of the gods?"

"Not Hilde. Mummy."

"What nonsense you talk."

She laughed, and he saw she had no idea of the truth she
had stumbled so close to. "It's obvious she's fond of you.
Everyone is. But it was Athena who helped heroes. Don't
forget that."

Since her encounter with her father, Louisa Vermeulen-
Sickerts had given her full attention to the question of how
to leave her family without destroying it. She loved her parents too well to escape their care by any means that would
shame or wound them. She could not elope or run away.
Neither could she bear the idea of joining forces for life
with any of the young men she and her sister danced with.
Besides, she knew that to live independently of her father
she would have to leave Amsterdam.

It had taken her some time to see that the solution to her problem was right before her. She did not dislike Piet Barol. She thought him unscrupulous but admired his guile more than she let on to Constance. He was a man who could make things happen, and their not being in love was surely an advantage. She had too much experience of her sister's chaotic affairs to believe in the longevity of romance. It would be wiser to trust Piet's self-interest, which would never let her down.

She took his hand. "Let me come to Cape Town with you."

"What?"

"Marry me."

"What on earth?"

"Please, Piet. I cannot live my life in this house. I must escape."

"From whom?"

"From my family, much though I love them. Let me come with you. I'll not be a burden."

Piet's astonishment was so sincere he could not mask it. He took his hand from hers, afraid that someone would see.

"It is not a very romantic proposition, I grant you." Louisa was aware that a passionless proposal might offend a man as vain as Piet Barol, but she could not lie. "You do not love me, nor I you. But many marriages prosper without that fickle commodity. We are both intelligent and ambitious. We are amused by one another. Together we would make a formidable pair."

"You do me a great honor, but—"

"I could not run away. It would cause my parents too much pain. Yet to stay here, to live this frivolous life forever, will cause *me* too much pain. My father says a woman may fulfill herself by helping a man succeed. I am capable of more, but it is a place to start." The skepticism on Piet's face made her promise recklessly. "I should not mind if you took a lover. I have no inclination to children, but would bear you one if you wished. You—I—I will have a sizable dowry. You may keep it all for yourself."

This last concession struck quite the wrong note. "I would not consider that," said Piet with dignity; and then, more gently, because he could see what this offer cost her: "It is hopeless, Louisa." It was the first time they had used each other's Christian names. "Your father would never permit it. I am from quite a different class."

"So was he, once. He loves you, Piet. You are the only man he would let me cross the world for."

"What about Constance?"

"Constance will fend for herself. Papa's troubles gave her a shock. She wishes to be married by Easter. She has told me so."

There was silence in the deserted corridor. Piet frowned to imply that he was giving this wild proposal his full consideration. In fact he was not remotely tempted by it. He could never marry one of Jacobina's daughters, no matter how platonic the understanding. And a lifetime of being silently judged by Louisa Vermeulen-Sickerts was not worth any amount of money.

"Please," said Louisa, humbly.

"I cannot," he answered. "It would not be right. You will find some other means to win your independence. I know you will. Forgive me."

To have offered herself for sale was one thing. To have had the transaction declined was another. Louisa, who rarely blushed, went very red in the face. She stood up. She felt she should say something superb to Piet Barol but did not trust herself to speak. Instead she bowed and walked down the stairs. She wasn't dressed for the cold, and it was snowing outside. The idea of retracing her steps to change was impossible. So was the thought of any interaction with a member of her family.

She went through the dining room and into her great-aunt's house. Egbert was playing the piano. She tried the library door, which was locked. She went up the stairs. All the rooms on this floor were locked, too. She tried every door, rattling their handles as though sheer force of will could open them.

Someone must clean these rooms, she thought. How do they get in? She began to look in all the places one might hide a key, lifting every ornament with increasing irritation. Finally she picked up the ugly gray vase that sat on the radiator cover and shook it. A key fell out. She tried it on all the doors in succession and one opened. It was the door to her great-aunt's bedroom.

Louisa was a little in awe of her great-aunt Agaat. Even though she was hundreds of miles away she hesitated before entering her private quarters. Agaat did not approve of children. She had not relaxed this attitude as Constance and Louisa reached womanhood, and in any other mood Louisa would not have contemplated this audacious trespass. But today was not like other days, and she passed through the door and locked it behind her.

Now her feelings overwhelmed her entirely. She threw herself across the chaise longue and sobbed. She was furious and afraid. Constance would marry soon and have her own house. She would be left with her parents until she accepted the offer of a polite young man and moved two streets away. Constance's lack of enthusiasm for earning her living had sounded the first note of permanent discord between them. Louisa had not ceased to love her sister ardently, but she respected her less. For the first time in her life she felt truly alone.

Added to which was the embarrassment of being refused by Piet Barol! He who had gone to such lengths to charm *her*! It was bitter indeed to be spurned by one she had so subtly patronized, in whose goodness she had never believed. I suppose he's pleased with himself now, she thought, the stuck-up, self-aggrandizing— She threw herself on the floor and beat the carpet with her small fists, in unconscious imitation of her childhood tantrums. It took half an hour for her anguish to drain. Finally she sat up. "I will live my life as I wish!" she shouted. She did not know how she might accomplish this feat, which no other girl of her acquaintance seemed even to have imagined. But the promise she made herself was one she would not break. She dried her eyes and stood up. As she did so her foot connected with something solid in the carpet's pile.

It was a tiny button covered in slippery, apple-green silk.

Three hours later, Piet Barol began dressing in superb spirits. He put on the tailcoat he had worn to Constance's birthday party and knotted his white bow tie eight times to achieve perfection. His cheeks were rosy from his bath; his hair shone with brilliantine. He opened his door to find Egbert waiting outside.

The child held in his hand a small velvet box, in which was a set of gold-and-onyx shirt studs he had helped his mother choose for Piet. He had spent all afternoon devising what to say, but now his eloquence abandoned him. "Please don't go, Mr. Barol."

He held out the velvet box.

Piet took it from him and opened the card. *From all of us, to wish you well*, Jacobina had written. "My dear Egbert." He crouched down, so that their heads were level. "You are ready for me to go. You have beaten your enemies forever."

"What if they come back?"

"If they so much as dare, you must defy them at once. That's the way to break them. It was you who found that out. Don't you remember?"

"It was both of us together."

"I was honored to collaborate with you. Shake my hand, as one man to another."

The boy did so, his grasp surprisingly firm. He was on the edge of tears but held them at bay. In a small brave voice, he said: "Will you teach me one thing more before you go?"

"With pleasure. What is it?"

"How to skate with my sisters."

"Of course. We'll go tomorrow, first thing."

Having orchestrated the banishment of Didier Loubat, Gert Blok was feeling better disposed towards handsome young men. "You do look splendid," he said, encountering Piet on his way downstairs. "May I say, Mr. Barol, that you will be as warmly missed below stairs as above them."

Piet shook the butler's hand. "It has been an honor to watch you at work, Mr. Blok. I hope to have an establishment of my own one day, and will endeavor to replicate the excellence I have encountered here."

Gert Blok had worked so long for a man accustomed to faultless service that his achievements were rarely praised. He was touched. "Any man would be fortunate to win a place in your household, Mr. Barol." He stood back for Piet to pass.

Piet met Constance outside the drawing room, but she barred its door to him. "There's a surprise in there. You must wait for it. Cocktails are downstairs tonight." The surprise was a Louis Vuitton traveling trunk, just arrived from Paris. It was a sign of her affection for Piet that Constance had disobeyed the impulse to keep it for herself and give him cufflinks instead. They went down the stairs to the octagonal parlor, which had been transformed into a bower of oleanders.

Constance had invited to dinner the two most agreeable young men in her circle who were, as yet, without wives, and her plans for the evening included a deft exhibition of her skills as a hostess. She nodded in agreement when Piet told her how lovely everything looked.

Maarten was waiting for them and poured the champagne himself. "What a beauty you are, my dear." He kissed his daughter as he handed her a glass. "You won't find such loveliness in the colonies, Mr. Barol."

"I dare say not, sir."

Jacobina entered, in a tight-waisted gown of amethyst silk. She had not trusted her hair to Hilde and the attentions of a professional hairdresser, anxious to win her patronage, had put her in an extremely good mood. She was glad to look her best for the departure of Piet Barol; glad, too, that he was going at last. There would be no more tutors, no more trysts in the house next door; no more flutterings of treachery as she slept beside her husband, her body still tingling from the attentions of another man. She kissed Piet's cheek and told him how sorry they all were to say good-bye to him.

It was five minutes past seven. The guests were asked for seven-thirty. "Now where the devil is Louisa?" Maarten looked at his watch. "Constance, go and fetch her."

"I expect she's dressing, Papa."

"Well, hurry her along."

Constance left, and when she returned it was clear to Piet that she was annoyed. "She's not well, Papa, and asks to be excused. She sends her compliments, Mr. Barol."

"Not well? She was in radiant health this morning."

Maarten had drunk two glasses of champagne, and Louisa's absence poisoned the gaiety they had fueled. "Fetch her down."

"It would be better to leave her."

"Nonsense. Fetch her down."

She is embarrassed to face me, thought Piet. The idea was not wholly unpleasant. He thought of the many nasty things he had overheard Louisa Vermeulen-Sickerts say to her sister about him, and then about the day she had tried to break his neck on her mother's horse. To have refused her, and done it kindly, was magnificent. "Please, sir. If she's not well . . ."

"You are good-natured as ever, Mr. Barol. But I won't stand for prolonged sulks. Constance, fetch her down."

Constance was gone longer this time and Maarten drank another glass of champagne. Again she returned without her sister. "Really, Papa, she has a fever. She should have some soup and go to bed."

"She was *perfectly* well this morning, was she not, my dear?" But Maarten did not wait for his wife's reply. "I am afraid, Mr. Barol, that my daughter is displeased with me and chooses to make her displeasure plain on this happy night. Well it will not do." He went to the foot of the stairs and bellowed her name.

Louisa appeared a few minutes later, wearing a monk's habit of oyster cashmere with a cowl over her dark hair. "You sent for me, Papa?"

"Whatever do you mean by this?"

"By what?"

"Our guests will arrive at any moment. You are not dressed to receive them."

"You did not instruct me to dress. You merely called my name so loudly I thought some grave crisis had overtaken you."

It was a long time since anyone had been insolent to Maarten Vermeulen-Sickerts. It enraged him. "Go upstairs at once and change."

Louisa wished strenuously to disobey her father, but a strict and careful upbringing had left her without the necessary courage. Seeing her hesitate, the idea of being magnanimous was irresistible to Piet. "No harsh words on my account, sir. If Miss Vermeulen-Sickerts wishes—"

"Very well, Papa." Louisa did not intend to owe her solitude to Piet Barol. She turned on her heel and left the room and despised herself.

The doorbell rang and the first guests were announced. Among them, to Constance's relief, was her friend Myrthe Janssen (shortly to be van Sigelen), who could always be relied on to cheer people up. Soon laughter and high, excited talk were bouncing off the room's stone walls, and the family recaptured its spontaneity.

Louisa came downstairs, inscrutable once more, and they went into dinner. The table had been opened to its fullest extent and Maarten had sanctioned the use of the Sèvres porcelain. Piet was directly opposite Frederik van Sigelen. It amused him to see that this ungenerous young man could not for the life of him fathom why anyone should go to such trouble for a servant. This heightened his pleasure at the *saumon Dorne Valois*, baked in lobster butter and decorated with *coquilles* of oysters. As the poached purée of Bordeaux pigeon was served, he remarked that he would shortly be sailing on the *Eugénie*. "I remembered your ardent recommendation."

"I'm sure even steerage is more comfortable than on other ships."

Myrthe Janssen looked at her plate. She was already beginning to dislike her fiancé, whose malice made her uneasy for her own future. "How thrilling to be going to New York," she said, lightly.

"My destination is Cape Town, in fact, Miss Janssen. The ship is making a special voyage."

"But I know all about it." Myrthe laughed the merry laugh she was known for. "Frederik's parents are going too, aren't they darling?"

"I believe they were invited. Albert Verignan, who owns the line, is a personal friend. But my father cannot be away from Amsterdam so long."

"Oh Mr. Barol, what fun you'll have. I'm told there's to be a fancy dress ball on St. Helena."

"Only for the first-class passengers." Van Sigelen tapped his glass and a footman bent to refill it.

"My means don't extend so far." Piet smiled. "I was fortunate to get the last berth in tourist."

Frederik saw Myrthe's warning look and forbore from asking Piet where he had got the money. "I'm sure it will be worth every centime."

"If it's not, I shall have you to blame."

As she left the table after the last course, Constance whispered, "Join us soon, Papa." And after the port had gone round once the assembled men surged up the stairs. In the drawing room Piet was presented with his trunk and made a witty and affectionate speech of thanks, which was met by a request from Maarten for "one last song at the piano, Mr. Barol."

"Something jolly!" called one of the young men, who had inveigled himself onto the sofa beside Constance.

"A song of farewell," said Myrthe Janssen.

Piet bowed. "Figaro's farewell to Cherubino, then, from the *Marriage of Figaro*." He struck it up merrily. Everyone knew the tune and there was much thumping of feet. "No more, you amorous butterfly, will you flutter around night and day," Piet sang, "disturbing the peace of every beautiful woman." The words made him think of himself, for he had conquered Jacobina, and resisted Constance, and provoked from Louisa a proposal of marriage.

His performance was met with rounds of applause and calls for an encore. He resisted modestly but at length allowed them to persuade him. "This was a huge hit in Rome a few years ago. If you want a farewell scene I can't think of one more moving. A man is in his cell, awaiting execution. This is the letter he writes his lover, a dazzling beauty named Tosca." He played a sprinkle of notes, feeling pleasantly invincible, and at once the atmosphere altered. Those watching were seized by a glorious, uplifting sorrow. "Oh! sweet kisses, oh! languid caresses!" Piet sang, and for a moment in the crowded room his eyes met Jacobina's, and they said good-bye.

Louisa saw them. She blinked and looked again. Piet was now concentrating on the piano and her mother had turned to a friend. All was as it should have been. Louisa accepted a cup of coffee from Hilde and tried to turn her mind to her own troubles, but certain facts abruptly forged a hazardous whole: an ugly dress, a potent smell, a green button lying on a blue carpet.

She said nothing as the guests began to take their leave and did not join her parents and Constance and Piet as they saw them off downstairs. As soon as she was alone she went into her mother's dressing room and opened her closets. The little green button had been fretting at the limits of her other sorrows; now she was sure she knew the dress it had come from. If the garment was undamaged she would know she was wrong.

But the gown of apple-green wool was not in the wardrobe. Nor was it in the laundry or the sewing basket. Louisa had a couturier's natural inventory for clothes and traced her way through a fortnight of her mother's discarded garments. Everything was there, either cleaned or about to be, but not the apple-green dress she had worn the day Constance and Egbert and her father went to the country. She bit her knuckle. Surely that was the day her mother had appeared in a hideous mauve concoction. This *was* in her wardrobe. She took it out. It was not at all Jacobina's size. When she put her nose between the ruffles of its neck she was met by the unmistakable smell of her great-aunt Agaat. Why should her mother wear her great-aunt's clothes? And why should she have damaged her own dress, apparently beyond repair, in Aunt Agaat's bedroom?

Louisa Vermeulen-Sickerts had no acquaintance with the odors of masculine arousal. This did not mean she was oblivious to them, and now she remembered the odd smell Piet had brought with him into the entrance hall that day. She began to understand other things, too: why Piet had not been dismissed for shaming the family by carrying Egbert into a crowded street; why he had been permitted to behave with total freedom, as no tutor before him had done.

Jacobina, Maarten, Constance, and Piet re-entered the drawing room to find Louisa standing by the fire, very pale. They were pleased with the evening and themselves. His daughter's pallor inspired penitence in Maarten. What if she really had a fever? He was about to order a hot chocolate for her to take to bed when she said: "Where is your green wool dress, Mama? The one with the small train?"

Jacobina had given much thought to how to dispose of sixteen yards of satin-lined wool—no small challenge in a house full of servants and sweet smells. She had decided against burning it in her aunt's bedroom fireplace, which someone would have to clean. Neither could she burn it in her own room, for fear of the smell. She had considered dumping it in a canal, but what if it floated? In the end, she had stolen down to the kitchen at two o'clock in the morning and stuffed it into the furnace. All this flashed into her head as Louisa spoke. "It's in my cupboard, I suppose."

"No it's not. I've checked."

"Why ever did you do that?"

"Because of the way you and Mr. Barol looked at each other when he sang about sweet kisses and languid caresses."

"What an idea, darling!"

"I found a button from that dress in Aunt Agaat's bedroom this afternoon. What were you doing there?"

"No one goes into that room, as you very well know."

"Well someone did, wearing a dress that now cannot be found." Louisa spoke levelly. "You were wearing it the day Constance and Egbert and Papa went to the country. You went next door in it, after lunch. Why did you come back in one of Aunt Agaat's dresses? And why did Mr. Barol follow you, smelling like—like—someone who has taken strenuous exercise?"

This last detail had the ring of truth. Maarten Vermeulen-Sickerts said "Louisa!" but he was looking at Piet Barol. And on Piet's face, where he expected indignation, he saw fear.

"Where is it, Mama?"

"I don't keep track of all my clothes."

"Have you destroyed it? Was it ripped or damaged in some way?"

Now Constance lost her temper. "Do shut up, Louisa. Are you drunk?"

"I am upset, Constance."

"But why, my sweet?"

"Because Piet Barol has seduced our mother."

Maarten took charge. "My dear, let us go to bed." He offered his wife his arm. "Louisa, I will deal with you severely in the morning. You have had too much wine. Mr. Barol, my apologies."

But he left the room without shaking Piet's hand.

Jacobina went with him. She knew she should protest, but truth boldly stated is hard to contradict to those who know us best. She climbed the stairs behind her husband and her silence confirmed to Maarten what the terror in Piet's eyes had already told him. Both of them feigned calm. Jacobina called for Hilde and began to unpin her hair. Maarten went into his dressing room and took off his clothes.

He was eight years older than his wife: stocky and strongly built. He did not pay much attention to his appearance and the studied avoidance of personal vanity had taken its toll. His legs were greeny-white, almost hairless now. He turned sideways to observe himself in profile. His belly was the size of a woman's in the sixth month of pregnancy. He thought of the marvelous suits Jacobina had bought him long ago, which he would never wear again: suits that now hung in the closet of Piet Barol. He sat down on a stool, dazed by his daughter's revelation, and waited for a surge of rage to carry him through to morning.

But instead a very different emotion took hold of him. To his surprise, and at first against his will, he began to see things from his wife's point of view.

Maarten had never considered that his sexual abstinence might have a cost for Jacobina. Now he saw that it inevitably did. Piet Barol was a tempting proposition to a woman. Was she not human, after all? She had enjoyed the carnal side of love in their first years of marriage. What if she missed it? What if Piet had laid siege to her, as he had once done, and reminded her of the attentions she no longer received from him? He put on his nightshirt and rang the bell. When Mr. Blok appeared, he spoke a few low words to him and went into his bedroom.

Jacobina was already in bed. They had shared this same bed for twenty-eight years and the moment of settling into it beside her was often the happiest of Maarten's day. He had never told her this. As he repeated the familiar movement, the fact that he had lain so close to her for ten years without once embracing her no longer seemed admirable. He was an intelligent man and loved Jacobina deeply. Abruptly he understood how wounding these bedtimes had been for her: the long sequence of days brought to a close by nothing more intimate than a chaste good-night kiss. He remembered the occasion, many years before, when she had asked for what she wanted; the way he had refused her, proud of his own restraint. What sorrow he must have caused her!

He turned towards his wife. Jacobina was propped up on her pillows, eyes closed. She had made her pain clear to him in many subtle ways. He understood this now and was overcome by remorse. To have put his own salvation before the happiness of one whom he had vowed to cherish was abominable. He leaned closer to her. Jacobina could sense him. She could not imagine what he was doing. She was torn between apology and accusation. That *Louisa* should know! Her clever, self-contained Louisa. The little girl whose dolls she had once helped dress. It appalled her. She felt the mattress tilt. Surely he would not hit her? She had several times been slapped in the face as a child by the sullen English governess who succeeded Riejke Vedder. Her body tensed. But to her astonishment, which was followed by an outpouring of long-seasoned love, Maarten did not hit her.

He kissed her neck and said, "Forgive me."

For the first time since their son's birth, Maarten Vermeulen-Sickerts ran his hand under his wife's nightdress. He buried his face in her hair and inhaled. Jacobina's smell was familiar to him, complex and sweet and reassuring beneath her Parisian perfume. It excited him. He pressed against her and his fingers edged up her thigh. They tickled her and she jerked away.

"*Kiss* me there," she whispered.

With creaking joints he shifted place and pushed her nightgown to her waist and obeyed.

Maarten had never been as assured in bed as he was in business. He had too little experience to trust himself, which made him an anxious, perfunctory lover. Fortunately Jacobina was no longer as unsure as he was. She suggested what he should do and shifted her body until his tongue found the right spot. Maarten was grateful for direction. It was the first time anyone had used forbidden words to him and they charged his imagination. The impact his attentions were having on his wife gave him confidence. Each time he came close to spending Jacobina pulled away, and calmed him, and so subtly asserted her authority.

Jacobina had expected many things from Maarten, but not penitence. To receive an acknowledgment of the part he had played in her transgressions inspired an explosion of love, for his acceptance of her humanity was more profound than any man-made law or church-made vow. The idea of refining with him the lessons she had taught Piet Barol, night after night for the rest of their lives, overthrew her fears of the future. She pulled her nightdress off, then his. His body was not as hard as Piet's, nor his skin as smooth and taut; but it was *his* body, and *his* skin, and for this reason alone she loved them.

While Piet Barol packed his trunk on the floor above,

prevented by Mr. Blok from taking anything that had once belonged to their employer, Maarten Vermeulen-Sickerts hoisted himself over his wife. As Jacobina opened to him he almost came, but did not. He began to press into her, tenderly but surely. She opened her eyes and smiled.

If God exists, thought Maarten, then He is here.

They made love for hours. They fucked and kissed and explored their once-familiar bodies in a wonder of rediscovery. They did not hear Piet take his trunk down the stairs or pass through the entrance hall for the last time. As he walked to the station with nothing but his tailcoat, his trunk, a set of onyx studs, the clothes he had come in, and two sketchbooks full of careful drawings, they lost themselves in each other, forgave one another, and like a Phoenix from a lustful fire their friendship emerged, purged and renewed.

Piet had been sitting on the cold stone floor of the ticket hall for three hours, waiting for the first Leiden train, before they were finished. It was almost light. As they lay with their faces touching, Maarten's arms around her shoulders, Jacobina said, "What about Louisa?"

"We shall go to your dressmaker's this morning and order another gown, identical to the first. We will say that the original is being laundered in the country. When the new one is ready, you shall wear it as if nothing has happened. Every time you do, I will take it as an invitation to make you my own."

"I am yours." She kissed his shoulder. "I never wasn't. I'm glad he's going."

"My darling," said Maarten, "that young scoundrel has already gone."

THE EUGÉNIE

iet Barol did not hope for comfort from his father and did not confide his transgressions or their humiliating exposure. For eleven months he had thought of Herman Barol only with gratitude for being away from him. He considered this as they shook hands in the sitting room full of furniture his mother had chosen, now woefully rearranged. It had been Nina's teaching room and the heart of her territory. In the seven years since her death her spirit had gradually leaked from it. Now, though the pretty little chairs and discerningly chosen lamps remained, there was nothing of her left but her portrait, which still hung above the piano.

Piet resembled this painting too closely to be received with anything but suspicion by the woman with dandruff and chilblains who for many years had been his father's housekeeper and was now his fiancée. Herman announced his imminent nuptials over breakfast as Piet was contemplating the sight of Marga's chapped fingers on his mother's tea service. He wished them joy. He doubted he would see his father again after sailing on the *Eugénie* and felt easier to know he would be cared for.

Indeed, Marga Folker cared for Herman Barol with an absorption that brooked no competitor for his affections and was glad to know that her beautiful stepson would not long remain with them. Herman did nothing whatever for himself except dress. Marga cooked and scrubbed and polished and swept and organized the ledgers that in earlier years it had been Piet's task to fill with methodical accounts of undergraduate perfidy. She was not favored with external charms and this had left her with half a lifetime's pent-up love. The spectacle of her showering it on Herman, who accepted it without remark, was distasteful to Piet.

He embraced them both and took a boiling kettle from the stove, to which he added icy water from the well in the backyard. The tin tub the Barols used for a bath was in its usual place behind the kitchen door. He took it upstairs. It was not long or deep enough to permit the simultaneous wetting of balls and knees and he washed as quickly as he could. He was out of practice and had added too much cold water.

The discomforts of this procedure reminded him forcefully of the circumstances of his youth and the necessity of breaking free of them. He dried himself, dressed, and went into the bedroom that had once been his parents'. Nina had brought the mattress with her from Paris at her marriage and had often stayed in bed until eleven o'clock in the morning. It was from this bed that she had dispensed to him a wisdom that ran wholly contrary to her husband's view of life. It was here, too, that she had nursed away his childhood illnesses and sung to him arias from Bizet and Mozart—who were, she said, the only composers who understood women.

Nina Michaud had decided to marry Herman Barol at the end of a painful love affair and had imagined that she could make for herself a companion as diverting as he was steadfast. His Dutch reserve had made a marvelous contrast to the glossy seductiveness of the rakes who pursued her in Paris, and she had left behind the dangerous delights of that city with relief. It had taken her months to understand that

Herman was quite unlike the man she had imagined him to be, and years to accept she could not change him. Disillusion, when it came, hit her hard. Nevertheless, she did her best to refrain from complaining of her husband to their son and slipped into doing so only by imperceptible degrees. It was when the eight-year-old Piet began to imitate Herman for her amusement that she understood she had gone too far to bother with stopping. The child caught to perfection the heavy tread of his father as he clumped to the chamber pot to relieve himself. Since Herman did so two or three times every night, at a volume to wake any sleeping soul, she and Piet found his impersonation intoxicatingly amusing. So, too, Piet's imitation of Herman's snoring and sudden sleep gruntings, his monotonous exhortations to errant students.

Nina had done all she could to educate her son for the life she had glimpsed, and lost. To have ended his first sally into the great world so dismally seemed to Piet a betrayal of all she had sacrificed for him. He stood in her bedroom, shivering and wishing he could confess and seek her guidance. But here too her spirit had vanished.

Christmas and New Year's Eve came and went. Having been deprived of his fine clothes Piet attempted to stock his wardrobe from the pawnshops of Leiden; but Christmas money had allowed all but the neediest to redeem their best suits and he found only two shirts, both with stains under the arms.

As his departure neared, his dissatisfaction with himself intensified. He thought with amazement of his duplicity in Amsterdam and started to hate himself for injuring a family who had only ever shown him kindness. Egbert weighed horribly on his conscience. He had coaxed the boy into the world of human feeling and become his first friend. To have left without so much as a good-bye was dastardly. Twice he sat down to write him a letter and gave up only because he could think of nothing to say.

Piet did not know that Maarten's evident delight in his wife had convinced even the skeptical Louisa that she was wrong. Nor did he know that Jacobina's appearance in an identical apple-green dress, four days after Piet's departure, had made her daughter burst into tears at breakfast and confess her hatred of him, and the true reasons for it, and beg her mother's forgiveness.

This scene was excruciating for Jacobina but she did not shrink from the hypocrisy it required. She was extremely sharp with Louisa and rebuked her for drinking in public. Then she said, "Let us hear no more about it," and later, in a kinder voice, "I forgive you, my darling." As she spoke she looked at her husband, and the love in his eyes allowed her to forgive herself also.

None of the Vermeulen-Sickertses would ever forget Piet Barol, but as soon as he had left them they began to think of him much less often. It was he who could not shake himself free of them. Their shades pursued him in his dreams, and on the third day of the New Year they were joined by Nina in a ferocious nightmare. He had shared everything but his amorous adventures with his mother. Now her outraged ghost knew all and told him he had failed her.

He woke from this dream in a fit of self-disgust that would not lift. He wanted to hurt himself and slammed his fist against the wall—impulsively, at two-thirds of his full force. The pain was stunning. It made him understand that he did not really wish to break his hand. A more profound expiation occurred to him: to renounce all he had been and start anew. He inched from the wall the loose brick behind which he had stored his treasures as a boy. All that remained in this cavity was a French passport in the name of "Pierre Barol," which Nina had obtained for him in Paris nine years before and about which Herman Barol knew nothing. With the sense that he was exchanging his soiled identity for a fresh one, he packed it in his trunk and went downstairs.

Piet took the sleeper for Paris on the sixteenth day of the New Year and arrived early on a dreary morning, while the brass lamps were still burning beneath the vast glazed roof of the Gare du Nord. His trunk was intended for people with porters at their disposal. As he dragged it through the starched, elegant crowds, he began to hate it.

The boat train for Le Havre left the following day after lunch. He had come a night early, despite the expense of a Parisian hotel, because he could find no way to say good-bye to his mother in the house now so scrupulously scrubbed by Marga Folker. They had been in the city once together nine years before, when he was fifteen and she thirty-five—ostensibly to visit one aunt and attend the funeral of another. In fact Nina had hoped to leave her husband and escape with her child to France. It had taken years to gather the courage to conceive this plan and implement its first stage. It took *tante* Maude Michaud twenty minutes to destroy it with the opinion, pronounced as fact, that Herman would pursue her for the boy and wrest Piet from her forever.

In the end Nina had not dared. Instead she spent sixteen years of savings on five days of sophisticated hedonism with her son and returned to Leiden defiant. They stayed in a rickety pension on the rue des Martyrs, beneath the blinding white marble of the Sacré Coeur. Nina had chosen Montmartre so that Piet might observe the perils of *la vie bohème* at first hand; also so that he could imagine the horrors of the Commune and see the church built to atone for them. They went to *tante* Henriette's funeral and made a day's worth of family calls. Otherwise they were entirely alone, immersed in each other as in a love affair.

Nina chose three restaurants. The first was a back room with bare wooden benches and crates of lobsters delivered from the *patron*'s brother in Normandy. Here she taught Piet how to drink a carafe of Chablis over a lunch of shellfish while entertaining a pretty woman (herself in an adorable new hat), without feeling giddy or unwell or talking too loudly. The next she chose for its rabbit, which was everything a simple country meal should be. The last was a grander establishment close to the Palais Royale where they ate *timbale de sole* stuffed with chopped truffles.

This meal cost so much that nothing was left for tickets to the opera. They walked through the Louvre and along the pale white paths of the Tuileries, humming together the great duets of Halévy, Gounod and Bizet. It was a night for French composers, Nina said. They reached the Place de la Concorde and paused before the traffic on the Champs Elysées. They had two francs over and Nina knew just the place to spend them. She led Piet up the rue de la Paix, past a perfumier whose scents were so potent neither their crystal vials nor the shop's closed doors could contain them. "You must face the world as an equal," she said, drawing him on and climbing the shallow, blue-carpeted steps of the Ritz Hotel with her arm in his.

The doorman did not question them. They had a coffee at the bar and watched the crowds of *élégants*. After some time, a gentleman with curled whiskers invited them to a matinée the following day.

"He takes me for a *demimondaine*," she whispered when the man had retreated, his invitation refused. "It's because I've nursed my coffee so long."

"What's a *demimondaine*, Mummy?"

"Come, I'll show you."

They strolled to the Place de l'Opéra and stood beside the steps of the Garnier as the evening's audience arrived.

With great precision, Nina pointed out the leading courtesans of the day and the subtle but significant ways they distinguished themselves from their lovers' wives.

Piet spent the night wandering the pale, magnificent city, lost in memories of her. With his mother he might have shared his misdeeds at Herengracht 605. Her absence left him to bear his regret unaided, and its burden was so heavy he did not join the conversation on the boat train the next day but hid behind a newspaper feeling profoundly alone.

He cheered briefly at sight of the ship. One could not feel entirely deflated on a crowded quay before her. The *Eugénie* had a black hull and a superstructure of dazzling white, repainted for the tropics. A strip of scarlet showed just above the waterline; she had four funnels, black with scarlet bands, and above her anchor gleamed the golden shell and crossed *L*s of the Loire Lines.

High above him on a private gangway, the first-class passengers were entering the ship. He could hear their band's sparkling music. To his left, the long lines queuing for third class and steerage looked so much happier than he was that he could not feel superior to them. He thought of the sum he had spent on his own ticket and tried to be optimistic, but the tourist-class vestibule, carpeted in violent swirls of green and red, dismayed him. So did the stewards' demeanor. As one led him to his stateroom with the air of doing him a distasteful favor, the pleasures he had renounced in Amsterdam recurred painfully to him.

"*Votre cabine, monsieur.*" The steward opened the door, handed him a receipt for his trunk, and departed with it.

At the Loire Lines offices in Amsterdam Piet had not thought to ask for the specifications of his accommodation. Now he saw he had been unwise not to. His cabin had no porthole and was very hot. Intended originally as third-class quarters, it had been converted to tourist class to cater for additional demand. But its superficial comforts—a mahogany washstand, monogrammed linen, a copied Fragonard in oils—could not disguise its proximity to the engines. As these were fired it shook violently.

Piet sat down on his bunk, aggrieved. Fifteen minutes later, the door opened and a stocky young man with florid cheeks and slick-backed blond hair entered, complaining in a loud English voice. "It will not do. I was promised—Yes, I jolly well *will* speak to the purser." He shook Piet's hand forcefully. "Percy Shabrill. An honor. Do excuse me." Percy Shabrill left again and began shouting in the corridor. Piet hoped he and his voice would find another berth, but it was not to be. He reappeared as the departure bells sounded, his cheeks redder than they had been before. "Damned Frenchies." He flung himself onto the opposite bunk. "They've given us the worst cabin on the bloody boat. Hope you don't snore, old fellow. I take a dim view of snorers."

"So do I."

They went up together onto the tourist-class promenade deck to watch as the ship left the harbor for the open ocean. The wind and the engines drowned the string quartet, but Percy's voice carried well over the competing noise. "That's me out of Europe for some time. I won't be back till they've invented an air balloon. I'm not mad keen on the sea." Percy was going to South Africa to join his brother at Johannesburg. His faith in his prospects emphasized to Piet how drastically his own confidence had dwindled since the day he had sold Maarten Vermeulen-Sickerts' silver man. Perhaps he should have kept him for luck. Percy leaned closer. "You ask how I'm going to get rich."

Piet had asked no such question.

"What's wrong with Africa? You tell me. It's bloody hot and there are too many darkies standing about with nothing to do. Well, I can fix all that. Chum of mine, dashed clever chap, had an idea about refrigeration. I bought the rights off him. There's a fortune to be made."

As they went back to their cabin, Percy expanded on this theme. "You build a cube out of chicken wire, then a bigger cube around it. Fill the gap with charcoal. Get a darkie to pump water over the charcoal on the half hour. As the water evaporates, the space inside the smaller cube cools. Quite good enough for most foods." He began to sketch this invention for Piet. He was not a talented draftsman. Soon the paper was covered in squiggles and arrows. Percy's eyes were shining with a convert's conviction. "See?"

Piet said that he did see.

"Can't fail, won't fail."

It was a relief to Piet that Percy's interest was wholly self-focused. When they went to dinner two hours later, he was still talking. Like their cabin, their table was small and inconveniently situated just behind the swing doors. The two other passengers assigned to it were an English lady named Miss Prince, going out to teach at a mission school, and a German widow whose recent bereavement appeared to have left her buoyed and cheerful. Their common language was English, since this was all that the two English people spoke. Piet's was proficient, Frau Stettin's less so, which meant that the burden of conversation with the others fell on him.

A wicked look or smile at the hideousness of it all from Miss Prince might have lifted Piet's spirits, but in fact she seemed rather impressed by Percy Shabrill.

He was sitting with his back to the wall and had a full view of the dining room. There were no bare boards, as in third class. There was a carpet and electric light, but for all that it was dingy and overcrowded and for some structural reason its roof was supported by pillars every few feet, which made it claustrophobic and cramped. His fellow passengers were dressed with the careful pretension of the rising middle class. They seemed greatly pleased by everything, as he might have been had he never met the Vermeulen-Sickertses or grown accustomed to their way of life.

But he had, and this robbed him of the naïveté necessary to delight in the second rate.

Other disadvantages swiftly emerged. Piet yearned for solitude, but this was not available to a man in a shared cabin on the *Eugénie*. Percy's constitution was delicate and he spent much of each day in bed. A full complement of 450 tourist-class passengers left the public rooms crowded, as the decks were too except in the foulest weather; and an unwritten convention entitled anyone to strike up a conversation on the slenderest pretext.

Frau Stettin was the least unbearable of his new acquaintances, because she was artless and sincere and happy to talk with very little prompting. Her cheerful voice, rambling on irrelevancies, was a soothing distraction from his self-reproach, and Piet exerted himself to inquire after her grandchildren and to remember their names and ages, with something of his old attentiveness. Miss Prince's moods were highly erratic. Only a disciplined childhood in a Warwickshire vicarage had trained her to present to the world a façade of calm, conventional womanhood. This façade expertly achieved, her conversation contained nothing to snag Piet's interest and meals eaten at her side passed slowly. He spent one afternoon expressing polite approval of the textbooks with which she intended to teach native children English. It appeared that she and her father had devised them and paid for their printing. "One so wants to help the kaffirs to be *useful*. Deep down, that is what they wish for themselves," she said, opening a section titled "Phrases for the Home" which included the constructions *May I direct you to the drawing room?* and *Her ladyship is indisposed.*

"It would be hard for a kaffir to manage without such knowledge," he observed, thinking how unjust it was that this woman should have the freedom denied to Louisa Vermeulen-Sickerts. Miss Prince detected nothing at all ironic in his tone and prattled on, warming to her theme of native self-improvement. As he listened to the stories of her colonial acquaintances' troublesome servants, and the importance of training their children to do better, he searched the room for someone to share and appreciate the ghastliness of his situation, but confronted nothing but well-scrubbed faces beaming good cheer.

Percy Shabrill's voluble self-certainty, even when gripped by seasickness, sapped Piet's remaining reserves of optimism. It seemed a dangerous folly to be crossing the world without an idea of what he would do at the other side, and this thought preoccupied him as he played bridge with Frau Stettin or listened to Miss Prince's theories on education. Though he had vowed to spend no money on board, restraint was difficult in practice. Only the food was included in the price of passage. When a steward appeared after dinner with a tray of brandies, already poured, it was embarrassing to refuse. He accepted one, and when the others exclaimed over its excellence he did not tell them how awful it was.

On the third day out there was a violent storm. The impact this had on Percy was briefly cheering. It pleased Piet to see him laid so low and for once the reading room was empty after lunch. But the next day, as they passed through the Bay of Biscay, the seas calmed and the crowds returned. He woke early, roused by the rattling of his cabin. The ship was picking up speed and with each knot the vibrations grew more violent. One of the shelves was inadequately screwed to its bracket and clattered unendurably.

He dressed and went to breakfast, followed by his grumbling cabinmate. The eggs were fried in the English manner and had been left too long in the warming tray. As he sawed into one he observed that Percy and Miss Prince had taken a close interest in each other, and their clumsy flirtation was as irritating as the rubberized yolk. Piet spent the morning playing piquet for low stakes and losing. Then he went to his cabin. It was mercifully empty. He lay down on his bunk and closed his eyes.

Piet had not cried since his childhood, but when Percy opened the door ten minutes later he felt briefly as though he might. Percy was speaking of Miss Prince in low, ardent tones. He gave every sign of taking Piet into his confidence until lunch. Piet excused himself and went on deck, past the ranks of deck chairs, the shuffleboard players and strolling couples. At the aft section was a spiked trellis, separating tourist from the roomier portion assigned to first class. He went there and leaned over the rails, staring at the sea. His expression was so tragic that a bold little girl asked if he was all right.

"Thank you," he said. "My eyes are just stung by the wind."

And then he heard his name.

Like a wish granted by a fairy godmother, Didier Loubat had materialized not two feet away. In a tailcoat with the line's shell and crossed Ls on the lapel, he was standing on the other side of the barrier. His hair was shorter than he had worn it at Herengracht 605. He looked older and more glamorous.

"Don't show you know me." He took a soft cloth from his pocket and polished a spot of rail. "You look awfully glum."

"I am."

"Life on board not up to your standards?"

Piet turned out to sea, as if unconscious of his friend's presence. "It's dreadful in every possible way. I should have gone steerage and saved my money."

"I can change your mind about that." Didier returned the cloth to his pocket. "You can't see any part of steerage from first class, and it has no open deck. If you'd been in there I'd never have found you. As it is, I've been freezing my balls off hoping to catch sight of you." He began to fold up a deck chair, pretending to have trouble with it. "Now listen carefully. The tourist-class reading room will be empty while everyone's at lunch. If you go through the service door outside it in twenty minutes, you'll find yourself in a corridor with a grille gate at one end. I'll meet you there. Go to your cabin and put on a better tie."

"What if we're caught?"

"You'll be set off the ship at the next port. I'll be dismissed. There are worse places to be stranded together than Madeira. Believe me, first class will be much more to your taste."

Piet shook his head, still looking out to sea. "You've already lost one place because of me. Unlock the gate and disappear. I'll come through alone. That way only I end up in Madeira if things go wrong."

This was not at all the outcome Didier sought. However, the conversation had lasted too long already. "All right. Once you're through the grille, slide it closed behind you but leave it off the latch. Walk down the corridor. Open the door, go up the main staircase. I'll be in the Winter Garden at the top. It's fairly quiet until four."

Half an hour later, wearing one of his two good shirts and feeling more cheerful, Piet Barol slipped into the deserted corridor behind the tourist-class reading room and let himself through the open grille at its end. He was about to open the baize door to first class when a steward came through it.

"May I help you, sir?"

Piet was aware that the faintest trace of nerves would betray him and imagined Constance Vermeulen-Sickerts waiting upstairs. This allowed him to say "I was exploring. How big is the ship?" with convincing naturalness.

Maurice Moureaux had spent twelve years working on liners and knew his business. It was not uncommon for passengers in other classes to attempt intrusions into first class, if for no other purpose than to steal an ashtray and earn a colorful boast. He took personal delight in seeing these men (they were always men) thrown off at the next port. He was unerringly accurate in spotting an invader, which meant that he wholly trusted his instinct in the matter of the gentleman standing before him, encountered though he was in a service corridor.

"Almost twenty-four thousand gross tons, sir." His tone was an expert counterfeit of enthusiasm. "Seven hundred and thirteen feet long, seventy-five wide. We're at a full complement of two thousand and twenty-six passengers in four classes."

"What's she like to work on?"

"A privilege." In fact the crew accommodations on the *Eugénie* vibrated unbearably, and Maurice Moureaux had far preferred his previous ship. As he looked at Piet Barol, however, he thought that this voyage might have its compensations.

Piet saw his look and understood it and was not embarrassed, which made Moureaux bolder.

"There are almost three miles of passageways and the noise below the passenger decks gives you some idea of the power of the engines. Would you like to see the staff quarters, sir?"

It was thus—subtly, unmistakably—that a range of services not mentioned on any menu were referred to between the staff of a Loire Lines ship and a select circle of passengers. All the first-class stewards were attractive and Maurice was no exception. He was in his midthirties, wiry and youthful, with a sharply defined face he could bring to life with a dazzling smile when he chose. He chose to do so now, since the chance to enjoy himself had arisen so naturally.

"At another time, perhaps." Piet, who had read all of this, smiled with polite regret. "But I am meeting a friend in the Winter Garden."

"Of course, sir." Moureaux bowed. "Permit me to escort you there."

Didier Loubat was pleased that his first encounter with Piet Barol should take place in a woodland glade traveling across the waves at twenty-four knots. He liked the Winter Garden's cool, white pillars; the ranked masses of greenery positioned for maximum discretion. Gilt birdcages hung from the ceiling, the doves inside as white as the walls. Their cooing made it possible to speak in absolute privacy.

Unlike Piet Barol, Didier Loubat was not accustomed to taking charge of his own destiny. In the days after leaving the Vermeulen-Sickertses he had tried to resign himself to never seeing Piet again, tried and failed, and so conceived this bold plan of a rendezvous in midocean. Because he had never yet applied himself to intervening in the narrative of his own life, he was not prepared for the euphoric rush this first success unleashed.

The standards of service in first class were in every way superior to those in tourist, and Maurice Moureaux found nothing remarkable in the rapturous smile with which Piet was greeted by the Winter Garden's duty steward. He said good-bye warmly and left them, wondering who would have him. It was well known that there was "someone for everyone" on a Loire Lines ship.

Didier led Piet to a corner table, pulled out his chair and slid it beneath him, unfolded a napkin and placed it on his lap. In the undertone of an expert waiter, audible only to the person addressed, he said, "Everything's free. Would sevruga and blinis please you, Mr. Barol?"

Piet nodded. Didier brought the caviar in a silver dish above a tower of crushed ice, and as the black eggs popped between his teeth the despair that had threatened to overwhelm him retreated. "How on earth do you come to be here?"

"Just a job. Difference is I wake up in a new place every day." Didier had prepared this explanation and delivered it nonchalantly. "Whatever spell you cast on Mevrouw Vermeulen-Sickerts worked. Her reference was like a love letter. I always thought she disapproved of me."

"Obviously not."

"Were they sad to say good-bye to you?"

At this moment a passenger signaled for Didier, who went at once to attend to him. By the time he returned, Piet had considered candor and decided against it.

"They had a dinner for me and gave me a trunk. Nightmare to carry it, since I can't afford porters, but I was very touched."

"How much of the money have you gone through?"

"Too much."

"Well you can save here. Passengers only pay for alcohol, and I'll slip whatever you want onto someone's bill." Didier inclined his head. "Permit me to fetch you the wine list, Mr. Barol."

In contemplation of this catalog of treasures, Piet's mood improved further. The room was filling now and Didier more regularly engaged. Piet tried not to be caught staring as he drank his way through an excellent bottle of Petit Chablis. On the ceiling above him three pretty nymphs were caressing one another. Between two pillars on the opposite wall a woodland bacchanal was taking place.

"They're not afraid of bare flesh," he remarked, when Didier next returned.

"No. And neither are the passengers."

"Randier than the guests at the Amstel?"

"Much. There's nothing to do all day on a ship but scheme and flirt."

The natural and immediate restoration of their old banter stilled Didier's nerves. He fetched a duck soufflé and boasted of his opportunities for sexual intrigue, feeling mildly ashamed to begin their encounter with a half-truth. Though he described an engaging series of female conquests, in fact it was the line's male passengers who had shown him approving attention. Didier had accepted a judicious selection. There had never been any question of payment for these encounters, but though his presence had been voluntary he had not sought the intimacy of a second meeting; he had given his heart already. "This is only my third voyage, but I've already lost count," he said. "People do as they please in the middle of the ocean."

"These women invite you to their cabins?"

"While their husbands have a massage or a swim. But the ship is full of nooks and crannies. It was designed for mischief."

"Lucky devil."

Didier grinned. "Let me get you an ice, then you'll have to be off. Monsieur Verignan will be along shortly and you're at his table."

Jay Gruneberger had spent a very pleasant half hour watching the gorgeous young men, one dark, one blond, flirting with each other on the opposite side of the room, pleasant even though he was beginning to feel old and their bloom confirmed it. He was forty-two, in committed good condition, his arms and shoulders still well muscled though his trousers, once a favorite pair, were biting painfully. His face was almost ugly, with full sensual lips and a hawk nose; he would never again have the thoughtless slenderness of youth. Though his expression was one of a man lost in abstract thought, he was watching the young men intently.

When the dark one rose to leave Jay stood to follow. He was surprised to see that the blond one led the dark one. Had they agreed an assignation? It was clear that some intimacy existed between them. He reached the door a discreet distance behind them, keen to learn its nature, but his escape was blocked by a torrent of effusive greeting.

Albert Verignan, founder and chairman of the Loire Lines Company, was a man of influence on both sides of the Atlantic: a plotter who achieved his ends with a guile that did not endear him to Jay Gruneberger, who in all but his sexual life was as straightforward and honest as good manners permit. They greeted each other with noisy amity. With a regretful glance at Piet Barol's retreating back, Jay allowed himself to be detained in one of his host's characteristic tête-à-têtes.

Verignan was deftly complimentary. He praised the cut of Jay's suit and the genius of his wife. "I have never known anyone with such an eye for spectacle, for beauty, for detail, as Rose!" he exclaimed, though he meant that he knew of no one besides himself with such rare talents. "She has chaired the committee superbly—though she might bankrupt me yet, mind you." He looked down modestly, as he always did when introducing the subject of his own generosity. "She has insisted on having a five-hundred-foot terrace blasted by dynamite from the rock. The line's timetable has been overthrown and a new route to South Africa added. Really, I should be very cross. But how can one resist her?"

"You have acted wisely not to try."

Verignan laughed good-naturedly. He knew that Jay Gruneberger did not like him and was determined that he should. Verignan had been a young man when the Prussians invaded France in 1870 and had witnessed the end of the Second Empire on the battlefield at Sedan. The destruction wrought by their advancing armies had left him with a virulent hatred of Germans, which decades of rivalry with the Hamburg-America and Norddeutscher Lloyd Lines had greatly concentrated. He approved of the entente cordiale with Britain, but though Georges Clemenceau seemed a decent patriot he could not forgive him his attempts to impose an eight-hour workday and an income tax. Verignan had lost hope that democracy, with its compromises and debate, its half measures and delays, would rise to the kaiser's challenge. He had made a fortune by following his instinct and it told him now that an unchecked Germany spelled disaster for France.

The hour called for a hero. And every hero has his maker.

Verignan had chosen his man already, an ambitious young deputy named Colignard. He should be elected democratically and seize power when he had control of the army, as both Napoleons had done. Verignan doubted very much that France could meet the German threat alone, whoever led her. A grand alliance of France, Great Britain, Russia, Poland, perhaps even the United States, would be necessary to check the kaiser's ambitions. Bringing it about was just the sort of challenge Verignan relished. He understood the seductions of glamour and had devised the voyage to introduce the elites of his favored nations in a setting as conducive as possible to the forging of friendship—a setting, moreover, that would remind them of the priceless contributions France had made to the world. He intended that the ball he had planned should be reported in every illustrated newspaper on earth.

Verignan had chosen St. Helena so that clever journalists might detect a symbolic Anglo-French reconciliation almost a century after the Battle of Waterloo. Its extreme remoteness was a further attraction. The idea of showing five hundred people who thought they had seen everything something they had never seen satisfied his feeling for publicity. So did the notion of transporting them miraculously from the depths of winter to a scented summer's night. Since he himself was paying for the three hundred waiters, the eighty chefs, the four thousand bottles of champagne, the fireworks, the orchestra, and the dynamiting of a hollow in the rock where the dancing could take place if the weather was fine, the enormous sum raised could be spent directly on needy, photogenic children in each of the countries that formed his imaginary alliance.

These plans shimmered in the air as he remarked how pleasant it was to be with a ship full of friends, and Jay Gruneberger thought wistfully of the men Verignan's arrival had prevented him from following. He emphatically preferred the dark one.

Noting his abstraction, Verignan remembered hearing that his companion was vulnerable to certain kinds of blackmail. He preferred to gain his ends by charm but was prepared to resort to darker strategies if necessary, since Jay Gruneberger was listened to in quarters whose support would be vital. Whatever must be done for the peace of Europe, he thought.

Auguste Colignard was brought over to be introduced. He was square jawed and inspiring, his manner subtly flirtatious: a man for posters. Jay was compelled to drink a cup of tea with him and spent the afternoon roaming the ship in search of the dark beauty he had missed.

But he had quite disappeared.

O ver the next five days, Didier Loubat's long-mounting infatuation with Piet Barol became a roaring love. They met every morning and were not once challenged. Sometimes they spent six or seven hours together before Piet's return to tourist class, longer than they ever had in Amsterdam, and the pleasure Piet took in his company made Didier wildly happy. He was a junior steward, assigned as needed. The bounties of the earth were available to first-class passengers at any hour, and wherever he went he took his love and rained delicacies upon him.

"You never speak of your parents," he observed on the sixth day out as Piet sprawled in the depths of a smoking room sofa, nursing a twenty-five-year-old brandy though it was only eleven a.m. It was an overcast day with an unsteady sea and the paneled room with its cozy fire was almost empty. A copy of Winterhalter's portrait of the Empress Eugénie presided over the fireplace, her gown rather more revealingly cut than in the original.

"With the Vermeulen-Sickertses to absorb us, it never occurred to me."

"Will you miss your father?"

Piet contemplated the liquid in his glass. "I don't suppose so."

"Not miss your own father?"

"He's not a very sympathetic man."

"Is he a drunkard?"

"Heavens no. He's not vile in that way. In fact, he doesn't approve much of indulgence in any form. My mother used to say he lacks the gift of joy."

Didier loved his parents and was well loved in return.

That Piet should have no mother, and a father who never embraced him, made him want to care for him forever. Monsieur and Madame Loubat were well accustomed to their son bringing handsome friends home for the holidays. They treated them with great kindness and put them in Didier's bedroom without remark. As he led Piet from the Renaissance through the reigns of Louis XV and XVI, following his roster from smoking room to salon to the veranda café, he grew ever surer that his mother would love Piet as her own and imagined telling her of him without shame.

The unifying theme of the ship's decoration was the sea, and Verignan's decorators had not missed a single opportunity to allude to it. While Didier worked, Piet sat in a haze of contented drunkenness and counted how many gilt shells and crossed Ls he could see. It was an extremely pleasant form of self-sedation. Sometimes a single fireplace yielded as many as twenty. In the panels of a double door in the salon he counted eighty-three. It made him feel sophisticated to disapprove of this fussiness and of the embroidered antimacassars, the too-showy reliance on gilt, the ostentatious hats of certain female passengers. But the effect was undoubtedly arresting, and its splendor helped to dull his memories of the Herengracht.

Both young men were so absorbed in each other and themselves that neither noticed the regular presence of a worldly, well-built male passenger in his forties, with a neat beard and a hawk nose. Jay Gruneberger wondered whether the dark one was a poor sailor, because he never appeared at meals—but no, he was eating with great delight whenever he saw him. He could find no explanation for his regular absences. Nor for the blond and the dark always and only appearing together. He watched them and saw the look on the steward's face when his friend spoke. More than once he was tempted to intrude on their conversations and introduce himself, but he was too well known and too happily married to initiate contact until he could be certain of their discretion.

On the ninth day of the voyage, Didier was on lifeguard duty at the first-class indoor swimming pool. He had put a pair of bathing trunks on a passenger's bill and given them to Piet, who looked magnificent in them. The pool was one of the glories of the ship, decorated in the stylized motifs the first Napoleon made fashionable after his Egyptian campaign; as grand and shadowy as a Pharaoh's tomb.

The sight of Piet Barol in bathing drawers heightened Didier's sense of urgency. They had only eight more days in this world-no-world on the ocean; the approaching shore threatened everything. It was a calm day. Ropes and swings had been attached to the ceiling to be climbed up and dived from. Piet made rather a display of himself, climbing hand over hand halfway to the roof, the muscles in his back writhing like serpents; knotting the rope around his feet; diving down again.

His performance drew applause. He had a steam in the Turkish hammam and then a dip in the iced plunge pool. By the time he reentered the changing room, his body was red and tingling. He was aware of his skin, a pleasant tautness in his limbs, and then, abruptly, of having had no contact with another human being since his last delicious afternoon with Jacobina. He needed to piss and went to the urinal, wondering how he might get some of what he needed. He had just pulled his vest down to free himself when Didier entered the room.

Didier went to a locker and undressed quickly, knowing that if he were caught in the passenger changing room he would be dismissed. The impulse to be naked near his friend was imperative; it dimmed all risk. Piet glanced round and

saw Didier facing away from him, changing from one bathing suit into another. He turned back to the wall, but at
the reaches of his vision he was aware of the lightly muscled
body he knew so well. It brought to mind their first conversation; the flicker of instinct that had told him Didier might
be persuaded to ease certain intimate frustrations.

He had desisted on that occasion and not thought of it
again. He had never combined such things with deep affection. For the first time he understood that it was possible
to do so if one dared. Didier had stopped moving. Piet felt
himself watched and looked down at his prick, now stiff and
insistent in his hand. He was embarrassed but also afraid—
because he did not want to have a love affair, and he understood that Didier would do nothing for him except out of
love. Nevertheless he could not piss. He waited, trying to
calm himself, and a door opened.

A well-built man with a neat beard and a hawk nose
entered. At this intrusion Didier came to himself, collected
his trunks, and went through the door into the stewards'
room. The bearded man went to a sink and washed his
hands. When he had gone, Piet went into a lavatory stall
and dealt with himself vigorously.

That night, Didier stood by a silver-gilt dessert trolley
thinking of the afternoon. The room in which he was
stationed was two decks high, a miniature theater in gold
and turquoise and red velvet. Where the seats and boxes
would have been on land were tables with shaded electric
candlelights. An entire opera was staged on each voyage,
generally on the second-last night at sea. On this journey
the performance was scheduled for the following evening to
avoid clashing with the Bal de la Gloire on St. Helena.

It was Didier's responsibility to serve wafer-thin slices of cake without disturbing audience or performers. Tonight's dancers were making so much noise this required no concentration. A middle-aged lady beckoned and he went to her, deep in thought. Passengers occupying suites were placed closest to the stage. The English couple staying in the Henri de Navarre did not care for music; their table was empty almost every night. If Piet came after dinner and it was empty again, he would be safe for the rest of the evening.

Didier conveyed his plan the next morning as he served his friend coffee in the veranda café. "Wear the tailcoat the Vermeulen-Sickertses gave you and your gold-and-onyx studs."

"But what if they come to their table?"

"Dinner's served before the music starts. If they're not there for that, they won't be coming at all. I'll open the grille for you at ten."

Percy Shabrill was in their cabin when Piet returned to it. "Nineteen orders so far and still five days to go. I must say, there's a good crowd on this ship." He was entering details into a ledger, self-consciously. Piet's extended absences had begun to disconcert Percy, who suspected his cabinmate of having an entrée not available to him. It made him louder and more boastful, and his thundering conviction tugged on Piet's spirits.

As Percy told him that he had already done enough business to pay for half his passage, Piet could only admit that he had employed his time much less profitably. It was amusing to sit all day in a sumptuous room, talking to a friend and eating and drinking more lavishly than he could ever afford to do again, but Percy's vigor made him ashamed of retreating from his responsibilities.

"And what will you be doing in South Africa?"

It was the first personal question Percy had asked him, and Piet had no answer. "I'll see what's needed when I get there."

"Confident devil. You mean to say you've no concrete plans? No connections?" Percy chuckled, secretly unnerved. "You're a braver fool than I." He went back to his ledger, but the word "fool" hung in the humid air of their cabin and seemed to Piet to be precisely what he was. He lay down on his bunk and pretended to read. Percy's purposeful bustling depressed him further. He watched Percy dress in silence and said he was seasick and could not eat. The dinner bell rang. At last he was alone—but at Percy's departure his inner furies turned on him and made the hot, expensive, rattling room a little hell.

At nine o'clock he took out the tailcoat he had worn to Constance Vermeulen-Sickerts' birthday party and the box of studs Egbert had given him hours before the final catastrophe. He washed and put them on without joy. When he was dressed, the discrepancy between his inner and outer selves troubled him. Confronting him in the mirror was a young man in glorious good health, apparently favored by nature and fortune. His glowing face gave no hint of the self-disgust within; neither did his clothes suggest the alarming truth that he had no funds to keep them. They would have to be pawned as soon as he reached Cape Town.

He went to the reading room. It was empty; so was the service corridor behind it. As he went through the baize door into first class, he was struck by the total *silence*. The rattling of his cabin had seeped into his bones; its sudden lifting was a miracle. He was standing in a corridor hung in pale blue brocade embroidered with waves and shells. He went down the passage, his leather soles sliding over the thick carpets, and as he passed the reading room a steward emerged and bowed. "The singing's just starting, sir, if you were hoping to catch it." He opened the door into the stair-case hall. "Lift or stairs?"

Piet did not trust the notion of an elevator. "I'll walk, thank you."

The staircase was flanked by pillars of painted marble. Across the ceiling nymphs with very little on were being pursued by muscular Tritons. At intervals in the balustrade the line's shell and crossed *L*s were pricked out in gold. The ship was empty, and the absence of chatter and clat-tering heels heightened the impact of its magnificence. Piet paused on the second landing under the great gilt clock. As it struck the hour, he climbed the last flight to find Didier waiting for him, flushed but grave. He nodded and led Piet beneath a dome of turquoise and gilt to a table set for one by the stage.

The *Eugénie's* director of music believed in taking his audience by surprise. The instant the last dessert plate was cleared, while the room was still full of talk and laugh-ter, he lifted his baton and plunged it into darkness. Piet had never seen *Carmen*, but knew it from the first high-spirited leap of the overture. A surge of gaiety swept the room. Accustomed to provincial orchestras heard from the cheapest seats, Piet had no notion that a group of musicians might make a sound as rich and subtle as that achieved by the *Eugénie's* band.

The stage filled with handsome men in uniform. Albert Verignan employed well-known singers for the solo roles, but stewards with musical training doubled as members of the ship's chorus. Piet recognized some of them from Didier's tours of duty. A young woman appeared in a blue dress with dark plaits over her shoulders. He could not see her face as the soldiers surged round her, lustful and impu-dent. They were touching her and pulling at her dress; for a moment there was danger beneath the music's catchy jollity. "Who are you looking for, my beauty?" sang their leader.

"Me?" She had an exceptional voice. When the crowd parted Piet saw that she was about his age, with a finely wrought face and devilish eyes. She announced that she was looking for a brigadier named Don José.

It was Stacey Meadows' habit to address this line directly to one of the gentlemen sitting closest to the stage. She offered no intimate favors but was not above accepting devotion and pawnable trinkets from the men who occupied the *Eugénie*'s grandest suites. To be met by the bold, delighted stare of Piet Barol separated this night from the many others on which she had reprised the role of Micäela, a country girl too innocent to interest her, sent by an officer's mother to give him a message and some money and a kiss. As the soldiers begged her to stay with them, she resisted with dazzling indignation. They threatened. One singer pressed his body against her, in contravention of the limits imposed at her insistence during rehearsals, and she freed herself emphatically while delivering a blazing B flat.

Piet Barol was transfixed. He watched her flee the stage, and the vague desire that had been mounting for days flared explosively. To touch a *young* woman! To use all he had learned from Jacobina on someone his own age! The possibility ignited his senses. He was suddenly aware, more deeply than he had been before, of the marvelous room; of the enthralled, well-dressed crowd, as it slipped beneath the music's sorcery. How splendid to be where he was!

He knew the opera's piano reduction intimately. To hear it played by musicians of distinction was a revelation. A crowd of children appeared, to general applause—so extravagant, so typical of Verignan, to bring fifteen adorable infants halfway around the world for a few scenes in an opera. Then the girls from the cigarette factory sauntered on, barely dressed, limbs and necks glistening with oil. A crowd of young bucks pursued them as a number of male passengers intended to do directly after the curtain call. Carmen's entrance unleashed a roar of recognition and welcome. Germaine Lorette was in her late forties, squat and thickset, with a large nose and a voice of astonishing, undulating power. She moved with such arrogance there was nothing ridiculous in the handsome youths begging her to love them.

Piet had accompanied many amateur mezzo-sopranos as they tried their hands at "L'Amour Est un Oiseau Rebelle." Lorette's insolence was riveting. She picked a flower from her corsage and tossed it at Pierre Lauriac, the tenor playing Don José. He was twenty years younger than she and as in awe of her as the crowd was. The promise of sex filled the room; radiating from Carmen's scorching glance, reviving the audience's recollections of the cigarette girls' smooth, oiled limbs, and their exquisitely made-up mouths singing of sweet cigar smoke and the transports of lovers.

An unspoken "when at sea" rule was taken for granted by all but the strictest watching moralists, and a glorious lasciviousness took hold of them, preserved from vulgarity by the music's sophistication. Across the darkened room knees pressed against neighboring knees, hands clasped beneath tables. Even couples who had been married twenty years smiled at each other and were charmed by one another's faces, lit by the soft red light of the shaded lamps.

Sitting at the captain's table, bored by his fashionable companions and glad to be silent at last, Jay Gruneberger saw with pleasure that the strapping young man who never came to meals had made an exception tonight. He shifted his chair to get a clear view of him. Piet's lips were slightly parted and the rosy light made his cheeks shine like a farm

boy's. Jay looked for the blond one and found him staring at
his dark friend. Didier's face had forgotten its professional
neutrality. Oh to be young and in love, Jay thought.

Didier hardly heard the music and took no interest in
the figures on the stage. He was in a state of quiet ecstasy.
To have followed Piet on his adventure and rescued him
from tourist class, to have brought him here and given him
the gift of an opera, made him immensely proud. His gaze
flickered occasionally over the tables, but no one had the
temerity to interrupt Germaine Lorette's first aria. Otherwise he looked only at Piet.

Stacey Meadows returned. During her brief absence from
the stage she had artfully heightened her makeup, and when
she reached for Don José, she was standing several feet
to the left of where she was meant to be, right before Piet's
table. "Your mother sent me," she said.

"Tell me of my mother!"

The duet began, tenor and soprano standing alone on the
empty stage. Unlike Germaine Lorette, Stacey Meadows
did not overpower her partner. As she told him she was his
mother's faithful messenger, Piet had to look away. Nina
had sung him to sleep with these words as a child. "Tell him
his mother dreams of him night and day, that she misses
him and hopes for him," Stacey sang. "She forgives him and
is waiting for him." Her voice soared over the shimmering
violins as she promised to give Don José the kiss his mother
had sent him.

But Piet did not see her deliver it.

He was in tears.

Pierre Lauriac took a deep breath. "I see my mother!"
Sharing the stage with Germaine Lorette had unnerved
him. He was trying too hard and the tightness in his throat
made every leap perilous.

Piet's shoulders began to shake. He had chirruped the

part as a little boy, but only as a man had he come close to achieving its true beauty. "Even from afar my mother protects me." Lauriac was close to Piet's age and standing not five feet away. The words summoned Nina, pale but frivolous in the hours before her death, making light of the pains in her chest. Piet's eyes met Stacey Meadows', who was pleased to see that the power of her performance had made this handsome stranger weep. It added sensitivity to his outward advantages. She turned to Don José, annoyed to have an imperfect partner at such a moment, and smiled so reassuringly that his singing dramatically improved.

"Tell her her son loves her and venerates her." Piet's lips followed Lauriac's as they sang. "He repents today."

The bright figures on the stage sparkled and lost their distinctness. Stacey Meadows turned from Don José, her eyes on Piet's—and deep within his mourning was the exhilarating knowledge that the woman on the stage was not his mother. Indeed, she was just the sort of messenger Nina would have chosen. He looked back unflinchingly, and it was as though they sang of cherished memories to each other, and for each other alone.

Didier watched this exchange and found it highly arousing. That the man he loved could seduce a pretty opera singer simply by staring at her made him proud. Perhaps they might share her, as Piet had refused to do with the Amsterdam whores. He did not require Piet to abjure women; merely to accord him the rights and status of First Friend.

Didier was better able to understand Piet's tears than Stacey Meadows. Piet was alone in the world, his mother dead, his father indifferent. And yet he was *not* alone! As Didier watched him struggle to master himself, he knew that the moment had come to tell him so. He had dreamed of it and feared it; now he felt confident in the face of it. In his pocket were the keys to the first-class swimming pool, purloined from the board in the purser's office. Beneath one of its loungers was a bottle of green Chartreuse and a cashmere blanket, taken from a stateroom. It would not be missed now that they were in the tropics. They would have the pool all to themselves until five a.m. They could plan what to do in South Africa and fall asleep side by side. (He had taken care to provide only one blanket.) Perhaps they might honor the possibilities of their stroll home from the Karseboom. In the right circumstances Didier had persuaded many men to kiss him. He waited impatiently for the interval, relieved that the minx in the blue dress did not return. There would be time for her later.

Tonight belonged to him and Piet.

The second act ended with an explosive finale in which Germaine Lorette made the crystal shake with her advocacy of the wandering life and the intoxications of *la liberté*. Piet took it as a resounding affirmation of his decision to leave all he knew behind. He was not superstitious, but only the coldest, least imaginative rationalism could fail to be moved by the message of maternal forgiveness he had received. He felt radiant with well-being. In his dreams Nina had cursed him; now she had blessed and absolved him.

When Didier appeared, bearing a bottle of champagne in an ice bucket stamped with the line's shell and crossed *L*s, he wanted to rise and embrace him. Instead he looked away and lowered his voice when he said: "You're the best friend a fellow could have."

Didier uncorked the bottle. "I saw you and the girl with the plaits making eyes at each other. Promise not to keep her all for yourself."

"I never make promises about women."

Didier poured. "I get off duty at one, and I've got the swimming pool keys. There's more drink there. I hid it this afternoon with foie gras sandwiches and iced cakes." He set his shoulders back. *Do it now.* "We can spend the rest of the night together. No one will find us." As he spoke, he held the bottle very close to Piet's glass, and their knuckles touched.

This contact gave the words their full meaning. Piet had sensed its possibility as they stood in the changing room together, felt an animal answer in himself and chosen not to confuse it with love. Now he understood that his friend had done the opposite. It took the edge off his joy. He had a slight, pulsing erection, but it was not Didier's presence that had caused it but the thought of removing Micaëla's tight blue dress and unplaiting her braids. For a moment Piet could think of nothing to say. He did not wish to injure his friend, but it seemed the time for euphemisms was past. "We know each other too well for that," he said gently.

"Of course." Didier bowed and retreated. He went to his post at the sweets trolley and busied himself slicing a *tarte aux pommes.* An overweight lady of sixty, strictly observing her nutritionist's injunction to have "just a little of what you fancy," summoned him and asked for a tiny slice: her eighth since lunch. He served it to her and bowed.

"Are you not well?" She was a sympathetic person, with a grandson about Didier's age.

"I'm quite all right, madam. You are kind to inquire."

But Didier was not at all all right. He left the room, went through the kitchens and out onto a stretch of open deck where the empty bottles were stored. He wanted urgently to be alone. When he was, he hid himself behind a vat of scraps as a large rat ran from the rail into the kitchen. The pain was ferocious. He did not know how to escape it. It choked him, made him bend double. He began to cry. What had he based his confidence on? Nothing. Piet was his friend. His graciousness, when others might have taken offense, confirmed his affection.

But affection is not the same as love, and it was love Didier Loubat wanted from Piet Barol. Sex too, if possible, but love first and foremost. Now Didier knew he would get neither. He felt pathetic and embarrassed and then brutally sad. Life would now return to snatched encounters, diverting in themselves but conducted without feeling. This could never again be enough.

He dried his eyes. He could not have Piet. The sooner someone else took him the better. He opened a bottle of fizzing mineral water and splashed his eyes with it. Then he patted his face with a tablecloth, took the goods elevator down three decks and emerged opposite the reading room. He opened the baize door and went down the corridor to the grille he had so often opened for Piet. There was no vindictiveness in what he did; only the conviction that it was better to suffer completely on this night already so full of sadness. He knew Piet Barol would not be caught. He would find his way into someone's bed and escape being cast off, a branded stow-away, on a piece of rock a thousand miles from any other. There was a vein of stoicism in Didier. In this time of peril his sensitivities turned to it and he resolved to do what must be done.

He closed the grille and locked it.

The curtain call was sublime. Don José had fortified himself with three excellent cognacs backstage and they mixed in his blood with the elation of having somehow seen the evening through. Germaine Lorette was contrite for having overshadowed him so completely. As he went to bow she told him he was the best Don José she had ever worked with. She kissed Escamillo, who was an old friend, but said nothing to the little slut playing Micaëla, who was altogether too gifted and too thin to merit praise. When she heard the cheer that greeted Stacey Meadows she strode onto the stage before it had even half died and sank to her knees with the grace of a child, though her joints were arthritic and she weighed sixteen stone. This trick of sudden fragility had driven audiences wild for thirty years. She remained in the depths of her curtsy, eyes downcast, until every person in the room was standing and applauding her.

Piet Barol led them from the center of the first row. Jay Gruneberger watched his hands as he clapped and was glad. A steward tapped Piet on the shoulder and gave him a slip of ship's notepaper, on which the words *Follow the man who brings this* were written. "From Mademoiselle Meadows, sir. You'll want to come now, before the crush. May I guide you?" Piet looked for Didier, to show by a smile that there need be no awkwardness between them. He was not there. For several moments he hesitated, hoping he would return, but the thought of refusing this invitation did not enter his head.

He rose and followed the man through a side door.

A large crowd of male passengers was making the same pilgrimage. Though the backstage dressing rooms were formally out of bounds, access to them could be achieved by a discreet tip, and those with permanent mistresses in the chorus had nightly invitations. Piet was borne along with a boisterous crowd of the richest men on earth, which he took as an excellent omen of his own prospects. They reached a steel door and made a show of forcing it. Inside, in their flimsy costumes, gypsies and cigarette girls were smoking and undressing. They feigned horror at being disturbed, but in fact most of the invaders were known to them and welcome, and those who were not hoped to be and were scrupulously charming. After the first intrusion the door opened constantly, admitting flowers and champagne and flush-faced men.

Piet stalked the crowd looking for a blue dress. It was often said of the chorus girls on the *Eugénie* that they looked as good in person as they did onstage. He passed through them admiringly but was not distracted.

She made him wait twenty minutes. When she entered, she was wearing a wrap of pale pink silk and her dark curls were free of their braids. Both of them were pleased with how the other looked, relieved that the music and the low lights had not caused an embarrassing misjudgment.

He went to her and bowed, raised his eyes to hers and smiled.

"Do say you speak English."

"I speak English."

"*Very* good. All this French talk makes me so tired." She went to a rack of clothes, and for a moment he thought she meant to change in front of him. Other girls were undressing; he tried not to see them or to hope that she would. She did not. She took a scarlet dressing gown from a hanger and said, "You might as well get us something to drink."

There was plenty to drink. They stood beside an open bottle of champagne, delivered to another passenger and forgotten when his lady summoned him.

"Do tell me you aren't a gigolo."

"Of course I'm not."

"It's just that your clothes are so new and so chic. The effect is marvelous but not authentic."

Stacey Meadows was wary of too-perfect strangers, though she was also drawn to them. She was now twenty-six. Three years earlier, over tea in a New York hotel during a visit to that city with her mother, she had met a French vicomte with adorable manners. This charming gentleman, just touching fifty, had offered to show them the sights. By the afternoon of their second day together he had roundly banished Stacey's virginity and left her thrilled with words of love. He had promised to marry her and given persuasive reasons why she should not tell her parents of his intentions; had paid for her passage to Paris and a suite at the Grand Hotel. Three days before her boat docked he had married a Belgian railway heiress. She learned of it soon after her arrival and in a flaming rage took herself to a music hall and got a job and thanked God for sparing her a pregnancy with that man's child.

Stacey's voice had been much praised in the front parlors of small but comfortable Chicago houses. It found instant favor in Paris too, and she got a teacher who knew what to make of her gifts. She neither spoke to the vicomte again nor took his money. As she became better known, she felt glad to have been flung so far from her respectable life in the Midwest. She wrote to her parents and told them she was well but did not apologize for running away, and it was only to her brother Fred that she gave a forwarding address. The day she posted this letter she went to an audition at the Opéra Comique and was accepted into the chorus. Barely two seasons later she had a soloist's part on a highly publicized voyage on a famous ship, with Germaine Lorette in the title role. "So you are well dressed and self-made and you cry during affecting scenes at the opera," she said. "I do approve."

"My mother and I sang your duet together. You gave it so well I felt she was speaking to me."

"You should be scolded, not forgiven. I can quite see that."

Elsewhere in the room girls were sitting on men's laps, squealing as their corsets were unlaced. Piet did not wish to seem unsophisticated, and Stacey's presence after three hours of tantalizing imagining inspired him to follow the example of the other men. He leaned forward and kissed her neck.

The sting in his cheek made him gasp. Stacey rose. It was best to impose discipline from the beginning; otherwise all was chaos. Since the decisive shattering of her illusions she had had no patience with sentimentality, but the *vicomte's* expert induction had left her with a very great liking for clean-smelling men with beautiful lips. Having encountered just such a one, she felt that a little anticipation would make their first embrace infinitely sweeter. She decided to postpone it. "You may call tomorrow after tea to repent. I have a quiet hour while my braids are plaited. We can talk without this mayhem."

"I'll do my best to come."

"I'm sure your best will be enough."

But the chorus dressing rooms were not accessible from tourist class. "If I don't come, you must know that I wished to but was detained. May I see you in Cape Town?"

"I will be there as long as the ship."

"Permit me to look you up, then. What is your name, mademoiselle?"

"Stacey Meadows."

"I shall find you, Miss Meadows."

"And I shall let myself be found."

Observing the exit of Piet Barol, Jay Gruneberger did his best to extricate himself from his conversation with Mrs. Cornelius Schermerhorn. He had unwisely told this lady, who was a passionate amateur botanist, that his wife grew several rare species of bromelia in the hothouses of their estate on the Hudson River. Mrs. Schermerhorn had gone to great lengths to get *Bromelia balansae* to flower, and never once been successful, and she was halfway through a detailed account of each effort (continued in Jay's ear throughout Germaine Lorette's standing ovation) when Piet disappeared. Jay did his best, but the subject was close to Mrs. Schermerhorn's heart. It was fully three minutes before he could get away.

By the time he had done so, there was no sign of the stranger with the patrician profile. Jay was considerably annoyed. The *Eugénie* would dock at St. Helena the next day, and his wife would join him, having gone out on Albert Verignan's yacht a fortnight earlier to oversee the final arrangements. By fashionable standards the Grunebergers' marriage was a deeply contented one, and Jay felt for Rose a tender affection that would not countenance seductions she might observe. She was the child of his parents' oldest friends; he had known her since she was six and would not wound her. This meant that his opportunities to follow his own inclinations were limited. When the craving was insuperable he satisfied it hastily and opportunistically, generally in the male lavatories of railway stations and other insalubrious venues. Some of the men he met in these places asked him to pay them, and once or twice he had succumbed to this temptation and emerged from a dingy hotel two hours later, his overcoat pulled over his face, feeling soiled and regretful. For several days he had been imagining a seduction of an altogether more discriminating kind, conducted in the superb comfort of his accommodations on the *Eugénie*. To have the possibility presented and then snatched away seemed unjust. He went to the landing above the grand staircase, which offered an excellent vantage point.

Once again the lad had vanished.

Though Jay and Rose Gruneberger figured prominently in lists of "New York's most invited," and were always described as "popular" and "in demand" by the society press, Jay had no close friends. Twice at Yale he had confided his attraction to his own sex, and both times his confidant's revulsion had withered their intimacy as surely as salt poured on a snail will kill it. The boys who had fallen in love with him at his New England prep school were now married fathers and when they met made no mention of earlier realities.

Jay's pride did not permit self-pity. He kept his loneliness in quarantine, confined in a vault reinforced by unsentimental discipline. He was able to ignore its existence for months at a time, but tonight he felt it seeping from its confinement. He went out onto the promenade deck. It had rained during dinner and the teak boards were slippery. Now the air was exotic with the scents of the tropics. The moon was a night off its fullness and sent an orange summons across the waves towards him. It was absurd to spend such a night without a lover. He escaped its beauty and went indoors, but the band's merry music made him sadder.

Jay Gruneberger's business associates admired his capacity to engineer a situation to his satisfaction. The foundations of this ability were intelligence and persistence. He had felt certain he could speak to the fellow at least and ascertain from this encounter whether more might be hoped for. Now he abruptly lost the energy to mount another useless search. He went instead to the salon and ordered a cocktail. They would either meet or they would not. He left it in the lap of the gods.

Piet left the chorus girls' dressing room smitten. He was not depressed by his failure to achieve a more instant union with Stacey Meadows. Delay could only heighten their coming together and he admired her strictness wholeheartedly. As he walked down the corridor he felt euphoric. A year before he had been a junior clerk in Leiden, obliged to sleep in a musty alcove and shit in an outhouse. Now the most powerful men in the world took him for one of their own. He thought sympathetically of Didier and wondered whether he should find him at once and make things all right. He decided against it. His friend would feel patronized by immediate sympathy. He would look for him tomorrow and laugh their awkwardness away.

Piet had a great gift for experiencing the present. It seemed a waste to burden it now with thoughts of the future or the past. He had the run of the world's finest ship and the clothes and manners to enjoy this glittering world undetected. Who knew when such a situation might arise again? He resolved to drink the cup of pleasure deep and hurried on.

The grand staircase was crowded. He had not had dinner and was pleasantly light-headed with hunger. He sauntered down the stairs, thinking of food, and looked into the smoking room where sandwiches of rare roast beef could be obtained at any hour. But the fug of a hundred postprandial cigars made his head spin. He left by a door in its west wall and found himself in a broad passage he had never been in before. The marble here was not painted. It was cut in vast slabs and covered floor, walls, and ceiling: a frothy cream jagged with shots of blue. At its summit was a gilt elevator and a menu stand embossed with the words GRILL ROOM.

He pressed the button firmly.

With an elegant whirring the cage came down—lined floor, walls and ceiling in marble. It did not seem that the chains that pulled it could support such weight, but the presence of a respectful attendant prohibited a display of nerves.

"You'll want to hurry, sir. Last orders are in fifteen minutes."

Piet stepped onto the platform and the doors slid shut. The lift began to rise. Up and up they went, through three decks, then four: each was crowded with people. It stopped on the fourth and a gay group joined him, the ladies in magnificent jewels. He was aware of their approving notice, and when one dropped her fan he retrieved it and was prettily thanked. The doors opened onto a vestibule painted like an afternoon sky, the rays of a gilt sun pointing towards the grill room's entrance. The party with him were greeted rapturously and led to their table.

"May I have your cabin number, sir?" Maurice Moureaux held his pen above the register. "There is a supplementary charge for the grill room. It will be added to your bill."

Over his last six transatlantic voyages, Maurice Moureaux had formed an understanding of some convenience with a *plongeur* in the first-class kitchens, a cocky Marseilleise of no education but great wit, with an immense prick. The purser disapproved of shipboard liaisons and had transferred Jean-Anton to the *Joséphine* two days before the *Eugénie*'s departure, leaving Maurice with no erotic companion. He was fastidious. Since encountering Piet Barol in the reading room's service corridor he had found no one to his taste. To be able to ascertain his cabin number struck him as a piece of great good fortune. He repeated his question.

"My cabin number?"

"Or the name of your suite." Moureaux smiled his glossy smile and stood as tall as he could; he worried about being short.

For an instant Piet faltered, confronted by the decision between retreat and advance. He decided to advance. "The Henri de Navarre."

"And your name, sir?"

"Van Sigelen. Frederik van Sigelen."

"Come this way, Mr. van Sigelen. Will you be dining alone?"

Piet nodded.

"What a pleasure to see you again." Moureaux took a leather-bound menu and led him to a table by the window. In the long oval mirrors an orange moon glowed. The ceiling was glazed; Piet had never seen such stars. It was the most expensive room on the oceans, a private concession run by César Ritz. Only dishes that had been served to the kings at Versailles were offered here, and the amounts beside them were among the largest he had ever seen in print.

Moureaux unfolded his napkin and placed it on his lap. There was a dance floor at the far end of the room, surrounded on three sides by waves and stars. "I shall send the sommelier at once, sir."

A flutter of subsiding adrenaline made Piet shiver. He had dared and won—again! He felt triumphantly alive. Moureaux bowed and retreated; but moments later, as Piet weighed the merits of quail and turbot, the steward returned.

"I'm sorry, Mr. van Sigelen. The register has Mr. and Mrs. Rossiter in the Henri de Navarre Suite."

"Did I say Navarre? I meant Marie Antoinette."

"Of course." Moureaux hoped that the handsome young passenger had made this error to ensure that they spoke again. He asked Piet whether he had explored the ship to his full satisfaction.

"She's a glorious machine."

"I should be happy, at any moment, to show you over her."

"I'll remember that."

The band began to play the Waltz of the Flowers. It was a piece of music that summoned for Moureaux the glory of his youth in St. Petersburg, when he had been the most admired waiter at its composer's favorite restaurant. As the clarinet swirled, he was again twenty-two and incontrovertibly desirable. He bowed and returned to the register. When Piet stood and followed him his heart beat faster.

It was clear to Piet Barol that he should not be present for much further examination of the passenger list. "I've left my cigarettes in my cabin," he said nonchalantly. "I'll just go and get them."

"Permit me to have a packet sent to your table immediately. Which brand may I obtain for you?"

"I have them hand-rolled in England. I'll get them myself."

It was possible to deduce a great deal about a person's inclinations from the contents of his wardrobes. Moureaux was glad to have this opportunity to conduct a discreet examination. "Allow me to fetch them for you."

"They're in a locked case. I'll go."

The gaiety of the music inspired daring. "I could accompany you, if you wish."

"That's not necessary."

"Very well, sir. The kitchen will be closing shortly. I shall ask the chef to wait for you. May I take your order?"

"The turbot."

"Thank you."

Piet went to the elevator and pressed the button.

Moureaux began to prepare his bill and to wonder how he might contrive to bring him breakfast in bed one morning. He felt dreamy and romantic and could not find the name van Sigelen anywhere on the passenger manifest. He scanned the lists of suites. Catherine de Médicis. Henri de Navarre. Joan of Arc. Louis XIV. Marie Antoinette. By this entry were the words: *Schermerhorn, Mrs. Cornelius. Coffee should be iced after Malta.*

"One moment, sir."

The lift doors opened and Piet stepped into the car. He turned as the trellis shut, and in his glance were both insolence and fear.

Abruptly, Moureaux knew.

He was temporarily anesthetized by shock. As Piet sank out of sight he opened his mouth but made no sound. He, Maurice Moureaux, had fallen for a stowaway! It made him breathless, then furious. There was a ship's telephone on the desk; he lifted it and dropped his voice. *"Alert bleu.* Male. Midtwenties. Evening dress. Of good stature. Dark hair." As he gave this description he was aware of its inadequacy. "Send word to the stewards' mess. He has just gone down in the grill room elevator. Watch all exits. I shall come at once and identify him."

But by the time the operator had transferred this information and the grill room elevator had returned to take Maurice on his quest, Piet Barol had passed through the smoking room and found a staircase to take him down two decks. He moved efficiently and calmly. He did not make a stir. On this fine night the reading room and the corridor that led to it were empty, but as he walked towards the green baize door a group of men appeared. He slowed until they had gone. When they had, he slipped into the service corridor and began to run.

As he reached the grille the narrowness and brilliance of his escape struck him forcefully. In a state of extreme self-congratulation he pulled the latch.

It was locked.

Piet threw his full force against it. The gate remained impervious. He rattled the barrier ferociously, but human ferocity was no use against cold steel. For the first time the consequences of his illegal escapade became quite real. He would be expelled from the ship on an island hundreds of miles from any other, with no reputation and hardly any money. At all costs he must avoid that.

Who would help him? He could not ask it of Didier. The idea of throwing himself on the mercy of Miss Stacey

Meadows was more diverting and his confidence returned. She would be amused by his predicament and think more not less of him for his audacity. The idea that she might hide him in her cabin, perhaps in her bed, planted the seeds of triumph in this disaster.

But first he must find her.

Piet went back through the baize door. He had paid more attention to his fellow dressing room pilgrims than to the route they were following. He could only hope to remember it by returning to the starting point of the journey, which meant traversing the main foyer of the ship. He thought of Machiavelli's advice to act boldly with Lady Fortune and walked down the corridor towards a sound like a waterfall.

At the foot of the grand staircase, as if at a cocktail party in Paris, two hundred people were being amused by one another. From high above them came a sultry waltz, performed only on nights when the sea was calm and the breezes warm. He slipped into the throng feeling safer.

By the time he reached the main elevator, he was master of himself again. He took it up three decks and tried the theater's quadruple gilt doors. They were locked. He followed the corridor round, trying for access to the service labyrinth. There appeared to be no other way in. The only doors led to staterooms, their shell-shaped handles gleaming in the low light. He began to hurry. Everywhere he turned were rows of doors, barred to him. He went from one corridor to the next, the waves on the pale blue brocade walls repeating like the bars of a fanciful prison. He had begun to sweat and slowed down. It was essential to look untroubled. At last he found a door that gave onto the deck and went outside into the balmy night.

Of course. He should climb the barrier into tourist class. Where was it? He looked over the rail. Below him was the first-class promenade deck, full of strolling stargazers. It was darker where he was, a place for illicit couplings. He walked quickly aft, past the lifeboats. From beneath their covers came gruff panting sounds and the occasional gasp or laugh. He crossed the wet deck, looking for the portion of it assigned to his own class. He hesitated at the barrier. It had been designed specifically to deter such adventures and stretched sixteen feet towards the heavens, with no place for a foothold. Only by climbing right over the ship's back rail and somehow clawing himself round its farther edge could an assault be attempted.

Piet Barol was not a coward. Equally, except when goaded by Louisa Vermeulen-Sickerts, he did not seek out situations of physical danger. He had always felt a gentle contempt for men who could think of no other way to prove themselves. He looked over the edge. The great propellers churned the water far below, sending a trail of froth a mile long behind them. He did not relish the thought of hanging by one hand above them. The spokes of the gate were wet and would be slippery. He looked over his shoulder. He was unobserved. If he were to act, he should act now. But his body had ceased equivocating and was shaking its answer: No.

St. Helena was better than death.

He went inside. He remembered being led down a flight of stairs on his way to the chorus girls' dressing room. Perhaps from the deck below he would have a better chance of success. He found his way back to the elevator and took it down to the main landing, which was packed with revelers.

Ten feet away stood Maurice Moureaux.

Piet stepped sharply down the stairs away from him. Moureaux was with two other men. One of them descended the opposite branch of the staircase to cut him off on the next landing. Piet went more quickly, but without drawing attention to himself. It seemed that the stewards were also unwilling to make a scene. He reached the landing several steps ahead of his pursuers and extended his lead on the flight below. Now he was in a white panic. He thought of the rooms he had idled in with Didier. None would be empty now. None possessed the sort of furniture into which one might climb and quietly spend the night. He should have tried the lifeboats, but the way back was barred. Ahead of him were the doors to the salon. He went through them and flung himself behind a screen that sheltered a cluster of armchairs.

A well-built man with a neat beard and a hawk nose looked up from a copy of the *Gentleman's Journal*. "Do join me," he said. "I'm drinking alone."

Jay Gruneberger believed in luck. It was impossible to thrive without it. Sometimes he saw his inconvenient desire for other men as the price he must pay for being so favored by the Fates in other respects. He felt extremely lucky to be married to Rose, who was wittier and kinder than anyone he had ever met. He was lucky on the Stock Exchange and on the golf course. Two years before, on the day of his fortieth birthday, he had hit a hole in one in front of three hundred people who knew him well. He had felt great exhilaration on that occasion. It was nothing by comparison with what he felt now.

Piet Barol sat down. In moments he would be hauled from the room and publicly disgraced. He thought of Percy Shabrill watching him being taken onshore in a tender. He and Miss Prince would talk of nothing else for the rest of the voyage.

"Is something wrong?" The man with the beard had a deep, kind voice and an American accent.

"I'm not feeling very well."

"Seasick?"

It was at this moment that Maurice Moureaux put his

hand on Piet Barol's right shoulder, his long fingers digging deep into the muscle. Another steward took charge of his left one in a similar fashion and a third stood behind his chair. They were slightly out of breath. Moureaux kept his voice low, not wishing to alarm the female passengers. "This man is a dangerous stowaway, Mr. Gruneberger."

Piet stood up. His bravado was spent.

Jay smiled. "On the contrary, he is my private secretary. I have known his family for thirty years."

"I am under orders to escort him to the brig."

"I'm afraid I can't spare him. Would you bring us a menu?"

"His name is not on the passenger list, sir."

"I needed someone at the last moment and there were no cabins. He's making do with the sofa in my sitting room."

Maurice Moureaux knew Mr. Gruneberger was lying, and he also knew why. That he could do nothing about it was frustrating in the extreme. The junior stewards were silent, watching for his lead. "Fetch Mr. Gruneberger a menu, Laurent," he said at last. "I am so sorry to have disturbed you, sir. And you, Mr. van Sigelen. Forgive my error."

"Think nothing of it," said Piet.

The three stewards bowed and retreated. Laurent returned with a menu.

"Mr. van Sigelen will have the turtle soup. Bring it with a bottle of Sancerre."

"At once, Mr. Gruneberger."

Finally they were alone. Subsiding adrenaline and hunger and the gentle rocking of the ship made Piet half delirious. When he could speak he said: "I am greatly in your debt."

"Then you're an honorable fellow after all. *Are* you dangerous, as they say?"

It did not seem to Piet that there was anything to be gained from lying to his unexpected benefactor. "I broke into first class to see a friend who's a steward," he confessed. "We used to work at the same house in Amsterdam."

"You both left to come on the ship?"

"He lost his place because of me. Then I lost mine. We ran into each other on deck."

Jay Gruneberger suspected that this encounter had not been wholly coincidental, but he did not propose to direct the talk towards a potential rival. "What did you do to lose your position?"

"I'm too ashamed to say."

"Then you must keep your counsel, Mr. van Sigelen. Though in my experience confiding a burden can ease it. I promise you discretion."

"My name is Barol, not van Sigelen."

"Glad to hear it. The van Sigelens I know are vile."

The waiter came with the wine.

"Drink it quickly. A glass will calm you."

Piet did as he was told and they shook hands. "At least tell me how you were exposed, Barol." Jay spoke as if requesting the day's gossip at his club. "Often the denouement is more interesting than the details of what led to it."

"I tried to eat in the grill room. I didn't know you had to give a cabin number."

"I don't mean on the ship. I mean in Amsterdam."

Piet hesitated. "Someone said something that was true. No one had thought of it before she said it."

"About you?"

"About me and someone else. A lady."

"A relative of the speaker."

Jay said it as casually as if he had heard the story days before. His precision was disconcerting and Piet drank another glass of Sancerre. When it was finished, he said: "Her mother."

"And I presume that you and this lady's mother . . ."

"Only once."

"You were caught at the first attempt? How very unre-sourceful." Gruneberger smiled. He never minded if a fel-low did not like other fellows. In some ways he preferred it, since recollection made infinite embroideries possible. It was often better than an unsatisfactory half hour concluded in mutual embarrassment.

Piet did not wish to seem wholly incompetent. "We met often. It was the last time that gave us away."

"I thought it only happened once."

"We only once did everything one might do."

"I see." Jay had a calm, authoritative way of asking ques-tions that elicited answers. At shareholder meetings, men who had spent years honing the art of subtle evasion found themselves lulled by his calm, courteous pursuit of knowl-edge. Piet Barol had not had a candid conversation for so long that the lure of one was strong. Under the influence of a stranger's gentle prompting he found that there was much he longed to share. He did not mention the Vermeulen-Sickertses by name or give any details that might establish their identity, but he told Jay all that had happened on the Herengracht.

The experience was immensely relieving. When the San-cerre was finished they had a cognac and by now the room was noticeably emptier. The most worldly person Piet had ever met was Maarten Vermeulen-Sickerts, who was as con-servative as a medieval monk by comparison with his new confessor.

Like the rest of fashionable New York, Jay Gruneberger was never sincerely shocked. He took Piet carefully to the epicenter of his drama, guiding the narrative to the details of what exactly he had done with his employer's wife. Being told this story by an engaged and passionate Piet Barol, lean-ing forward in his chair, the scent of sweat rising from him, a cognac balloon in his vast hands, was to Jay Gruneberger a form of pleasure so heightened, so rare and refined, that it far excelled the merely erotic. He had a mind capable of considering many perspectives, so while he absorbed every detail of Piet's story he was also able to float into a vaguer place, where all he heard were the low notes of his voice and all he saw were his face, glowing and happy again, and his thick neck and his dark blue eyes.

At length a regretful steward told them that the salon had closed.

"You'd better take the sofa in my sitting room." Jay made the suggestion in the tone he used when offering a colleague a ride home from the office. "There's no way of getting you back before morning."

"I don't know how I'll ever get back."

"My cabin steward will be on duty at breakfast. I've known him fifteen years. He'll take you to your own part of the ship and no one will be any the wiser."

"They'll do an inspection and find me."

"That won't happen now I've vouched for you. That's the Loire Lines' great thing. They never embarrass one."

"Then I accept with gratitude."

They left the room and went down a wide corridor. "I take this suite because it's quiet. The disadvantage is it's a damned slog when you've had a few and there's no private deck."

Jay had waited in his secluded corner of the salon as long as he could, hoping that his friends would have gone to bed by the time Piet Barol accepted his hospitality. He was relieved to encounter no one he knew—though he was ready to introduce his new assistant with aplomb, should he be required to. In the end he was not. They stopped outside a pair of double doors flanked by four pillars. Above

them, beneath the line's shell and crossed *L*s, were the words
CARDINAL RICHELIEU.

The decorative centerpiece of the Richelieu Suite was
a copy of the famous portrait by Philippe de Champaigne, from which the room's predominant colors were
also borrowed. Champaigne's Richelieu was ruthless. The
Eugénie's copyist had caught his robes of rose and gray but
softened his expression, the better to complement the atmosphere of the ship. He surveyed the room like a discreet
and approving voyeur. It was wonderfully quiet, with dark
mahogany paneling to chest height. Piet and Jay sat down
on a sofa upholstered in pale blue velvet and their talk
ran on. Having relieved himself of his story, Piet had developed a sincere interest in his rescuer.

Jay Gruneberger was not used to self-revelation, having had cause to master the habits of discretion. But their
unusual introduction and the frank cordiality it led to
allowed a spontaneous trust to arise between them. Piet's
questions were as perceptive as his own had been. He found
himself describing his childhood in Cincinnati, his meeting with his wife when she was six and he eight. He had
often told the story of how he and Rose had climbed trees
together long before falling in love. What he did not often
say was that his father and mother had despised each other
and used their only child as a foot soldier in their strife. He
confided this in Piet Barol and learned a great deal about
Herman and Nina in return.

"You should have chosen New York!" he said with feeling, when their talk reached Piet's plans for his new life.

"That was my first thought. I decided on Cape Town
when I knew the boat was coming here. I wanted to sail
on her."

"If you'd seen New York once, you'd not have changed your mind. It's worth a thousand times this tacky little ship."

As he listened to Jay's descriptions of a city he would never know, Piet Barol found himself thinking about Stacey Meadows and the challenges and advantages of being loved by her. "Where's your wife?" he asked.

"Rose has been on St. Helena this past fortnight. She's the chairwoman of the ball committee and doesn't hold with delegation."

"You must miss her."

"Immensely. She's coming on board tomorrow afternoon. I've had to bring her gown from New York."

"What's the theme?"

"*La gloire*. Choice of a man named Verignan."

"Who are you going as?"

"I'll show you." Jay stood up and opened the door to the bedroom. After half a bottle of Sancerre and a cognac he was no longer as content as he had been merely to look at his new friend. Neither was he so moved by the alcohol, the lateness of the hour, the fullness of the moon, as to abandon all caution. If the boy doesn't come in, he thought, I'll leave it at that.

But Piet did come in.

Jay took his costume from a mahogany cupboard. Rose had had it made for him and every detail showed the attention and care he so valued in her. She had chosen the uniform of a union colonel in the Civil War and personally supervised six fittings. Jay had a sudden urge to show Piet Barol how good he looked in it. Very matter-of-factly, he took off his tailcoat and his collar and began unbuttoning his shirt. "One always eats too much on a ship. I'd better make sure it still fits."

Piet did not know whether he should return to the sitting room or honor the sudden intimacy of the evening by staying where he was, as he would have done with a friend. He compromised by sitting on a chair at the foot of the bed, from which they could continue their conversation without facing one another directly. The first-class suites on the *Eugénie* had windows, not portholes, and the glass reflected the room. Piet tried not to watch as his savior took off his shirt. He had often been naked with fellows his own age but had never seen a much older man with his clothes off except his father; and Jay Gruneberger looked nothing like Herman Barol.

Jay boxed and ran and played tennis and every morning lifted forty-pound dumbbells until his arms ached. He was broad shouldered with a densely hairy chest. Though thickening in his midsection he looked superb in a room lit by soft lamps and an orange moon.

Jay knew that there are moments in life when risks must be taken or failure accepted. He was not ready to accept failure. He looked at Piet, wondering how to touch the boy without alarming him. Then he went to his chair, gripped his shoulders, and pressed his thumbs gently but firmly into the knots beneath them.

The effect on Piet Barol was paralyzing. Not three hours before he had contemplated hanging by one hand above the engines, and the tension of this untaken decision remained deep in his muscles.

"I see a wonderful Russian three times a week in New York. I'd happily share his expertise with you, Barol. Or I'll call a steward and have the sofa made up next door. Absolutely as you wish."

Since earliest adolescence, Piet's body had demanded pleasure of him and rewarded his efforts to seek it. Now it answered on its own behalf with a long relieving sigh.

"I thought as much. You've had a trying day."

Watched by the knowing cardinal, who was not at all deceived, Jay went to the bed, drew back the coverlet, and with four plump cushions made a resting place for Piet's head. "It's better if you're lying down with your clothes off." He was careful to sound indifferent. "That's how I always have it done."

Piet hesitated. Then he stood up and took off his tailcoat, his waistcoat, his tie and his collar. His shirt as he unbuttoned it smelled of sweat and fear, an olfactory reminder of the evening's adventures. The room was the ideal temperature for nakedness. As he pulled off his shoes, a deep weariness crept over him.

"If you put your head between the pillows, you should be able to lie almost flat. It doesn't do to twist your neck."

Piet did so. The linen smelled of roses and was deliciously soft. Jay stood over him, remembering his first sight of his back and giving thanks for his freedom to touch it now without fear. Piet had kept his drawers and his socks on. These last Jay removed. He had a secret passion for feet, and the smell of Piet Barol's caught in his nostrils and heightened his alertness. He surveyed the young man just as Jacobina Vermeulen-Sickerts had done, wondering where to touch him first. Though this was not at all his Russian masseur's practice, he swung himself over Piet and planted his knees on either side of his body. Then he applied the knuckles of his index fingers to his uppermost vertebrae.

It was the first time Piet had encountered physical pain that held the possibility of pleasure. He gasped at the intensity of it. "Breathe out very slowly," said a deep voice above him. Jay's hands were strong, and his back had so often been the focus of an expert's attention that he knew his way unerringly over Piet Barol's. Piet breathed out as instructed. Tendrils of fire singed his skin. He had never yet been in the care of a connoisseur.

As Jay moved up and down Piet's back, his hands never leaving his body, a wholly wordless and yet precise and attentive communication began to open between the two men. The ship had met a swell and was rising with it and falling, as if timing itself by Piet's breaths. This motion, and the darkness, and the scent of roses, and the rich combination of pain and its relief sent Piet Barol into a state whose existence he had not imagined.

When Jay lifted his legs and pulled his drawers down them and over his ankles, Piet barely registered this boldness. Certainly it did not offend him. He was in a place far beyond all questions of propriety. Now Jay put his elbows to work, setting them over the warmed knots of muscle and by infinite gradations placing greater and greater weight on them, so that Piet was almost crushed but at the same time lifted far above the aches in his body. These began to flow down his arms to his fingers and his legs to his toes and then to leave him entirely, as if they had never been.

When Jay's elbows reached his buttocks, they located precisely the store of a lifetime's spinal tension. As they pressed down, implacable and relentless, so Piet's cock was pressed into the firm mattress and an element of erotic pleasure began to twist through the tranquil darkness that enveloped him. Jay's elbows retreated, were replaced by fingers that gripped his thick legs, his calves, his ankles, and then—it sent goose pimples all the way to his neck—a warm, scratchy tongue ran over the soles of his feet.

This did intrude on Piet's formless blackness. But Jay acted with such confidence he did not resist, and his instinct to do so was dampened by the knowledge that the situation that now presented itself—in the middle of the sea, in the middle of the world, in the middle of the night—would never arise again. He said nothing when Jay kissed the back of his legs, his bearded chin sending shivers across his skin.

And when Jay's tongue reached his balls he let out a low ecstatic murmur.

Other boys had played with his prick or sometimes sucked it but had never touched him there; and the women he had seduced had been far too well bred to think of doing so.

Just when it seemed impossible that these sensations could improve further, Jay pulled Piet's buttocks apart and flicked his tongue over his arsehole. This piece of daring lit a deeply buried circuit in the young man's pleasure sensors. He opened his eyes. Rose-scented darkness and the outlines of two square pillows confronted him. He tried to speak but could find no words. Jay's tongue pressed farther and the electric connection between them, so far transmitted by knuckles and elbows, blazed through this new synapse. Piet thought of all he had done for Jacobina, without thought of reward. It seemed he was to be repaid after all.

He was. As the orange moon sank into the sea and the sun extinguished the stars, Jay Gruneberger's tongue overthrew the last of their mutual inhibitions and explored the unvisited places of Piet's body to its owner's full satisfaction. Both men, at once intimately joined and quite alone, alive in their own beings, entered into a state of rapture more profound than either had ever known.

It was light when Piet could bear it no longer, and the violence of his ejaculation was most satisfying to Jay Gruneberger. He wiped Piet down with a towel and rejoiced in what he had accomplished. Then he took off his uniform and lay down beside him.

Without exchanging a single word they fell asleep.

Jay's cabin steward kept an extensive record of the preferences of the hundred or so passengers who requested him personally on each voyage they took and knew not to bring Mr. Gruneberger's breakfast until rung for. Jay was woken by the heat of the sun, and for a moment his exploits hung in his consciousness like a marvelous dream. He opened his eyes. Beside him, fast asleep on his side, lay Piet Barol.

Jay got up and put on a dressing gown. The sound disturbed his companion, who stretched to his fullest extent, yawned loudly, scratched himself, and woke.

Jay's stomach tightened. He could not bear to betray all they had shared by parting awkwardly. "Morning, Barol," he said cheerfully. "Sleep all right?"

There was a moment's silence. Then they both smiled and all uncertainty evaporated. Jay handed Piet a dressing gown and poured him a bath. Piet took it while breakfast was ordered and emerged to find a linen suit laid out for him beside a table set for two. He was taller than Jay, and the trousers were too short, but with a belt to hold them at the top of his hips and a sweater to disguise this arrangement he looked every inch a first-class passenger dressed for a day of elegant lounging.

"We'll have you back in your cabin before lunch, with no one the wiser." Jay lit a cigar. "But what of your life plans, Barol? Do you have connections in Cape Town?"

"None, I'm afraid."

"So what will you do?"

"That question weighs on me."

"What are you good at?"

"I can draw. It's not much of an accomplishment."

"That depends on how well you do it." Jay was looking at Piet's hands. He wanted to see them at work before they parted. "Sketch something for me."

"What would you like?"

"A memento of our evening together."

Piet thought for a moment, then took a sheet of ship's notepaper and in ten minutes had caught the mahogany bed with its twisted sheets and the wily prelate who surveyed them. He signed it and gave it to his host.

"You should be an artist."

"No money in it."

"Then sell people things. There aren't many who can express themselves in words and pictures, as you can. What would you like to make, or have made, that other people might like to buy?"

"Furniture, perhaps."

"Then that's settled. If you do it right, you can make a fortune. My wife's decorator certainly does. Let me tell you how to make a name for yourself."

Percy Shabrill was lying on his bunk when Piet returned to their cabin, locked in a violent interior tussle between curiosity and resentment. Resentment prevailed. He forbore from asking Piet where he had been in case this should give him an opportunity to boast of an enviable adventure. Instead he told him with studied unconcern that he had secured a further three orders for his refrigeration system. "We'll be within sight of St. Helena by teatime," he remarked when he had finished. "Miss Prince tells me there was a prison full of filthy Boers there during the South African War."

"And now there's to be a party."

"Not for us. Harbor's too small to dock at apparently. I'm just about sick of this bloody ship." He yawned. "It's only first class who're getting off at all. Should be a jolly view if it's not too rough."

"Wake me to see it." Piet turned to the wall and closed his eyes.

Piet woke just before sunset, dressed and went on deck. Percy had spent the afternoon with Miss Prince and had not thought to rouse him. Nervous with envy, clumps of tourist-class passengers were talking over the frail sound of a string quartet sent to console them. Frau Stettin had worn her best dress, which was pink and white and altogether too young for her. "Ah, the memories of my youth!" She gripped Piet's arm to steady herself. She appeared to have drunk a quantity of champagne.

A flotilla of small white boats, each identical, was making for the ship from a long, low piece of volcanic rock floating in an endless ocean. Above it a sky shot with amber and vermilion swirled like a toreador. "Oh look!" cried Miss Prince, as the first of the sloops approached.

Jay Gruneberger gave his wife his arm. He was intensely proud of her. The spectacle of the white crafts bobbing on the sea with the sunset behind them would live on in the memory of every witness. The cheers from the third-class and steerage decks made this as plain as the sullen silence of tourist class. Even the first-class passengers, well versed in worldly delights, felt pleasant tingles of anticipation at this tantalizing overture.

Rose had interpreted *la Gloire* altogether originally and come as Water: glory itself, the giver of life. Her dress was a bewitching blue, deep and shifting against the expanse of the ocean with pearls sewn like bubbles in its folds. Together the Grunebergers stood out emphatically from the throng of gaudy empresses and Napoleonic generals.

Jay had long since ceased to savor the privileges of his life, but the risks Piet Barol had run in order to sample them made him appreciate them afresh. It was, after all, agreeable to be invited to a party that the world would discuss for weeks. It was agreeable always to have one's name remembered, to be made way for, and included, and flattered, and quoted. To dance under the stars with Rose tonight and exert himself on her behalf would be splendid. He felt profoundly calm and happy.

He was turning his attention to Elizabeth Schermerhorn when he saw the blond steward who had been Piet's constant companion. Didier was operating the tiller of a nearby cutter, his features taut and controlled. In his eyes Jay recognized at once the anguish of rejection. He was familiar with unrequited adoration and it was clear Piet might inspire it. The question was: had he returned it in this case? He thought of the young men's familiar intimacy with each other; then of the ease with which he had persuaded Piet to spend the night in his cabin.

Jay Gruneberger had a fine instinct for human motivation, but it was obvious from Piet Barol's stories that his matched it.

Who had been playing the more convincing game?

He had promised himself he would not look for him, but the fireworks exploding above the ship gave him the excuse to turn and he could not resist. Piet was at the very front of the crowd on the tourist-class promenade deck, between a rather plain young woman and an old lady in a bizarre confection of pink and white. He waved.

Everyone on the little white yachts was scrupulously ignoring the two thousand people watching them and Jay could not return this greeting. For a moment their eyes saluted one another. Then Jay poked his tongue an inch through parted lips and turned away.

Piet was woken at first light by the laughter of revelers returning to the ship. At once he thought of Didier. He dressed and went to the trellised barrier where they had first met. His friend was often on early duty at the veranda café, which opened onto the first-class promenade deck. He would find him and behave quite naturally.

Not a soul appeared. Verignan's party had gone off exceedingly well and none of his guests had gone to bed before dawn. Piet waited an hour by the barrier, to no purpose. He was about to go to breakfast when a woman in a floaty white dress appeared and sank gracefully onto a lounger on the other side.

It was Stacey Meadows.

The heightened sensuality of the last few days roared over him. She was staring out to sea, superbly self-possessed. He watched her furtively, having no means of reaching her. As he contemplated the defiant set of her chin against the vast ocean he thought of Don José's fatal mistake: to bind himself to a person who did not understand him and never would. It was the same error his mother had made. He considered his amorous adventures thus far, not one of which was worth a lifetime's devotion. Then he thought of the note Miss Meadows had sent him, which suggested an intelligence as self-determining and imaginative as his own.

He went to breakfast beset by an insistent desire that nothing—not Frau Stettin's conversation nor the amorousness of Percy Shabrill and Miss Prince—could tame.

The last days of the voyage passed with agonizing slowness, the physical imperatives of Piet's body competing with a mounting anxiety to which he had no answer. His sleep was fitful and he barely ate. What on earth would he do in Cape Town? He could think no further than his encounter with Miss Meadows, in which alone of all the uncertainties he faced he had the utmost faith.

On the morning of the final day, Table Mountain came into view through swirling mists. Despite the earliness of the hour the decks were crowded. Percy had proposed to Miss Prince the evening before and been accepted. He had kept Piet up all night talking of rings and houses and the style in which he intended to keep his wife.

Piet avoided them as best he could, having offered his congratulations over breakfast. The mountain ahead humbled him. It seemed the altar of a god or a deity itself: above the impudence of human contemplation. He returned to his cabin to find his bill waiting. Since his expulsion from first class he had found its habits hard to break and had resisted less and less the insidious pressure to buy things. Now he saw that he had been persuaded to consume eight cocktails and four brandies. He had had his tailcoat laundered in anticipation of its sale, and the amount charged for this service was many times greater than any sum he could hope to raise on it. He took from the safe the black steel box he had brought with him from Amsterdam and found its wad of notes far thinner than he remembered. At first he thought he had been robbed, but a few minutes with a pencil and a scrap of notepaper confirmed otherwise.

He recalled Didier telling him that a stroke of luck is not the same thing as being rich. The extravagance of his ticket, a night at the Karseboom, the sleeper to Paris, his hotel there, taxis to transport his wretched trunk, and now his wasteful expenditure on the ship had drastically depleted Maarten Vermeulen-Sickerts' gifts. For a horrifying moment Piet thought he might not be able to pay the account. What ignominy to have to borrow from Percy! He counted the notes with dread, and when he had separated what he owed only three remained.

He went on deck again. A blazing heat had incinerated the mist. Ahead of him was a chaotic port—foreign and energetic and wholly indifferent to him. He could barely survive a fortnight on his remaining reserves. What then? He did not know and could not think.

He found a deck chair and sat heavily in it, hiding from the daunting view. He heard the anchor break the water and a bell ring. With a shudder that made the ladies sway, the engines went into reverse and the boat stopped. His anxiety intensified. He knew that confidence alone could save him, but his capacity to manufacture it had deserted him. The band began to play "La Marseillaise."

"At long bloody last. Land!" Percy Shabrill was upon him, absurdly dressed in a tweed suit and plus fours—as if for a golfing holiday in the north of England. Having sold eighteen refrigeration systems and seduced a woman right beneath his cabinmate's nose, he was inclined to be generous with Piet Barol. "As soon as Dotty and I are settled, you must visit us."

Piet knew that this might be his only refuge from the doss-house and the realization was bitter indeed. Nevertheless he thanked Percy and took down his brother's address in Johannesburg.

"Just look at all those darkies. Enough to give you nightmares."

And with that Percy was gone.

The decks began to clear. Heat and fear made Piet dizzy. At length he went below. A steward appeared. "Letter for you, sir. Stand by for disembarkation."

Piet did not wait. He felt that another encounter with Percy Shabrill would break him. He pushed his way to the vestibule doors, glad that Didier had written to him. He was badly in need of a friend. As he stepped onto the gangway he saw Didier standing on the quay, directing the first-class passengers towards the customs shed. "Loubat!" His voice carried over the swell of noise.

Didier recognized it and turned deliberately towards its source, as if putting his hand into a flame. Years of training allowed him to keep his face absolutely expressionless as he looked for the last time at Piet Barol. Then he shook his head and went into the shed.

The swell of the crowd could not be restrained. It carried Piet to the end of the gangway and onto land that rocked disconcertingly after nearly three weeks at sea. Only the alchemy of friendship might have transformed this disaster into an adventure. The sudden revocation of Didier's was crushing. Piet joined the throng at the passport window and took the letter from his pocket. Perhaps Didier had explained. But the note inside the vellum envelope was not from Didier Loubat. It read: *Find elegant premises in the best district. Take a room at the Mount Nelson hotel and introduce yourself widely. Exploit your European glamour. Good luck. J.G.* and was accompanied by a check for a thousand pounds.

I hope it's not a love letter you're reading with such radiant concentration." Stacey Meadows was standing beside him in a dress of peppermint-green satin. "I should be rather jealous if it were, though I'd forgive you if you'd let me join the line. I was late getting off and I've lost my parasol. I can't stand in the sun with this mob."

"It would be an honor, Miss Meadows." He offered her his arm.

"You *do* look pleased with yourself."

"Only delighted to run into you."

"My invitations are not often ignored."

"I tried to come but was prevented. May I explain over luncheon?"

They went together to get their luggage. Stacey had a great deal more than Piet. A Loire Lines porter took it for them to the customs hall where an official asked for their papers, taking them for man and wife. Piet handed over the passport his mother had given him long ago. Stacey Meadows presented hers. When both had been stamped she said: "I couldn't possibly lunch with you. I don't even know your name."

"Well, that is easily solved." He took her hand and kissed it. "My name is Pierre Barol."

The consuls of France, Great Britain, the United States and Russia were waiting on the quayside to welcome the *Eugénie*'s first-class passengers, the Polish representative having been delayed on his train from Johannesburg. Verignan had hired every spare automobile in the city and had them repainted and stamped with the line's shell and crossed *L*s. The last was leaving the port when Piet and Stacey emerged from the customs shed into a jostling horde. Black porters were heaving trunks onto their backs. Indian boys in fezzes and gaiters asked for tips and picked pockets when they could. One or two dark-skinned gentlemen were examining the contents of the *Eugénie*'s hold in suits as smart as any Piet owned, and this sight shocked him most of all. He had expected to find the natives in appropriately exotic dress.

The same impulse that made Piet Barol mistrustful of elevators and other novelties now expressed a strong preference for a driver who resembled the cabmen of Europe. Stacey waited in the shade while he obtained the only remaining vehicle driven by a white man, a barouche upholstered in burgundy velvet, slightly frayed, and drawn by a pair of high-stepping grays. Its driver was a helpful and dapper Cockney who took them for persons of the greatest quality. Once lifted in and comfortably ensconced, Miss Meadows said: "I did enjoy watching you get the best carriage, Mr. Barol."

Stacey Meadows did not intend to rot her life away in the

chorus of the Opéra Comique and was well aware of the fate of girls in her position who made no plan before losing their looks. She refused, absolutely, to strike the Faustian pact of the courtesan. For some time she had been on the lookout for an alternative insurance against the indignities of middle age in the demimonde. She had rarely encountered a mate as suitable as the heroic figure at her side, his glance so smoldering she barely noticed the blazing yells, the street cries and gay colors of this city at the far end of the world. She decided to address his likely disadvantages immediately. "I see from your passport that you are French. I suppose that makes you as unreliable as you are diverting."

The carriage turned into Adderley Street, a thoroughfare lined with buildings as handsome and solid as any in Amsterdam. Piet had imagined roads of mud, but the avenue was well paved and dissected by tramlines. Among the seething crowds were people as elegantly dressed as Sunday strollers in the Vondelpark. Much was reassuringly familiar, but the diamond-sharp brightness, the smells of spices and salt water, the vast mountain guarded by a rock in the shape of a watchful lion, declared the newness of this world and its possibilities. His courage revived, and with it his conscience.

"It is not my real passport, Miss Meadows."

"Indeed?"

"You may rest easy. I am Dutch by birth and we are a most dependable race. My mother was French. I traveled on papers she once obtained for me."

"Are you a fugitive from the police?"

"From myself, only." The thrill of sitting beside a clever woman with a large check in his pocket did not override Piet's distaste for the subterfuges of the life he had left behind. He decided not to begin with a lie. "I was not a first-class passenger on that ship. A friend of mine was a steward and let me in to see the opera because he knows I care for it so."

Stacey's face fell. "Do you mean to say you have no money?"

"This morning I had barely sixty guilders to my name. Now I have a thousand pounds."

"So you *are* a thief!"

"Far from it." Piet showed her Jay's letter and told the story of his discovery, his flight from the stewards and his rescue by a passenger of means, who had invested the capital to start him off in business.

"You must have been very persuasive with this American gentleman." Stacey Meadows looked at him skeptically. The moral certainties of her Chicago upbringing had been thoroughly overthrown during two seasons at the Opéra Comique, which had taught her a great deal about the range of human inclination. She knew many men who preferred their own kind, more or less openly, and had long lost the habit of disapproval. But the animal part of her nature was disappointed and slightly surprised to learn that her companion might be one of them. His poverty allowed her to be direct. "I don't mind the slightest bit—but tell me—what did you do to earn such a sum? I know very well why moneyed men take an interest in people like us."

Piet, who never did so, blushed deep scarlet.

"I thought as much. Did you enjoy it?"

He hesitated. "In a novel sort of way. The alternative was being put off the ship at St. Helena and spending my life there. I looked for you first, you may be sure." He told her of his desperate hunt for her cabin. When he had finished she was smiling, despite herself, and he snatched her wrist and kissed it.

The fervor with which he did so reassured Stacey

Meadows, who decided to overlook a desperate act. Though she withdrew her wrist she was very pleased.

The carriage trundled beneath an ornamental arch and entered the Company Gardens beside a palace of rose brick and blinding stucco. Ahead of them stretched a shaded avenue from which paths twisted seductively into lush vegetation. A Greek temple faced the mountain, brilliantly white against the sky. Wherever they looked were flowers they had never seen—explosions of purple on long, swaying stems, trees hung with fanfaring trumpets in pink and red. They were both silent at the wonder of it, and in that silence Stacey Meadows thought quickly.

She had assumed that her companion's income matched his beauty and was disconcerted to find this was not so. His candor, however, even on the most delicate topics, set him apart from the smooth-talking beaux who usually pursued her. She thought of the way Germaine Lorette had sabotaged her curtain call and a longing to escape the cutthroat competition of artistic Paris seized her. To do so with a worthy collaborator might be more diverting than marriage to a magnate who would doubtless have objectionable female relatives.

She turned her subtle, strategic mind to the situation at hand. "It is wise to pretend to be French if you wish to make furniture and gain a rich clientele. You should exploit, as your friend suggests, your European glamour. What about Monsieur *de* Barol, *monsieur le baron?* A title would suit you admirably, and since you are starting afresh . . ."

"If one does that one might as well be a vicomte."

"An excellent suggestion." Stacey withdrew from her purse the little platinum band her first seducer had given her in New York and slipped it onto the wedding finger of her left hand. She felt that her embrace with this delicious young man had been delayed quite long enough, and that once it had taken place she would be clearer in her mind. They proceeded up Government Avenue in tingling silence, her invitation well understood by them both. They passed the prime minister's house and a museum of natural history that resembled a French château, crossed the traffic on Orange Street and entered the fragrant grounds of an imposing hotel built on the foothills of the mountain.

The drive was thronged with the vacated motors of the *Eugénie*'s first-class passengers, and the sun struck their eyes so sharply that both of them emerged from the barouche with lids half shut. A doorman appeared immediately with a sun umbrella. In a lobby full of the sweet scents of luxury Stacey wrote *The Vicomte and Vicomtesse Pierre de Barol* in the visitors' register. This, and the quality of the Louis Vuitton trunk the bellboy brought in, inspired the manager to issue instructions for a suite on the first floor to be prepared rather than the room with bath that Piet had engaged. He begged them to take a glass of champagne punch on the terrace while it was being made ready.

The Mount Nelson's garden was decked in the flags of France, Britain, Russia, Poland and the United States. Jay Gruneberger had been keeping watch at the fountain for an hour, wondering whether Piet Barol would follow his advice and come to the hotel. He half wished not, but had been unable to resist making the suggestion and providing the young man with the means to act on it. He saw Piet as soon as he appeared on the terrace with a young woman in a peppermint-green dress and knew at once that there would be no repeat of their shipboard revelry. He was more relieved than regretful. His hand stopped shaking and he turned to Albert Verignan, who had been attempting all morning to wheedle from him a repeatable pronouncement on the international situation.

"There will be no European war," he said, partly for the pleasure of annoying his host. "Anyone can see it would mean the end of the world."

Piet and Stacey were shown upstairs to a private parlor that opened onto the largest bedroom Piet had ever seen. It was wonderfully light and pretty, with a paper of pink and blue spring flowers and a bath in which it was possible to lie at full stretch without touching the ends. Beneath their windows the city beckoned like a temptation. "We will plan your assault on this colony after lunch," said Stacey, removing her hat. "But first things first."

Three days of rapturous lovemaking followed, during which the Vicomte and Vicomtesse Pierre de Barol spent twenty-seven pounds of Jay Gruneberger's money and drank an awful quantity of champagne. The girth and enduring solidity of Piet's cock were attributes of which Stacey made full and inventive use. As he watched her lower herself onto him, squealing as she found the angle she wanted, he thought how infinitely preferable this was to the *froideur* with which Jacobina Vermeulen-Sickerts had treated him.

He used the expertise he had gained from that lady to excellent effect, and the frankness of Stacey's compliments redoubled his eagerness to please her. It was the first time either of them had had such opportunities for uninterrupted pleasure and as the days and nights slipped into one another their ecstasies became tender. In calmer interludes Piet learned the story of Stacey's *vicomte*, her flight from her family and her hatred of Germaine Lorette. At her prompting he confided the circumstances of his childhood and his expulsion from Herengracht 605. This perilous honesty forged a bond that sex—in bed, in the bath, on the sofa of the sitting room, over the desk as its crystal inkwell rattled—cemented and confirmed.

By the morning of the fourth day Piet's cock was red and swollen, thoroughly chafed by its addictive exertions.

"I'm bound to be pregnant," remarked Stacey to the jasmine-scented breeze as they sat over breakfast on their balcony.

"Then we must marry at once."

"I rather hoped you'd say that." She reached for a silver pot of hot chocolate and turned to him with a serious expression. "To be practical for a moment. You must foreswear all other women. You may flirt as much as you like. Indeed it may be necessary for you to do so. But you are never to touch beyond the wrists."

"Agreed."

"And men too. St. Helena or no St. Helena."

"I promise."

"Certain people will dislike you on principle. It is the disadvantage of being charismatic and good-looking. Many more men will hate you than women. They will be my special responsibility. Instead of holding you back, they will be decisive in our success. I do not see how we can possibly fail."

"We will certainly do better together than apart."

"Of that," she murmured, taking his hands in hers and kissing them, "I have no doubt at all."

To be continued

ACKNOWLEDGMENTS

I am deeply grateful to all those who helped me to imagine and write *History of a Pleasure Seeker.* I first told the story to Pieter Swinkels and Jolanda van Dijk, of De Bezige Bij, and later to my wonderful Dutch editor Peter van der Zwag. The Fonds voor de Letteren and the NLPVF made possible an extended stay in Amsterdam, where Bert Vreeken and the staff of the Willet-Holthuysen Museum were extremely generous with their knowledge and time. My Dutch researcher Irene Lannoye worked tirelessly translating documents and advising on names and other details; without her this book would have taken ten years longer to write. I am grateful, too, to William H. Miller Jr. for his superb work on ocean liners, Brian Fernandes, Marianne Schonbach, Fleur van Koppen, the Van Loon Museum, the Goethe Institute Amsterdam, the Athenaeum Bookshop, Daniel Viehoff, Pieter Rouwendal, Harriet Sergeant, Anne-Catherine Gillet, Will Hartman, Nancy Herralda, Andrea Wulf, Michael Bawtree, Dominic Treadwell-Collins, Lyle Saunders, Annika Ebrahim, Anne-Marie Bodal, Fanny Adler, Peter Adler, Ian Ross, George Shilling, Victoria Wilson, Irène Némirovsky, Kirsty Dunseath, Kathleen Anderson, Patrick Walsh, Jane and Tony Mason, Benjamin Morse, the staff of the National Library of South Africa and the Mount Nelson Hotel, Cape Town—and, of course, to Fryderyk Chopin, J. S. Bach, Georges Bizet and Coco Chanel.

To hear the music, learn the historical context,
and look into the world of *History of a Pleasure Seeker,*
e-mail Piet@Barol.com for exclusive bonus material.

A NOTE ON THE TYPE

The text of this book was set in Garamond No. 3. It is not a
true copy of any of the designs of Claude Garamond (ca. 1480–
1561), but an adaptation of his types. It probably owes as much
to the designs of Jean Jannon, a Protestant printer working in
Sedan in the early seventeenth century, who had worked with
Garamond's romans earlier, in Paris, but who was denied their
use because of Catholic censorship. Jannon's matrices came into
the possession of the Imprimerie nationale, where they were
thought to be by Garamond himself, and were so described
when the Imprimerie revived the type in 1900.

TYPESET BY
Scribe, Philadelphia, Pennsylvania

PRINTED AND BOUND BY
Berryville Graphics, Berryville, Virginia

DESIGNED BY
Iris Weinstein